COYOTE KILL

To _____ I hope you like the book.

Karen
Sept. 28, 2007

COYOTE KILL

A Carol Ward Mystery

KAREN R. WILSON
Author of FOR JUST CLAWS

iUniverse, Inc.

New York Lincoln Shanghai

COYOTE KILL

A Carol Ward Mystery

iUniverse books may be ordered through booksellers or by contacting:

iUniverse
2021 Pine Lake Road, Suite 100
Lincoln, NE 68512
www.iuniverse.com
1-800-Authors (1-800-288-4677)

Because of the dynamic nature of the Internet, any Web addresses
or links contained in this book may have changed
since publication and may no longer be valid.

This is a work of fiction. All of the characters, names, incidents,
organizations, and dialogue in this novel are either the products of the
author's imagination or are used fictitiously.

ISBN: 978-0-595-44271-3 (pbk)
ISBN: 978-0-595-88601-2 (ebk)

Printed in the United States of America

To Camille and Boots, my two office workers
who never missed a day on the job.

Chapter One

The coyotes snarled and lunged, moving quickly, weaving in and around each other, fighting over the carcass. Excited yips came from those on the fringes of the main pack. Not sure which I'd counted and which I'd missed, I guessed the entire band to be at least a dozen. Moonlight shone from their pale backs.

My legs ached from sitting in my neighbor's cramped pickup truck, waiting for the coyotes to show up, me unbelieving, her swearing she'd seen them the night before. It was twilight when we pulled off the two-track road, pointed the truck into the woods, and shut off the headlights. My eyes had slowly adjusted to the darkness, which was coming earlier now that we'd entered the autumnal equinox. "Want to see what they're fighting over?" I asked, lifting the passenger-side door handle.

"Are you out of your mind? I can see tomorrow's headline now. 'Carol Ward, 47, of Hadley, Mich., killed in coyote attack.'" Denise tucked a stubborn lock of thick chestnut hair behind her ear.

"They'll run off when we shine our flashlight at them." How could she be content to sit in the truck? A lone coyote raised his head at the sound of my door handle, his yellow eyes glowing. I released the handle and waited.

"It's probably a deer or a turkey," she said, noncommittally, as if it really didn't matter to her one way or the other.

"How can you be so sure?" I asked. The loner turned to watch the others again. He stood apart from the pack, the rest of them intent on their tug-of-war. Then, dropping his head, he picked up what looked like, in the moon's glow, a softball, his sharp teeth clamped wide around it. He stood still for a moment, his nose up, catching the wind, then loped off with his prize, heading into the black of the deep woods.

"Too bad we didn't borrow Sheriff Morton's night binoculars," Denise said.

The last thing I wanted was to get involved with that man. "Except then he'd want to know what we're doing and why, and then pretty soon we're not doing anything at all. We're being lectured," I said. "Again."

"He lectures *you*. He trusts me." She took a pack of cigarettes and a lighter from her denim jacket.

"*He trusts me*," I mimicked under my breath. I pulled my glasses down from the top of my head, working them free where they had become snarled in my shoulder-length dark hair. My night vision wasn't bad with the full moon, but I needed help with distances, just like the rest of the over-forty crowd. I followed the loner as far into the woods as I could. "That's no deer skull he's carrying," I said, squinting. "It's round, not oblong, and there's no bone on a turkey that big."

She took a quick drag on her cigarette, blowing the smoke out an inch of open window. "Let's get Todd and Jack."

This was not a caper our husbands would be interested in, especially considering what night it was. "On a Monday night? You've got to be kidding. Remember a little nuisance sport called football?"

I asked. If there wasn't ever another ball game played in the history of the universe, it would be just fine with me.

"What's so important about finding out what they've got? Why can't we come back tomorrow, in the daylight, or on the weekend?" Her fingers gripped white on the steering wheel. "The coyotes could have rabies, or distemper ... or anthrax, or ..." She rolled her window down farther. "Do you hear that? They're growling and fighting, Carol, and I'm not wanting to be their next snack!"

"Blink the headlights and blow the horn. They'll run," I said, sounding more sure of myself than I felt. One side of me agreed with Denise; the other side didn't want to lose this opportunity. By tomorrow, whatever carcass they had would be history. "We'll make sure they're gone before we get out of the truck."

She stubbed out her cigarette and folded her arms in front of her. "Nothing doing. I'm staying right here."

She could be annoyingly stubborn at times. Reaching over, I pulled the headlight switch on and off several times, the lamps illuminating the dark woods like bizarre strobes. The coyotes raised their heads, scanning the truck. Two took a sideways leap toward tree cover. The rest of the pack stared intently, figuring out who we were and what we wanted. I got out of the truck, but stood behind the open door, waiting, hoping Denise got out too. One glance told me she wasn't budging. "Shoo!" I yelled, and threw my arms up. The pack scattered. Their dun colors melted into the woods and were lost in the towering pines.

There was no going back without losing face. Cautiously, I stepped forward. The place where the coyotes had been feeding seemed closer now that I was outside the truck. I pointed my flashlight on the ground in front of my boots. The dirt was soft, it crumbled beneath my feet. Dead leaves were scattered where the coyotes had dug in with their hind paws, tugging at each other. An earthy sandalwood scent hung in the humid September air.

"I'm going to get Todd!" Denise said, starting the engine.

"Don't leave me here!" I pleaded. The truck was about thirty feet away, and would take more than a quick jump to get back to it. Without its shelter to retreat to, I was in trouble.

Then she screamed. I stopped, confused, and turned around, away from the direction of where the coyotes had disappeared into the woods. "They're coming back!" she said. "Look! On your right!"

Shadows moved at the edge of the tree cover. I saw a pale snout and heard a low and drawn-out growl. I pivoted, but my left boot sank, catching on a root or a branch. I stumbled and fell, the flashlight rolling out of my fingers. I heard the pack's raspy breathing. *Rabies.* "They're only dogs," I told myself. "They want to sniff and see if I've got food." *Anthrax. Distemper.* My fingernails dug into the sandy soil in front of me, searching for the flashlight, but I knew I was wasting precious time.

The sound of Denise's voice reverberated in my head, unintelligible words that may as well have been in another language. I savagely tore at the root or vine that had somehow tethered itself to me and felt it give way. Then I saw the lone coyote's treasure, pale in the moonlight. He must have dropped it when I'd startled him. I scooped it up and ran.

Denise was out of the truck. She was standing on the driver's side running board; I could see her head above the cab. Fern and horsetail whipped against my legs. She ducked into the truck and lunged across the seat to fling the door wider. "Get in!"

She threw the truck into gear before I was all the way inside. The door banged against a tree at the edge of the turn-off, slamming shut. We bumped down the dirt track, over pot holes and the dried mud gouges left by four-wheelers. I flicked on my side of the cab light and found my thumb and forefinger poked through the eye sockets of a human skull, grit still clinging to it in the places where the coyote's saliva had wet the bone. Repulsed, I dropped it. It bounced across the seat, into Denise's lap. She screamed and tore her hands from the steering wheel, swatting the skull away as if it were an angry hornet. The truck swerved sharply to the right and caught in a cement-like rut, then bucked violently and jumped the rut, landing in the gully alongside the dirt road, nose down.

Chapter Two

Denise walked well ahead of me, gravel crunching under our feet. The torn sole of my boot flapped with each step. "I told you I'd seen them here last night, when I rode through the woods from your place," she said, smug in having proved the coyotes' existence. "Chevron galloped off like a scared jackrabbit and almost threw me." She stuck her upturned palm out. "Where's my five bucks?"

I dug into my wallet for the money but came up short. "I'll have to owe you," I said.

"I don't know why I let myself get caught up in your stupid hare-brained schemes," Denise said crossly. "Everything was fine until you had to get out and investigate. And now my truck is in a ditch with a dented door and God knows what else." She kicked a rock out of her path.

She was angry at me and I guess she had every right to be. It *was* my fault, once again. All because, just like she said, I was forever coming up with some stupid idea and dragging her into it.

Both horse lovers, we met while working for a hunter show stable called Fox Valley almost twenty years ago, and enjoyed the kind of misery-loves-company relationship that forms between workers when the pay is low, the hours are long, and the conditions are otherwise less-than-perfect. Now, by happenstance, she was my neighbor, too, or as near as what could be called a neighbor out here in the country, where it didn't always mean "next-door." In our case, it meant our homes were separated by a 4,000-acre equestrian park maintained by the state of Michigan.

"I'll fix the truck door," I said. "Last summer I painted the tailgate on my Ranger."

She turned to face me, her hands on her hips. "Don't you touch my truck!"

"Geez, it didn't look that bad," I said, assuming her remark referenced the quality of my work. I resumed watching the ground beneath my feet. Crickets, in loud cacophony, quieted as we walked by, then restarted their chorus after our passing.

"You know what you're like?" Denise asked as she walked backward, glaring at me. "You're like a little snowball at the top of a mountain, and by the time you roll all the way down, you've caused an avalanche and crushed an entire village."

"What the hell are you talking about? What village?" I asked.

"Oh, never mind, it does no good whatsoever to be mad at you, you're so …" she trailed off, searching for the right word. "Out of touch with reality, that's what you are."

"I'm out of touch? That's rich, coming from you. You're the one who wants to act like nothing happened back there. You're the one who said, 'Let's put it back where we found it. No one will know. Pretend we never found it.' It's a human skull. How can we pretend we never found it?"

"We quietly put it back and don't tell anybody. It's so simple, even you should be able to get it."

"That's just plain *not right*," I said.

"Since when did you get righteous?"

"When did you get so lazy?"

"Lazy? You've got a hell of a nerve calling *me* lazy. Who leaves her Christmas lights up year-round? Who fenced her lawn so her horses could graze it down and she didn't have to mow?" She got her cigarettes out again.

"We're talking about a human being here, not Christmas lights or a lawn!" I said. "Do you have to do that?" Denise chain-smoked when she was upset. She mostly just wasted the cigarettes, going through the motion of sliding one from the pack, lighting it, taking one or two puffs, only to snub it out a minute later. And though I suppose it wasn't any of my business, I did consider her a good friend, and friends don't let friends smoke—at least not without harassment.

She threw the cigarette down. "It'll be just like when we found Julie's body. The questioning, rehashing over and over. Signing statements. It was a nightmare I can't go through again."

So *that* was the real reason. Not that she was scared, or lazy, or even that she didn't care, but because barely four months ago, Denise and I found the murdered body of a teenage neighbor in the woods, not far from this very spot. "Like it or not, we *are* involved, just like we were then." A stone had worked its way inside my boot. "Dammit!" I yelled.

"What's the matter now?"

Plopping down on a boulder at the edge of the road, I took off my boot, turned it over and shook it out. "We need to decide what our story is, before we get to your house," I said, rubbing my sore heel. Mosquitoes, finding a stationary target, had begun to swarm.

"We slid off the road," she said. "That's it."

Didn't she trust her own husband? "You're not even going to tell Todd?" I asked.

"Nope," she said, swatting and slapping at the mosquitoes. "Let's get the hell out of here before we're eaten alive."

I could only wonder if the reason she didn't want to tell Todd was that she was afraid he would agree with me. We walked on in an awkward silence until a pair of lights came over the hill. "It's that new neighbor of yours, Richard, in his gas hog dually," she said. She stood in the middle of the road, flagging him to stop. "We slid off the road, okay?"

"Yeah, sure. For now, anyway." It was a decision I hoped I wouldn't regret.

It was Richard, all right. His name conjured up blue eyes as cool as icebergs. Long, slender legs in tight jeans. Jack and I had gone over to introduce ourselves when he first moved in. We saw no wedding ring, nor were we introduced to a wife. The following Sunday, Jack made the acquaintance of Louis, Richard's housemate, who had come down to the paper box in what appeared to be a woman's sundress, leaving Jack and I to form our own conclusions. Louis and Richard's relationship was now the gossip of our small, unequivocally bored and predominately female saddle club. It didn't matter to me one way or the other, but since it gave the rest of them something to do on rainy days, I figured the gossip served a purpose.

He drove an enormous old Chevy truck with cherry-red paint. Custom pin-striping ran the length of the vehicle. It probably got two miles to the gallon, having come from an era when gas was plentiful. A show truck. What he was doing driving these back roads that were little more than deer trails was anyone's guess. Hadn't he heard of stone chips?

"Evening, ladies," he said, leaning out the window. "Trouble? Or are you just walking for your health?" The angles of his cheekbones were perfect, like those of a model in an expensive sports car advertisement.

"A deer ran in front of us and we skidded off the road," Denise said, a little too rehearsed. "Now my truck is stuck in the gully."

"Oh the tangled web we weave ..." I muttered low enough for only her to hear.

She pointed back the way we'd come. "It's just over that hill, in the curve by the swamp."

"Think I can pull her out?" he asked.

It annoyed me that flailing motor vehicles were nearly always referred to in the feminine, as if they had misbehaved or had taken temporary leave of their senses, as if those two conditions were decidedly female. I smiled and kept my mouth shut.

"If you'll take us to my house, my husband can come back with the tractor," Denise said.

"Hop in. I can probably yank it out."

He left his truck idling, while he came around and ceremoniously opened the passenger side door for us. The old leather of the bench seat was cracked and stiff. In the places where it was split, dirty foam cushions were visible. The outside and the inside of the truck sharply contrasted one another. The outside was shiny and beautiful—the inside shabby and smelling of gasoline. Denise held back, so I slid in first.

"Carol, do you remember where you left our package?" Denise asked, suddenly upbeat and cheerful, as if our argument had never taken place.

"Package?" What was she talking about?

"You know," she said, jabbing me in the ribs with a well-disguised move. "The package we were delivering—the one that fell off the seat when we went off the road—remember? Where did you put it?"

Oh, *that* package. As far as I knew, it was still on the floor, where it had fallen when she'd slapped it away. "I believe you were the last one to have it," I said, irritably.

We came around the curve in the road. "There it is," she said, pointing to her truck. Muck had all but buried the front wheels. We stopped and got out. She gingerly picked her way down the bank and, probably afraid the skull would roll out and unsure of how she would explain that to Richard, opened the driver's-side door barely wide enough to squeeze in. Richard and I watched from the road above.

"Piece of cake," Richard called down to her. "Just make sure it's in neutral."

While they strategized, I stargazed. I followed the Big Dipper to the North Star. There was Cassiopeia, in her chair, and Cepheus. I shivered. Although the days were still warm, unlike the hot nights of summer, now the nights carried the damp and musky scent of early autumn. It was welcome relief after the unusually sweltering summer.

Richard turned his truck around and, after rummaging in his toolbox, lifted a thick rust-powdered chain from it. He wove the chain in and around the trailer hitch and hooked it back on itself, then carrying the hook from the opposite end, he slid down the embankment. With the chain outstretched, it was obvious that it would not be long enough. There were probably four more feet between the end of the chain and Denise's bumper.

"Want me to back it up more?" I called down to him.

"Be careful, the edge is soft," he said.

The big dually was a stick shift. Carefully, I put the truck in gear, hoping I remembered how to drive one. Inching closer to the edge, my foot hovered over the brake.

"Whoa," he yelled up to me. "That's good, right there."

He hooked the chain to Denise's truck, then scrambled back up the bank. "Keep the wheels straight," he instructed her. He got back into the driver's seat and moved his truck forward, until we felt the slack come out of the chain. I wondered if the old Chevy had enough power. Richard gunned it and the tires bit in. Slowly, Denise's truck came up out of the ditch. When it was on the road,

Richard unhooked the chain and heaved it into the back of his pickup, where it fell with a heavy thud on top of a shovel and rake. A chunk of damp clay fell from the shovel. A push lawn mower was wedged against the tailgate.

"In the lawn business?" I asked, pointing to the mower, and realizing that I didn't know what he did for a job. It seemed a good opportunity to make small talk and learn more about him.

"No, my house up in Davison still isn't sold and I'm going back and forth once a week to cut the grass." With a ragged towel he'd gotten from under the seat, he rubbed the rust from his hands. "Talk about a pain in the neck. With this economy the way it is, real estate just isn't moving."

"I'll bet. Too bad, we're looking to hire a lawn service. Neither Jack nor I have time to mow. The girl who lived in your house did our mowing—the one who died." I wondered how much he knew about Julie.

He shook his head. "She was young, wasn't she?"

"Nineteen," I said, hoping he wouldn't ask more questions. I always started out thinking I wanted to talk about it, then changed my mind. In some ways, four months seemed an eon ago, yet at the same time, not nearly long enough. I wondered if it would ever be long enough, and abruptly changed the subject.

"Jack and I temporarily rigged up a hot wire over the summer so the horses could graze the lawn down." It seemed the easiest way of dealing with the problem at the time.

Bathed in the glow of Richard's headlights, Denise performed a hands-on inspection of her passenger-side door as if it were an expensive Thoroughbred's bowed tendon. What she had done with our "package," I had no idea. She ran her fingers over the damaged paint. "Just a little scrape," she said. "Thanks, Richard, you saved me a ton of trouble."

"I'm headed home," he said to me. "I can drop you off, if you'd like."

If Denise thought this was the end of our discussion about reporting the skull, she was wrong. I'd been thinking it through, and my mind was made up. The only thing undecided was whether or not she came along with me when I went to the police. "I'll call you later," I said, hoisting myself into Richard's truck.

It felt awkward to be alone with him. What would we talk about? I knew almost nothing about him. I wondered if he felt the same way, because we bumped over the ruts at what seemed an amazing rate of speed. Stones flew from our tires, insects kamikazying into the windshield. Clutching the seat belt, I futilely attempted to jiggle the lock into place. The tools in the bed of the truck clanged and rattled and beat against the sides. Richard stared straight ahead, his neck muscles clenched.

"Geez, Richard, where's the fire?" I finally asked, grabbing the arm rest. He swerved sharply and I bounced off the seat, whacking my head on the roof of the cab. "Do you always drive like this?"

"Huh? Oh, sorry." He relaxed his death grip on the steering wheel and took his foot off the gas. I wondered if he'd totally forgotten I was there. "Sorry. I was thinking about something. You okay?"

I rearranged myself on the seat. "Yeah, sure. Don't worry about it," I said, smoothing the front of my jacket. There was less than a mile to go until we hit the county-maintained road, then just a quarter mile more to my house. "Thanks for pulling Denise out. It was my fault she ended up in there to begin with."

"Thought it was a deer." He looked at me quizzically.

I'd forgotten about Denise's lie. He made me nervous, staring at me like that, so I pretended to look out the window. "I mean the reason we were in the woods at all. She'd seen a pack of coyotes last night and I didn't believe her, so she bet me five bucks we'd see them again tonight."

"And did you?"

"Sure did. Probably a dozen or so." We pulled into my driveway. Through the living room window, the television flicker and glow could be seen. "Hope you sell that house soon. Taking care of two places is a drag."

"You got that right. Looks like Jack's home," Richard said.

"Monday Night Football." It seemed explanation enough. "What about you? Not a sports fan?" I asked.

He shook his head. "Not much on watching television," he said.

"Me neither. It's just a big waste of time if you ask me. Give me a good book any day," I said.

"There's a woman after my own heart." He started to get out and I wondered if he intended on coming into the house.

"Come in for a beer?" I asked.

"No, thanks, I'd better get home. But that door can be hard to open. I'll come around and pull it from the outside. It sometimes sticks."

"I can manage," I said, pushing my shoulder against the door. Nothing happened. "I'm not used to having things done for me, that's all." Now why had I said that? Sometimes the stupidest things came out of my mouth. But being waited on did make me nervous. I pushed again, harder this time, but he was already making his way around to the passenger side. Men opening doors for women as a courtesy was a stupid tradition. As long as I had two arms, I could open my own doors. Except this one, that is. Eager to get the stubborn door open before he got there, I whammed against it. Pain radiated from my collarbone up into my neck.

The door opened effortlessly for him. "Sorry about that, I need to fix it. The suspension on this truck is screwed up."

He must have mistaken the blank look on my face, which was really meant to disguise the pains which were now shooting to my forehead, for incomprehension, and said, "Makes the doors hard to open."

"Oh," I said, barely able to breathe.

"Say hello to Jack for me, will you?"

*　　　*　　　*　　　*

"Why not?" Jack asked when I told him Denise didn't want to go to the police.

"She doesn't want to get involved, and have a repeat of the nightmare with Julie, filling out reports, making statements …" I was peeling and cutting carrots to pack for tomorrow's lunch. "While you're standing there, will you get me a sandwich bag from the pantry?" I asked him.

He got the bag and held it open while I dumped the carrot sticks in. "Finding a skull isn't the same as finding a body. We don't even know who it is. Besides, she doesn't have a choice. If she doesn't tell Sheriff Morton, it's withholding evidence," he said.

"I tried to tell her that, but she wouldn't listen. You know how she gets. Then Richard came by, so the discussion ended."

"Pretty boy fag Richard?" Jack cocked his wrist effeminately.

"Don't call him that," I said, offering him a carrot. "You don't know that he's gay. And even if he is, what difference does it make?" Why was I defending Richard?

He came up behind me and nuzzled my hair. "It's not that I care either way. He can be whatever he wants to be, just in someone else's neighborhood, that's all. And provided he steers clear of me."

Burly and definitely not a pretty boy, Jack could have easily passed for one of the football players on the television screen, and somehow it seemed unlikely that Richard's amorous intentions would ever be directed his way. "I think we should tell Sheriff

Morton about the skull," I said. "There might be more bones out there. If Denise doesn't want me to involve her, I won't."

He took the phone from its rest and held it in front of me. "Get it over with. Call Denise and tell her what you just told me."

He was right, I knew. I didn't know why I was putting it off. Taking the phone, I punched in Denise's number, then looked up at the clock and realized too late that she might be in bed. Just one more thing for her to be mad at me about. She answered on the third ring. "Denise?" I asked.

"Yeah?" Was that an edge to her voice or was it my imagination?

"I'm going to call Sheriff Morton." My statement was met with an awkward silence. A sinking feeling made me wonder if I knew Denise as well as I thought. Was I pushing the boundaries of our friendship?

"And if he asks if you were alone?"

"I won't lie. First of all, I'm the world's lousiest liar and secondly, you don't lie to the police. You just don't do it." I waited.

"Great. I guess I can't stop you." Her tone was curt.

"Geez, I'm only doing what's right, that's all." Jack watched as I rubbed hot tears from the corners of my eyes.

"Do what you want, I know you will in the end anyway," she said.

"Do you think I *want* to do this? Do you think it's any easier for me?" Instead of answering, she slammed the phone down. "That got a definite thumbs down," I told Jack.

"You've got one more call to make. He stays up until midnight."

"I'm not sure I have his home number," I said, searching for an excuse. Sandwiched between a good friend that wanted one thing and my husband wanting another, I was torn. Tired and frustrated, I wished I could go to sleep and happily wake up tomorrow with none of this ever having happened. No skull, no truck in a ditch, and no unpleasant arguments. Jack slid the address book from the shelf and recited the numbers.

"Hearing from you at this time of the night isn't a good sign," Sheriff Morton said, annoyed at hearing my voice and probably wishing he hadn't picked up the phone.

"Is this a bad time?" Maybe he'd been eating. I knew how precious food was to him; it was his only outlet. The poor man was constantly on the latest fad diet, though he never seemed to shed a pound.

"That's none of your business."

The man was a nuisance to deal with. For some unknown reason, we'd never gotten along. And he certainly didn't try to make things any better. "Look, this isn't exactly fun for me either."

"Let's get to the point."

Would I be in trouble if I called him an unkind name? Something like fat ass or Porky? Would that be harassment of a police officer? And what would my sentence be? Thinking it might almost be worth it for a moment's gratification, I weighed it in my mind and decided against it. "I found something. Something I think you should know about," I started.

"You've been in those damned woods again, haven't you? I can't believe you still go there."

"Of course I still go there. There's nowhere else to ride." Why was everyone in a bad mood tonight?

"Cry me a river. What'd your latest scavenger hunt turn up?"

"A skull." The silence seemed like it lasted forever. I wondered what he was thinking. The word *busybody* had probably crossed his mind. I knew what he thought of me.

"What sort of skull?" he asked in disbelief.

"Human, of course. Do you think I'd call you at midnight on a weeknight to report any other sort of skull?" Sometimes I wasn't sure the man had a full deck.

"I swear, I don't know how you manage!"

"It's not like I'm out *looking* for skulls," I said. "It just sort of turned up."

"Where is it?"

Suddenly it occurred to me that I didn't know. It was somewhere in Denise's truck, unless she'd heaved it out the window alongside the road. Now how the hell was I going to keep her out of it? "Where's what?" I asked, stalling.

"The skull, for cripe's sake!"

"I don't know."

"Ms. Ward, it is very late and you have drawn me out of a nice warm bed for God only knows what, and now you want to play games. I am in no mood. Do I make myself clear?"

"Perfectly." Even testier than usual, I thought. "Someone else has the skull. Or at least she knows where it is."

"Why isn't that person calling me instead of you?"

He had me there. "You'll have to ask her. Denise. You'll have to ask Denise."

He sighed a long, drawn-out sigh that told me just how disgusted he really was. "You know the routine."

About now I figured he was probably rubbing his tired eyes the way he did, pinching them underneath his wire-rimmed glasses. "Yeah, sure," I said. "Do you want me to wait here or meet you at Denise's?"

"Denise's. I'll be there within an hour to get both your statements on tape." He hung up.

"She's going to be thrilled," I muttered.

Chapter Three

A couple of weeks ago, Jack mentioned that his builder employer might send him to Indiana to finish a warehouse complex subcontract. I'd put it from my mind, hoping that if I didn't think about it, then it wouldn't happen. But now it was time for him to go.

We ate breakfast in our sunny kitchen. I could see across the lawn, to where my horses stood at the gate waiting for their morning hay. On the surface, everything seemed so idyllic.

"The subcontractor went bankrupt. We've either got to finish the work or find another subcontractor," Jack said. He poured two glasses of orange juice. "There are huge penalties if the project doesn't make deadline, which is in six months."

Huge penalties equaled no year-end bonuses. That part I understood—but I didn't have to like it. "Six months?" I asked. My toast was dry and boring, a necessary by-product of being an easy keeper, the horseman's term for a horse that can survive on very little food. "Will I see you on weekends? What about the holidays?" It was early October and six months would take us into April. Unfathomable.

"If we really kick ass, we might be home by Christmas, but a lot depends on the weather. If I come home on the weekends, it'll just add to the length."

"What about my birthday?" I asked, immediately regretting the whining tone. "Sorry. I didn't mean it that way."

Camille hopped onto my lap and purred. She rubbed her silky white chin against my arm. A stray, I'd taken her in twelve years ago, when we first moved to the country. With each year there were more strays and now we had a houseful of cats—eight to be exact, nine if you counted Benny, the barn cat. Though the intention was always to find adoptive homes for them, in reality that was just a front to appease Jack. Who was I kidding? I never could have parted with a single one of them. They were as close to children as I was ever going to get.

"Your birthday is Thanksgiving weekend. I know we'll be back for that. We'll make it a long weekend, and do something nice, maybe go to the art museum. You'd like that." He ran a calloused hand gently through my hair.

Buy me off to shut me up. Thanksgiving seemed a long way off and I was so tired of him leaving. "I'll miss you," I said, thinking of how terribly inadequate those three words were.

"I'll miss you, too, hon, but the time will go by fast. You can come down too, you know."

"Oh, wouldn't that be romantic? A threesome with Ian in whatever flea-bag motel he's booked you to stay at." Ian, Jack's assistant, had the planning skills of an orangutan. "And what about the horses and the cats? I'd end up spending a fortune for a pet sitter and someone to clean stalls." Twenty-five years ago, no one had ever told me this is what marriage would be like. Work and worry and solitary nights.

The huge construction company Jack worked for sent him all over the country, either bidding on new jobs or managing those in progress. His time away usually ranged anywhere from a few days to a couple weeks, depending on how far away the job site was. Then he'd be home for two or three days before leaving again. Occasionally, it was nice to have an evening or two to myself. But most of the time, after I'd played all my Bob Dylan and Enya, and moved on to the Moody Blues and ended with Glen Campbell, I was tired of oneness. And this time it was not a couple of days, or even a couple of weeks. Now they were talking months.

This warehouse had been trouble right from the beginning; trouble with inspections, trouble getting materials, and now the subcontractor going belly-up. So it wasn't with delight that I drove Jack to the airport. I watched his plane until it was a small speck in the sky. Yes, he'd get a better bonus, I told myself, and yes, it would be good for the company. But six months? The oak trees lining the road wore brilliant yellow leaves that would be replaced with new green growth before Jack was home to stay.

And the house! Every squeak amplified; every noise sinister and startling. It would be a miracle if it held together in Jack's absence, especially the ancient plumbing. He'd pressed a list of phone numbers into my hand, names of capable, trusted repairmen—a plumber, an electrician, a furnace technician. But somehow, I wasn't comforted. Everything downstairs was so foreign, the mishmash of wires and pipes crossing each other in all directions, it seemed the basement was another planet altogether—one I didn't particularly enjoy visiting.

I dialed my friend Lida's phone number thinking a sympathetic ear was what I needed. She lived across town and, like Denise and I, also had horses. Since she and her husband Perry were retired, it was easy for her to arrange her riding schedule to meet mine. Sometimes in the summer she trailered over after I got off work, and we rode up to the ridge overlooking the meadow of goldenrod.

"She's visiting her sister in South Carolina," Perry said when I called.

"When will she be back?" I asked, trying not to sound nosy. She hadn't mentioned a word about visiting her sister last week when I talked to her. Normally she'd give me a call before she went out of town, just to let me know, or to ask me to check her animals while she was away. It seemed odd she hadn't done it this time.

"Next Tuesday."

Perry wasn't the most talkative person in the world, but today he was especially abrupt. In his defense, I wondered if maybe I'd interrupted one of his woodworking projects—a bookcase or a shelf, perhaps.

"I didn't know she was planning a trip."

"It was spur of the moment," he said.

Spur of the moment did not sound like Lida. "Everything okay with the animals?" I asked. "Need any help?"

"No, everything's fine."

"Have her give me a call when she gets back, will you?" I asked, wondering if she'd ever get the message. If he was in this much of a hurry to get off the phone, would he even bother to write it down?

"Yeah, sure, I'll do that," he said and hung up without saying goodbye.

What's eating him? I wondered, putting the phone down. Maybe they'd had an argument? That would explain why Lida suddenly felt the need for a vacation. I let it go and called Denise.

"Jack's gone, this time for six months," I said, and explained the out-of-state job. She was still peeved about the police statement, but if there was the smallest iota of compassion left in her, I intended to find and use it, to put us back on speaking terms. "I expect a major appliance to break down any minute," I said, looking at my watch. "He's been gone exactly two hours and six minutes."

"We're always here for you. And Richard is right across the road. Now you'll have the perfect excuse to visit more often—the damsel in distress," she said.

"Jack says he's gay."

"Huh?"

"How else do you explain Louis?" I asked. "Personally, I don't care if he is gay. I think he's just plain weird. Monday, after we left you, he took off about sixty miles an hour, flying over pot holes and ruts. When I asked him where the fire was, all of a sudden he jammed on the brakes like he'd totally forgotten I was there."

"That's strange."

"You're telling me. Anyway, I do need to talk to him. I think I lost an earring in his truck when I was scrambling with the seat belt. It's either there or in the woods where I fell. I've looked everywhere else." I got an Oreo out of the jar. "It had to be the silver and turquoise war bonnets Jack bought in Santa Fe. Handmade, of course … irreplaceable."

"Isn't that always the way? No one ever loses their junky stuff."

"Added to the fact that if Jack finds out, I'll be in for the lecture on how I don't take care of anything. The same lecture I got when I lost the diamond from my wedding ring," I said, plucking another Oreo from the jar. *No dessert tonight.* "Have you heard anything from Sheriff Morton about the skull?"

"He said to give him a call on Monday."

"Let's saddle up this afternoon and ride over there. We could look around, see if we find something else," I said.

"*Somebody* else, you mean?" Denise asked. "He said to stay away for a few days. He specifically said to tell *you* to stay out."

"Well, of course he said to stay out. Did you expect him to invite us into the investigation?" Although Denise could be annoying at times, her redeeming quality was her persuadability. "Come on," I pleaded. "Even if he finds out we snooped, which he won't, what's he going to do about it?"

"I suppose it can't hurt if we stay on the trail."

*   *   *   *

A state park made up of winding bridle paths separated Denise's gravel road from mine. Running through the middle of the park and connecting our roads was a two-track. Even during the good weather months, it was barely accessible by anything except four-wheel drive vehicles. When Denise and I rode together, she came from the west and I came from the east, and we met on this two-track. The terrain of the park was rugged, filled with steep, eroded hills and not of much use to anyone but horse people and die-hard mountain bikers. My chestnut mare, Feather, carefully picked her way over the dried, cement-hard tire gouges.

Chevron, Denise's new buckskin gelding, wasn't up to the more strenuous climbing yet, so we stopped often to let him rest. "The trees are gorgeous," she said, looking around at the gold and red and orange. After taking Jack to the airport, the day had turned warm. A soft breeze blew through the pines, spreading their clean scent.

"Indian summer," I said.

Denise slid a cigarette from its pack. Chevron twisted, pivoting off his near hind hoof. She lifted one rein, settling him, then cupping her hands around the cigarette, she held a lighter to it. "I love fall, but I hate winter."

"You don't get one without the other," I said, making the same bittersweet connection with Jack's job—money versus the loneliness. "That damn manure pile of mine is a mile high again. I'll have to burn it before snow comes," I said.

"You've already had two warnings. Next time it'll be a hefty fine." She took a long drag on her cigarette.

"Last time was not my fault," I said. "It spontaneously combusted."

"The end result was the same," she said. "It smoldered for weeks. You're lucky your neighbors didn't tar and feather you."

"If they don't like it, they can go back to the city, where they came from," I said. "Besides, what's the fire department going to do if I don't pay the fine? Confiscate the manure? Put me in jail? I'll be the first woman sent to prison for burning manure. Would I go to Jackson or Ionia?"

Denise pinched the end of her cigarette, then dropped it into an old prescription bottle she kept in her jacket. "Ionia—it's for the criminally insane."

"Smart ass. Actually, now that I think about it, I wouldn't go to either, since those are both men's prisons." I paused for a moment. "Have you ever stopped to think about how many more crimes are committed by men than women? Why is that?"

"Simple. It's the testosterone."

"Now you're blaming criminal behavior on hormones?"

"I figure it's got to be. What else do they have more of than us?" Chevron inched his rump close to Feather and swung out with his hind leg. Denise quickly flicked her spur lightly and he sashayed back into his own space.

"See, right there, even the animals do it," I said. "Why'd he get aggressive in her territory? She was just going down the trail, minding her own business. And he's a gelding, so you can't blame it on testosterone. Maybe it's not so much whether you're male or female, but rather how aggressive you are or aren't. More of a personality thing."

"But that theory leads us right back to gender, because the hormones are what cause the aggressiveness," Denise retorted.

"Who knows?" I said, shrugging my shoulders and dismissing the subject. We were almost to the clearing in the woods where we found the skull. The rocky path led over a steep hill and down again, where it leveled out to the road. "Listen!" I whispered to Denise, halting Feather. "Someone's down in the clearing, where the coyotes were."

"Let's go," she said. "We're not supposed to be here."

I wasn't as willing to buckle to authority. "You watch the horses. I'll go to the top of the hill."

Without waiting for her to agree, I quietly slid from Feather's back, touching lightly to the ground and passing the reins to Denise. I crept up the hill, briars clawing at my jeans and the bare skin of my arms, until I was nearly to the top. A wide oak tree hid me from view. Sweating from the climb, I crouched down, balancing myself against the rough bark of the tree.

Yellow plastic tape was stretched between the trees, sectioning off a portion of the clearing. Three workers with hand trowels knelt on tarps, overturning the black soil, then carefully sifting it between their fingers. A fourth person hauled full buckets of the sifted dirt to the edge of the clearing, where he dumped the dirt onto a mound. Sheriff Morton, standing next to one of the workers, reached down for something and held it up to the light, then laid it on a tarpaulin that was smoothed over the grass and anchored down at the corners with rocks. On the tarp, in neat rows, were bones.

I scrambled back down the hill to Denise and the horses. "They've dug a pit right where I fell. There're more bones. Lots of them." I took Feather's reins and tossed them over the mare's head. "Maybe it's an ancient burial ground," I said.

She twisted around in her saddle to face me. "Let's get out of here," she said.

"Leave if you want," I said, hoisting myself into the saddle. "I'm going down there."

"Don't be so nosy. You just had a run-in with the man less than a week ago." There she was with that authority thing again.

"So what?" I asked.

"I'll tell you so what: Let's say he gets a restraining order, or whatever it's called, and gets us kicked out of here? Then where are we going to ride?"

"He can't get us kicked out. This is a state park and I pay taxes." Actually, he probably *could* get us kicked out, but there were so many trails going in off the road, how could they monitor them all? Budget cuts in the parks department meant fewer personnel to police the trails.

"Stubborn old mule!" She neatly turned Chevron on his haunches and started in the opposite direction, down the hill.

"Mules just happen to be highly intelligent," I muttered. Her shoulders rose and fell in that "See if I care" way she had. I watched her ride away, then rode over the hill and down into the clearing.

Bathed in sunlight, the maple trees smelled like warm syrup. Between the trees and the road was the thick patch of horsetail and fern through which I had ran only five nights ago. A footpath had been beaten down, leading from the work site to the road. Feather's steel horseshoes and the creaking leather of my saddle announced us. She eyed the yellow plastic tape warily, giving the cordoned-off site a wide berth. "Wow," I said, feigning surprise. "More bones!" No one seemed to be paying attention to me, like I was invisible.

I sat on Feather in the clearing, waiting and watching. Finally, to no one in particular, I said, "I lost an earring the other night." No answer. "Right around here somewhere," I continued, hoping to get the sheriff's attention. "Mind if I look for it?"

The buttons of his shirt were pulled taut across his chest and in the gaps between the strained fabric, a white t-shirt showed through. There were half moons of perspiration beneath his arms. He wiped his plump hands on a handkerchief, then mopped sweat from his forehead.

"Yes, we do mind," he said. "This is a police investigation, not a used jewelry store. If we find an earring, we'll let you know." He pointed toward the road. "For now, I'd appreciate it if you would move along. We've got work to do."

Sheriff Morton was in his mid-fifties, balding and overweight. Even at his best, he was no Mr. Congeniality, but when he was dieting, which was almost all the time, watch out. He made the wicked witch of the west look downright cordial. "Sure, no problem," I said, not letting his irritability bother me. "Mind if I check Feather's girth first?" Before he could answer, I slipped off Feather and lifting the saddle flap, pretended to adjust the girth. One of the soil sifters, a young guy wearing blue jeans and a University of New Mexico athletic jersey, stood up. Arching backward, he stretched his arms overhead. "The soil's been disturbed recently, but whether from the coyotes or by someone else, it's hard to tell," he told the sheriff.

"How long will it take to get a report?" asked Sheriff Morton.

"If we get everything packed up and over to the university today, anywhere from a couple days to two weeks. Depends on what the professor has ahead of us."

"Put priority on it," Sheriff Morton said. "Tell him to call me if there's a problem."

Feather put her head down to graze in the sparse grass. I leaned on her shoulder, gently pushing her in the direction of the tarp where the bones lay. I committed to memory the arrangement of the bones on the tarp, by size and shape, straight ones arranged longest to shortest, odd shapes and fragments in the center. Four skulls were lined up like regimental soldiers on the edge. They looked like human skulls to me, just like the one I'd picked up. When I was sure I could remember the layout of the bones, I got back on Feather and rode home.

*   *   *   *

By the time I stood on the porch of Richard's cornflower blue Cape Cod, the sun glowed rosy golden, slanting low. The trees on the horizon were cast into silhouette. A cool twilight descended.

He'd made a lot of changes to the place in the short time he'd been here. The front door was now fuchsia and though at first I thought it an odd color choice, upon second glance, I decided I liked it. I'd always fancied having a Cape Cod, but when push came to shove and it was time to decide, I worried the stairs would be too much for my arthritic back and Jack's arthritic knee, so we settled on a ranch.

"Carol. To what do I owe this pleasure?" Richard asked, holding the door open.

I felt my face grow warm with embarrassment. I looked beyond him, into the foyer. The dark wooden floor had been stripped and re-stained. "I won't bother you but a second," I said, holding open my hand to show him the earring. "I've lost the mate to this. Did you happen to find it in your truck?"

He picked up the earring and turned it over in beautiful sun-tanned hands. A smile spread across his face and spilled over into a hearty laugh, his sandy hair falling forward. "Louis," he called up the stairs. "Can you come down here for a minute?" He turned, laughing, back to me. "I didn't mean to—"

I stopped listening. Handsome in a different way from Richard, Louis tip-toed down the stairs like Miss America, and in contrast to Richard's ruggedness, Louis moved with a mesmerizing, blue-blooded grace. Mahogany ringlets fringed a strong jaw line and perfectly complemented clear green eyes. When he got closer, I noticed he wore the match to my earring. It took an obvious effort to look away.

"Would you look at what the cat dragged in?" Richard teased.

"Oh, do be civil," said Louis.

"Carol's come for her earring," Richard said, showing Louis the earring in the palm of his hand. Then Richard added, for my benefit, "He found it when he was cleaning my truck, which, quote unquote, 'was a pigsty.'"

"Cleanliness is next to Godliness and all that," Louis said. He twisted a wisp of hair around his index finger and tipped his head. "Be back in a second." He galloped up the stairs so quickly it seemed he had been an illusion.

"It's quite an unusual earring," Richard said. "Where did you get them?"

"Santa Fe. Market day at the Governor's Palace," I said. On summer Fridays, Navajo, Zuni, and Hopi artisans staked a claim on the statesman's piazza, spreading handmade wares on colorful blankets. Turquoise dripped from earrings and necklaces and was set into massive silver belt buckles.

"Beautiful, perfect Santa Fe," Richard said. "Louis will be jealous. He's a painter. He says the natural light of the desert is perfect for painters."

Louis rejoined us, offering me the earrings on a small bed of pale tissue paper that smelled like sandalwood and crinkled when I put it in my pocket. "What's perfect for painters?" he asked.

"Richard was just telling me you're a painter. I am too. Watercolors," I said.

"Look at this one," Richard said, leading me through the foyer and into the living room. "Very Georgia O'Keefe-ish, wouldn't you say?"

Indeed, the painting was of a flower, and it was huge and it was abstract, but any resemblance ended there. Bursting from the center of distorted black petals, the stamens of the flowers were grotesquely oversized and brightly colored, some lemon yellow, others hot pink.

I wondered if oversized stamens and pistils—the reproductive parts of a flower—signified something. And the black petals? What did they mean? Clearly, Richard and Louis would be unimpressed with my plebeian depiction of the Great Lakes area. Pine trees, sand dunes, and harbors with lighthouses were so juvenile in comparison.

Louis stretched the sleeve of his black turtleneck over his hand and wiped a smudge from the glass. "What did I tell you?" Richard said. "He's obsessive about cleanliness."

"The centers of the flowers are so colorful, but why the black petals?" I asked.

"Black is the only true thing in this world," Louis said, not taking his eyes from the painting. "It is the combination of all, all colors, all senses, the beginning and end of all life. Pure and beautiful."

He was right in one respect, that black was the combination of all color. As for the rest, I had my doubts. "But isn't white the absence of all color and therefore the purest?" I asked.

Louis looked at me with new interest. "I knew it! I could tell when I first saw you … a classic watercolorist," Louis said. "I suppose one wouldn't find a tube of white on your palette?" he asked.

"Certainly not," I said. "Between the white of the paper and the dilution of the water, who needs it?" Had I become my college professor, with her unwritten laws and straight and narrow beliefs?

"What do you paint?" Louis asked. "Still-lifes? Portraits?" His thick, curly hair, the color as dark and rich as a sable coat, had a perfect quality about it, as if, in its unruliness, it was exactly the way it was meant to be.

"Landscapes. The woods, Lake Michigan's beaches and lighthouses, life in the Great Lakes," I said. An embarrassingly inadequate answer.

"You look at the same things as I do, yet what we see is different. And we paint what we see," Louis said. "If it was any other way, what need would there be for art?"

He had me there. To avoid further questioning, I veered toward another subject. "Speaking of the woods, the police have found human bones near where you pulled Denise's truck out of the ditch."

"Bones?" Richard asked.

"Lots of them. Skulls too." Somewhere a clock chimed, and it resonated through the house, like a lonely echo, reminding me of the solitary dinner that awaited me at home. What was the point of being married? Jack and I were never together.

Richard brushed his hair back from his eyes. "What are they doing with them? The bones, I mean."

Louis shifted from one foot to the other. He seemed to watch my every move in a way that made me feel uneasy, as if I were being scrutinized. No doubt I had been pronounced hopeless Midwestern hick.

"They're sending them somewhere to be dated. Carbon dated, I suppose, isn't that how age is determined?" I buttoned up my sweater. "I'd better go. When Jack's gone, I like to be in before dark."

"Your husband's gone?" Louis asked.

I nodded. "Went to Indiana to finish building a warehouse. Might not be back until Christmas, except for an occasional week-end or a stolen day here or there." I stepped onto the polished hard-wood floor of the landing. "Thanks for finding the earring."

"How do you manage the horses by yourself? That's a lot of work." Louis said.

It surprised me that he would care. "I'm used to it. I do wish he'd get a different job, though, one where he's home more. Sometimes I think he likes the traveling, so he can get away from me."

"Stupid man," Richard mumbled.

"Pardon?" I asked, wondering what he was getting at.

"Just kidding," Richard said.

"Unfortunately, this job pays better than average, and we need the money."

"Aren't you afraid all alone?" Louis asked.

"I'm not alone, with the cats racing from one end of the house to the other and fighting constantly." Their blank stares reminded me that not everyone knew my home was practically a shelter for homeless cats. "I take in stray cats," I explained. "Not that I specifically set out to do that, it's just the way it turned out."

"No kidding? How many are there?" Richard asked.

"Eight at last count. Nine if you include the feral who comes for the food I put out in the barn."

"Wow. How much food do they eat?" This time it was Louis asking the question.

"Forty pounds of kibble and sixty cans of soft food a month, plus all the extras. Hairball treats, catnip, and tuna once a week." I saw the incredulous looks on their faces. "I know, I know. I hear about it constantly from Jack. 'Those cats are eating us out of house and home,'" I said, mimicking Jack's deep voice. "What am I supposed to do? I can't turn them away, half-starved like they are when they come to me."

"They're hardly protection, though. A dog would be better," Louis said. His green eyes, flecked with gold, pulled me to him like a lure.

"It wouldn't be a good lifestyle for a dog, locked up in the house or a kennel all day while I'm at work." He was near me, his hand on the brass door handle. The scent he wore reminded me of the forest. It was a deep, earthy smell.

To the right of where we were standing, in a small mud room, was a stackable washer and dryer. "That's exactly what we've been looking for," I said, pointing to the appliances. "Our half-bath doubles as a utility room," I explained. "It's a pretty tight fit. But if we put the dryer on top of the washer, like that, it would free up that much space." I stepped into the laundry room. "Can it take a full-sized load?" I asked, pressing in the small lever that unlocked the door.

"Don't—," Richard said.

An avalanche of dirty laundry fell to the floor. "Oh, I'm so sorry!" I said, bending to pick up a pair of brown jersey gloves, stiff with dried mud, from the floor. The mud crumbled to a fine powder when I touched them. "I had no idea," I explained. "I wanted to see how much the machine held." A pair of dark socks were tangled in the sleeves of a white shirt and hung from the washer's opening.

"It's all right, really," Richard said, untangling the shirt and socks.

Louis jerked the socks from Richard's hands and picked up the jersey gloves. "How many times have I told you not to mix whites with darks?"

Obviously, this was a source of contention between them. "Oh, no, I didn't mean to get you in trouble," I said. "And now I've gone and made a mess too." A small heap of dirt lay on the floor underneath the opening of the washing machine. "If you have a broom," I said, looking around me, "I'll sweep it up."

"Don't worry about it," Richard said, good naturedly, taking a broom and dustpan from the hall closet. "I'll get it."

"Are you working on a garden for next year?" I asked.

Louis looked up from stuffing the light-colored clothes back into the washer. He dropped the dark socks and gloves into a hamper in the corner. "That's an odd question. Why do you ask?" He measured detergent, then poured it into the dispenser.

"It just seemed like there was a lot of dried mud on the laundry, that's all," I said.

He set the dials and pushed one of them in. The machine began to fill with water. "Now that you mention it, we *are* considering putting one out behind the barn," Louis said. "I love gardening, especially flowers. Of course, Richard, ever practical, goes more for vegetables."

"It's the only time Louis doesn't mind getting his hands dirty," Richard said, sweeping the pile of dirt into the dustpan.

"I'm sorry, it really wasn't any of my business." Things popped out of my mouth so quickly that sometimes I wondered if my brain and my mouth belonged to two separate people. "Thanks again for finding the earring," I said, heading for the door.

"Keep me posted if you learn anything new about the bones," Richard said.

"Are you interested in archeology?" I asked.

"No, not me. I'm just curious, that's all," Richard said. "Louis is the archeologist. He almost had his degree, then switched his major to art."

Chapter Four

Eight cats licked tuna from eight paper plates, each pushing his plate across the kitchen floor with his nose. The newspaper I read was folded and propped against the salt and pepper shakers on the dining room table. A thick drip of melted cheese fell from my sandwich, partially obliterating the headline that ended with "woman murdered." I scraped the cheese off with a fingernail and read the word "Third." Three women in as many months, all killed after rainstorms.

I wiped greasy fingers on a paper napkin and turned the page. Tomb quiet in the house, the ringing phone was like a burglar alarm in the dead of night. I jumped, dropping my sandwich into the tomato soup.

"Did you hear about the horses?" Denise screeched over the phone, Led Zeppelin blasting in the background.

"What horses?" I asked.

"Todd, can you turn that down? I'm on the phone," Denise yelled. "Haven't you seen the newspaper?"

"I just picked it up a minute ago; I'm still on the front page." Or what's left of the front page, the print smearing as I mopped up the soup with a paper towel. "And the television hasn't been on since Jack left." He hadn't even been gone a full twelve hours yet.

The music abruptly stopped. "Thank God!" Denise said, her voice returning to a normal decibel level. "Look on the back of the front-page section."

The photos were of horses, heads hanging, standing in stalls knee deep in muck. Bony hips protruded through coats covered in dried dung. My heart lurched, sickened. "Where is this?" I asked, my eyes quickly scanning the article.

"A racing stable near Ann Arbor. Hilldale Acres."

"Looks like Hellhole Acres to me."

"Thirty horses in training. The owners of the farm just packed up and left."

"Didn't the neighbors notice anything odd?"

"By the time they did, a couple of weeks had passed. Four horses were already dead."

My anger rose. "I'd like to lock up people like that and let them starve to death. Let them see what it's like," I said. Wasn't that the way it was supposed to be, an eye for an eye?

"Remember Sue, the lady who runs Horse Heaven, the rescue league?" Denise asked.

"Blond hair, fifty-ish?" I asked.

"That's her. She called this afternoon. She's got room for twenty horses, so she needs foster homes for the other six. She wondered if I could take them or knew of anybody else. Todd says I can take one temporarily."

I tried to think of anyone else I knew who might be equipped to handle an extra horse. "Normally, I'd suggest Lida taking one, but she's not home. She's visiting her sister out of state."

"Did I tell you I saw her and Perry last week, in the produce aisle of the grocery store? I was headed over to say hello, but when I got closer I could tell they were fighting over something. I didn't want to get in the middle of it, so I hung back ... pretended like I was looking over the grapefruit."

"What was the fight about?"

"Hell, I don't know, but talk about a knock-down, drag-out! Whew-ee!"

"Maybe that's why she decided to go to her sister's. He was strange on the phone today."

"He's an odd-ball kind of guy anyway. Sort of gives me the creeps. I've never gotten along with him all that well. Hey, what about you taking one of the horses?"

"Jack would kill me." At the bottom of the page was a photo of a gray horse, his big, dark eyes pleading. This was my chance to do something good and true and commendable. Something totally unselfish. Something I could be proud of. And I'd always wanted a gray horse, so why was I hesitating? "Jack will boil me in oil," I said.

"You've got two horses in a four-stall barn," Denise said. She paved the route to a guilt trip I was mapping.

"I know, I know. It's just that Jack's gone, and ..."

"Don't you see? That makes it perfect! Tell him you had to make a quick decision and he wasn't around, which is totally true. Want to run over there with me?"

It was only temporary, just until Horse Heaven found new homes for the horses. Those dark eyes jumped off the page. For once, I could do something totally unplanned and against all my better sensibilities. Something financially reckless. And Jack's absence did make the perfect excuse. It would serve him right, too, since he's never here to make the decisions. What could he say?

"I'll be right over."

*   *   *   *

The photos couldn't have prepared me for the stench inside the barn or the magnitude of the animals' suffering. The horses that were still able to walk were being carefully loaded into vans. Ropes were thrown over the rafters of the barn and with the help of pulleys, the horses that were down were gently lifted to their feet and stabilized in rubber slings made from old inner tubes.

A local veterinarian and a photographer were cataloging each animal removed from the farm, recording height, color, and gender, and making a quick sketch of their white markings. Most of the animals were young race horses in training. We found Sue in a stall, kneeling next to an emaciated animal lying flat on its side in the filth. It was the gray. His eyes were frozen, not even a flicker left. "Hey, Denise," she said, smiling when she saw us. "I hope you brought about fifteen trailers and twice as many strong backs." Across from Sue stood two men with wooden planks wedged under the horse's side. "This is Mike and Dave," Sue said, thumbing toward the men. "We're trying to roll the horse up, so I can slide the sling underneath, but every time we lift him, he just groans and sinks right back down again." She looked at her watch. "We might have to let this one go."

Mike began pulling the rope down from the rafters. His expressionless face made me wonder what he felt inside. There must be a fine line between caring and caring too much, having to shut down part of yourself so you could do what had to be done. So you could handle reality.

I wiped the back of my hand across my face. "The ammonia is so strong in here my eyes are watering," I said, hopefully explaining away my tears. The last thing I wanted was for them to think I was just another overly emotional woman. Then I had an idea. "If Mike and Dave wedge the boards under him and prop him up, and Denise and I hold him up from the opposite side, couldn't the four of us lift him enough for Sue to slide the sling underneath? He can't weigh much."

"Even if we do, there's no guarantee he'll stand on his own after that," Sue said.

"This one ain't gonna' make it anyway," Dave said as he nudged the horse with the pointy toe of his boot. "We're just wasting our time."

Sue stood and stretched, rocking back on her heels, then leaned against the wall. She looked exhausted. "We'll give him one more try." To us, she said, "Get two more planks out of my trailer. It's the red gooseneck out in the lot."

Denise and I high-stepped carefully through the mud of the parking lot. Away from the confined odors of the barn, the urine and manure and decaying flesh, the night air was fresh. The stars had come out. "If he won't stand, how will we get him into my barn?"

"Your barn! You've got to be kidding. Do you have to pick the one that'll be the hardest to rehabilitate?"

Those dark eyes told me he had given up, resigned himself to his fate, and that only made my fight for him stronger. Wasn't I always rooting for the underdog? "He's the one I want."

Denise stopped and grabbed my arm. "Whoa, one minute here. We're giving these horses foster homes, not permanent ones. Do you realize what we're talking here? Months, maybe a year or more, of special care, feed, medication, and vet bills. Big bucks. If you foster, the charity pays the bills."

"I'll work weekends to make extra money."

"If you do that, you won't have time to care for him. And even if you did find the time and money, there's no guarantee. After months, you might still lose him."

"I can't leave him. Did you see the way he looked at us?" I was such a sucker for an animal in need. If only I cared for people as much. But then, animals were way more loyal and way less judgmental. They always loved you the same no matter what.

She looked down, gouging the toe of her boot into the mud. "How the hell do we sling him up in my trailer?"

Denise's trailer was a two-horse ramp load, with mangers in the front and an escape opening from the right-side stall. "We tie one end of a rope to the partition running down the middle of the trailer, run it underneath the horse, then out the sliding window."

"Then where do we go with it? It won't work." She pulled her cigarettes out of her pocket and absently tapped the packet against the palm of her hand.

I kept quiet, knowing Denise never made a decision without first taking the time for a smoke. After she lit one and had taken a couple puffs, I said, "How about we pull the rope out the window and back to the trailer hitch?"

"Holy shit, do you know how dangerous that could be? What if he gets tangled in the rope?"

Once again, I was silently thankful for Denise's persuadability. "I'll ride in the back, on the left side, to make sure he doesn't."

"We need the other stall for my horse."

"Yeah, you're right. I forgot," I said, deflated.

We got to Sue's trailer and flung the doors open. Electrical cords, rakes, shovels, lead ropes, and buckets spilled from it. A burlap sack of oats leaned against the side of the truck, a feed scoop sticking out of the open bag. We rummaged through the mess, looking for the boards.

"Here they are," Denise called from the back of the truck. She climbed over the tailgate and lifted two planks from the bed of the truck, resting one end of each board on the tailgate. "Give me a hand."

Sliding the planks over the tailgate, I pulled them out of the truck. We each took one, heaving the ends up onto our shoulders, and started back. The closer we got to the barn, the stronger the smell became. I wasn't relishing going back inside. All the while, I was still thinking of how we could get the gray horse home.

"I could sit in the manger," I said.

"What?" Denise asked, confused.

"The manger. We run the ropes from the stall partition, under the horse, out the window and up to the hitch. I'll ride in the manger to make sure nothing happens."

"And if it does, how am I going to know, up in the cab of the truck? What if he freaks out?" She must have seen my pained expression. "Let's ask Sue. Maybe she can come up with an idea."

We brought the planks into the stall. Mike and Dave had positioned their boards under the gray, on the side he lay on, ready to lift him. Denise and I got into place and after the four of us had the horse propped up, we raised his belly just barely enough to give Sue room to snake her hands under him, and push the sling underneath and through to the other side. Then Sue came over to our side and attached the ropes to the pulleys. Everything was set to go.

We joined the veterinarian, waiting in the aisle. "Sometimes they scramble when they're up," he said. "Sometimes they don't. You just never know."

Sue wiped her hands on an old towel. "This one may not have enough left in him to give us any trouble," she said.

"Will he be able to be trailered?" I asked the vet.

"He might be one of those I recommend be left on the property a while longer, to get them stabilized before moving them."

"Can I take him when he's ready?" I asked.

"He'll be a lot of work," the vet said. "And you know there's always the danger of founder. Can't just start pouring feed into them. Seems like a nice horse, though."

*   *   *   *

Nothing lit the way except our headlights and lightning bugs cavorting in the ditches. We'd gotten the horse Denise was to foster into her barn and settled down in a freshly bedded stall, separated from Denise's own horses by an empty stall between them.

"I don't know how Sue does it," I said. "I'm exhausted and we were only there a couple of hours. She's been there all day and now she's spending the night in that awful place."

"She's a saint."

"Saint. That's a good name for the gray horse, don't you think?"

"Seems appropriate."

"The vet said I can probably bring him home sometime next week." I looked at my watch. It was already early Sunday morning. "Actually, this week, now." It was for his own good that he remain under the care of Sue and the veterinarian for a little while longer. Denise stopped at the end of my driveway. "Remember when we first started showing horses?" I asked. "All the elaborate planning we did so we never ended up anywhere that involved backing the trailer up?"

"How could I forget? Everything revolved around where we could or couldn't go with the trailer. It was like driving a car with no reverse. To tell you the truth, I still don't like backing up," she said. We both giggled and Denise started coughing. "Don't make me laugh," she said.

"Someday you gotta' stop smoking."

"Yeah, I know."

I got out and limped around the front of Denise's truck. My back ached. The smell of that horrible barn was everywhere. It was on my hair, my face, and my clothes. Poor Saint would have to endure it a few more days, but then he'd be home. At least he'd have some food in his belly and a clean bed of sawdust tonight. I waved her off, the lights on her truck swallowed up by the night.

I put my key in the lock and turned it, yawning. That's odd, I thought, no cats to greet me at the front door. No cats in the living room. Where were they hiding? "Kitties," I called, expecting them to pop out as I walked down the hallway. I dropped my purse on the bedroom chair and sat on the edge of the bed, too tired to undress. Then I flopped backward and fell asleep.

It rained hard in the night, torrents pelting the windows. A loud thunderclap jarred me awake. I stumbled to the bathroom. At first, the bathroom light blinded me, but then suddenly I was wide awake, with my heart pounding into my throat. I choked back a scream. Someone had scrawled *Mind your own business* on the bathroom mirror.

Blood-red lipstick, a color I never used, lay on the counter. I picked up the tube and turned it over in my hands. The bottom read Drop Dead Red.

Chapter Five

Louis answered the door wearing a woman's yellow terry cloth robe, belted around the waist with a sash of the same fabric. "Nice robe. I like yellow," I said, as if it were perfectly normal. There were more important things on my mind. "Richard around?" I asked.

"In the shower." He pointed up the stairs.

Somehow it seemed futile to ask him if he'd seen anyone or anything strange around my house the night before. Just what would this man consider unusual? "Somebody broke into my house last night. Jimmied the dining room window open and left a cryptic message on my bathroom mirror."

"Anything stolen?" Richard asked from the top of the stairs, buttoning the cuffs of a white oxford shirt. The front hung open, revealing the bronzed skin of his chest. Worn blue jeans molded seductively to his long, lean legs. While admiring his looks, I reminded myself that not only was I already married, albeit to a man who chose to be gone 75 percent of the time, but that Richard lived with a man who occasionally dressed as a woman.

Theft hadn't crossed my mind. Just knowing someone had been in my house gave me the creeps. How could I be sure they weren't still there, hiding in a closet or a dark corner of the basement? "I didn't notice anything missing, but then, I wasn't really looking either. I was more freaked out by the writing on the mirror."

My bedroom in the back of the house suddenly made me claustrophobic, so I'd slept in an easy chair in the front room. Jack's pistol had lain cold and heavy in my lap, while I dozed a light, worried sleep.

"What have you got to protect yourself?" Richard asked.

Hadn't we just discussed this, something about how a dog would protect me? Now I knew why the cats didn't show themselves when I came home last night. Cats don't protect—they hide. It's just their way. "Jack left me a handgun," I said.

"Did he teach you how to shoot it?" Richard asked as he sat on the polished wooden stairs, pulling on a pair of socks.

"Years ago. It's ready to go. Point and shoot, just like a salad shooter," I said, attempting humor.

"What was the message?" Richard asked.

"'Mind your own business,' written in lipstick," I said.

"What the hell is that supposed to mean? In lipstick?" Richard asked, incredulously.

"Sounds self-explanatory to me," Louis said, leaning against the stair railing. Curly black hair escaped from underneath the shawl collar of the robe.

Richard shot him a glance. "Care to expound on that opinion, Louis?"

"Well, she's obviously pissed someone off. 'Mind your own business' means just that. It shouldn't take any explaining."

"Any ideas of how it might have gotten there?"

Louis shrugged. "Beats me. But if you're asking me personally, I was here with you last night, remember?" His face held a look of feigned hurt. He went into the kitchen. "Coffee, anyone?" he called cheerily. "Hazelnut creme."

It smelled delicious, but straight Colombian was what I favored, strong and black. "No thanks," I answered. I'd spent the night in a state of semi-sleep, in which I imagined the entire time that I was still awake. I felt muddled and groggy.

Richard rolled his eyes back. "He's always making that damned flavored shit," he muttered, barely loud enough to hear.

"What'd you say?" asked Louis, who had suddenly returned and was pressing a steaming mug into Richard's hand.

"Nothing," Richard said, taking the cup. "Mind your own business," he mused. "What's the significance of that? Is anybody mad at you?"

"Not enough to break into my home." Only six months ago, Richard's house had been inhabited by two very different people, a mother and daughter, until the daughter was murdered. I unwittingly became involved in solving the case. There had been three people mad at me then, one of them Denise, who would never resort to breaking into my home. Why should she? Besides, she and I had been together last night. Another, an elderly neighbor, Marge, ditto on breaking into my home. And unless the residents of hell stalk the earth at night, there was no way the third was going to bother me again. I stopped believing in ghosts when I was eight.

"What color was it?" Louis asked. He drank from a mug that was zebra striped and was emblazoned with "Detroit Zoological Park" in bold black letters.

"What color was what?"

"The lipstick," Louis said.

"Louis," Richard said, scowling, "What the hell difference does the color of the lipstick make?"

"I just wondered, that's all," Louis said, apparently hurt. "Looks like someone got up on the wrong side of the bed." With a sneer and a whoosh of his robe, Louis flounced from the room.

"Don't mind him. Sometimes he's an ass," Richard said.

I sank onto the step next to Richard, glad to be rid of Louis. Call me old-fashioned, single-minded, or whatever, but there was something downright ludicrous in attempting a serious conversation with a man wearing a splashy yellow robe.

"He's jealous of you."

"Huh? Me? You've got to be kidding! What on earth for?" I was flabbergasted.

Richard's eyes were an incredible shade of icy blue, like the sky on a below-zero January morning. I was mesmerized, afraid to look away, and I remembered something I'd read about wild animals. How looking into their eyes became a struggle for dominance and the first to look away was the weaker, conceding defeat. I looked away.

He shrugged his shoulders. "He gets crazy every now and then. I blow it off and eventually it passes. Right now he's got this thing in his mind about you and me."

"You and me? That *is* crazy. I'm married, remember?"

"Unfortunately."

I laughed nervously. Was he flirting with me? Afraid that he had read my mind—and embarrassed by the prospect of that—I changed the subject. "Should I call the sheriff about the break in?"

"You haven't already?" he asked, surprised.

Actually, I had only given it a fleeting thought. "No, I wasn't sure ... I mean, I didn't know if I should. I don't want Jack to find out. He'd be all upset and come right home and then he'll get behind in his work. Next thing I know, I'm spending Christmas alone, too." The clock in the hallway chimed, startling me. "It's just that I have this ridiculous, creepy feeling that someone is still in the house. I know it's dumb, but I can't help it."

Richard put an arm around me, drawing me close. After the anxiety of the night, I closed my eyes for a moment and relaxed in how good it felt. I imagined he was Jack. "Would it help if I came over and checked things out?"

"Would you?" I practically gushed. "I'd feel so much safer."

*   *   *   *

As Richard checked the basement, I brewed coffee, using a coarse Colombian grind and my French press. I opened the cupboard and took out my Wedgwood cups, saucers and creamer set—wedding gifts from my mother. Dainty blue flowers covered the cups, their rims a delicate band of gold. Jack disliked anything fancy, so I rarely used them. The first time Jack drank coffee from the small cups, he was like a cowboy at an English tea party. Heavy, plain stoneware was more Jack's style; he was strictly utilitarian.

I stood back. The linen napkins were the exact shade of blue as the design on the china. Holding one of the cups up to the sunlight, the outline of my fingers was visible through the delicate porcelain. I put the cup back, turning the handle at exactly four o'clock, the way I'd been taught.

Richard tromped up the basement steps. "Looks fine to me," he pronounced. He ran his fingers through his wavy hair, an unruly sandy lock falling back onto his handsome face.

"Sorry it was such a mess," I said. "Jack's a pack rat—never throws anything away. 'Put it in the basement,' he says. 'Might need it someday.' He can't find a thing in that colossal junk heap he's got down there." It was the one area of the house in which he had free rein. I figured no one else ever saw it anyway. Well, *almost* no one else. I poured steaming coffee into one of the elegant cups.

Richard pulled out a chair and sat down. "Nice place you've got here."

"Thank you," I said, pleased. "Still think I should call the sheriff?"

"No, don't bother. I've checked the whole house," Richard said. "Just make sure you lock up when you leave and at night. And remember, I'm only across the road if you need me."

*   *   *   *

In the afternoon, Denise and I saddled the horses and rode north of the Pinnacle, where the trail narrows and winds to a sandy hilltop. It was a rare early October day that felt more like July, a pleasant reminder of summer.

Our cameras slung around our necks, we posed the horses and snapped photos of each other. Photos that added to hundreds of others like them, memories of horses we had and didn't have. Occasionally, we took the old photos out to poke fun at dated clothes or whine about how skinny we once were. I'd been sucking in my stomach for the camera since I was seventeen and still I'd never been as thin as I wanted to be. I loved food too much.

"What's hanging in that tree?" Denise asked, pointing to a tree on the other side of the trail.

It glittered in the sun. "A prism?" We rode closer to get a better look. "There's something else," I said, "It looks like a shirt." Denise reached the tree before me, Echo stopping to snack on tall grass along the way. He pulled hard against me when I tried to raise his head.

"What the hell?" Denise said, pulling a scrap of denim fabric from the tree. "An apron? What is an apron doing tied to a tree branch way out here?"

We had found odd articles in the woods before, usually attributing them to items fallen from a saddle bag or a rider's pockets; gloves or cigarette lighters, insect repellent and sunblock, an occasional dollar bill. There were other things in the tree as well: a child's blue plastic saxophone, an ornate beaded spider, a leather lace threaded through lettered beads that spelled, "Mom, I luv you."

"How strange," I said. "What does all this junk mean?" I slid off Echo and hooked the rein over the saddle horn to keep his head from the grass.

"Maybe it's a shrine, like alongside the highway where somebody died."

"Except nobody died here," I said. I bent down to pick up a small piece of paper, rolled up like a cigarette and held in place with a rubber band, which lay at the base of the tree. "Look, it's one of those notices the post office leaves when they can't deliver something."

"Like when they need a signature or something is too big to fit in your mailbox?"

"Yeah, only it says 'final notice,'" Suddenly, I sensed something stirring behind me and felt a breeze, as light as a breath on my back. I whipped around, but no one was there. "I'm getting the creeps. Let's get out of here." As I wound the notice back up, the rubber band broke; I cursed silently, twisted and knotted the elastic and put it back exactly where I'd found it. I slid my left foot into the stirrup and after hopping twice, hoisted myself into the saddle. I swung Echo around to the trail.

Without warning, the sand under his hoof gave way and he sank, as if he'd fallen into a hole. Jerking violently, he stumbled backward on the sandy hill, but now only fell deeper, his hind legs in the sand up to his hocks. He rolled over on his side, my leg caught under him.

We've fallen into a bog. But I knew exactly where the bogs were, the places to stay away from. Denise screamed. Echo struggled to get up and I tried to roll clear of him. His knee came at me and I turned my head, hearing a loud thump as his hoof hit my helmet. Pressing my hand into the sand, I pushed myself up, but the sand underneath fell away and I sank in deeper.

Then my fingers touched something cold. Thinking it was the tap root of the tree, I used it to pull myself out of range of Echo's hooves. It wasn't a root at all, but a hand, with a ring on the pinkie finger. We had fallen into a shallow grave.

Chapter Six

Echo stood and shook himself, the sandy loam falling from his coat like rain. The body beneath his hooves was only partially visible—a hand and an arm, and now the delicate bones of a woman's throat. I grabbed for Echo's reins, but loose dirt caved in all around my feet, swallowing my ankles like quicksand. "Dammit!" I yelled. Echo threw his head up and bolted. His hindquarters bunched up under him and he sunfished, bucking and galloping down the hill. "Sonofabitch!"

"Holy shit!" was all Denise managed to say.

"I'll kill that sonofabitch," I said, watching Echo's receding chestnut butt. I slammed my helmet down.

"Do you think it's anybody we know?" Denise asked, looking down at the body.

Somehow it seemed irreverent of her to call the corpse "it," like it should have a name or at least be "he" or "she." "I sure hope not." Echo high-tailed it around the bend and was out of sight. "That damned horse is lucky I don't carry a gun when I ride. There goes my cell phone. I don't suppose you've got one so we can call the police?"

"Nope. Sorry. You going up for a closer look?" she asked, her voice quavering.

"Not on your life. Don't touch anything." Then I remembered the postal notice and how I'd already left my fingerprints on it. "Why is this shit always happening to us?" I asked Denise, who was sitting on Chevron, looking into the grave. "I'm not riding with you anymore, every time I do, a dead person is involved."

"I could say the same for you," Denise said.

"And you're not leaving me here, all alone, like you did last time, while you go for the sheriff." Slapping the sides of my thighs, I dusted off my blue jeans. "Chevron ever been ridden double?"

She nodded. "His previous owner told me not to try it. He bucks."

Great. A bucking bronco. Still, it was better than walking or the alternative, which was staying here. I looked at the hand, sticking up out of the sand. "Crow hops or big bucks?"

She shrugged. "Guess we'll find out, won't we? I'm just letting you know, that's all."

Weather-wise, the day seemed so idyllic that it was hard to believe what we'd just found. The scent of the maples warming in the mid-afternoon sun was sweet. "Body hasn't been here long," I said, more to myself than Denise.

"What makes you say that?"

I sniffed. "Doesn't smell yet."

"Do you have to be so gross? Besides, it's still mostly buried." She slid from Chevron's back and, with trepidation, walked toward the corpse. Watching her, I wondered, did she have the guts? Would she brush the sand away from the face to see who it was? For once, my curiosity wasn't getting the better of me. I let her do the investigating.

"I don't think we should touch anything," I told her. "Let's get to a phone and report this."

She knelt near the base of the tree adorned with the ornaments, stretching over the grave to avoid the loose sand. Were the trinkets sacrificial? Were they the killer's calling card? I remembered something in the newspaper article about the murdered women. "Denise, it rained last night!"

She looked up at me quizzically. "Yeah, so?"

"Every time it rains, another woman gets murdered."

"You're right," she said, looking up at me, her face ashen. "But the newspaper never said anything about a tree with ornaments. If it were linked to the other murders, wouldn't the killer use the same methods?"

"How do we know he didn't? What if ..." I was thinking fast, my mind skipping ahead. "What if it was intentionally left out of the papers to trap the murderer?"

"What? How do you figure that would help anything?"

"The only other person that would know, besides the police, or whoever found the bodies, would be the killer. They could use it to trap him."

"Or maybe the other trees just haven't been found yet." Her shaking hand went slowly to the sand near the throat, as if she were deciding just how badly she wanted to know whose face was hidden by that thin layer of dirt.

I got that funny feeling again, like someone was behind me, their breath tickling the hairs on the back of my neck. "Let's go," I said. I wanted to leave this terrible place as soon as possible, on foot or on Chevron's back; it didn't matter anymore. I began walking down the trail. If there was one thing I didn't fancy, it was hiking the two miles back, but I'd just as soon do that as stay here. If she was as spooked as I was, she'd stick with me.

"Hang on," she called. "I'm coming!" She was struggling with the stirrup and hopping on one foot, her skin-tight blue jeans not allowing for much flexibility. When she finally got on, she rode Chevron up alongside me and took her foot out of the left stirrup. "Get up."

"Poor horse," I said, silently calculating our combined weights. "What a load."

"Maybe the extra weight will make him think twice about bucking," she said.

"On the other hand, it might cause him to buck more." The saddle shifted as I pulled myself up. I held onto the cantle, feeling like an awkward seven-year-old on her first pony ride. Denise's closely cropped hair smelled of strawberry shampoo. The sunlight dissected each strand into auburn and gold and mahogany.

"Any guesses who it is?" she asked.

I didn't want to guess. I was *afraid* to guess. "Hopefully no one we know," I said. "We did the right thing by leaving."

"What if we get blamed for leaving the scene of a crime? Is that against some law?"

"What else could we do, with no cell phone? We'll call the sheriff the first chance we get. There won't be time to blame us for anything," I said. Chevron's stride was smoother and longer than Echo's quick pony-like gait.

"Let's take the main trail back. It's quicker," she said. "Think Echo's back home by now?"

"I wouldn't care if I ever saw that damned horse again, except he's wearing my saddle and that I *do* want back." I was thoroughly disgusted with that animal.

I sat behind Denise's saddle, my legs around Chevron's broad flat back. She didn't suggest trotting or cantering to cut minutes and I was glad, since I wasn't sure of how efficient I'd be at staying on. My days of riding bareback had been over for quite some time.

When we got to the creek, it was swollen with last night's rain, making it too wide to jump. The approach was deep with muck. "Horseshoe graveyard up ahead," Denise warned. "Curl your toes around your shoes, Chev." She reined him over to the narrowest point to cross and lightly turned her spur in. He poked one foot into the mire, then balked when the oozing mud sucked him in halfway up to his knee. He jumped backward.

"I'll get off and walk across," I said. It was too much to expect of him, the river being twice as wide as normal and him carrying double weight.

"He should go when I ask," Denise said stubbornly. She spurred him again, this time harder and he surged forward. Both knees sank. He piaffed in the inky muck, lumps of it flying past my ears. My fingers gripped the cantle, but the leather was smooth, and it didn't offer much hold. Chevron reared and I slid off. My helmet, the strap of which I'd foolishly left unbuckled, flew off. I landed in a backward somersault, my head hitting the sharp edge of a rock. *Dumped twice in one day. That's got to be some kind of record.* Denise screamed and jumped off.

Chevron was trying to pull his hind legs from the muck. His front end came up off the ground again. A heavy-boned horse, probably 1,200 pounds, I thought he was going to roll over me. I tried to move out of his way, but the mud slowed my movement. One hind hoof came down on my hand, the other on my ankle.

Cool mud closed around me, encasing me like a mummy. Staying completely still, there was no pain. But when I began to crawl up out of the creek, a strange sick feeling gripped my stomach, like I'd had the wind knocked out of me. Sweat broke out on my temples.

"You okay?" Denise asked, kneeling by my side.

I didn't know. I wasn't quite sure of anything. It seemed that everything and nothing hurt at the same time. Denise was a blur.

"Holy shit!" she said.

"What?" I asked, alarmed by the tone of her voice.

"Look at your hand!" She pointed to it.

Things didn't seem to be in the right places. Things like fingers and the small fine bones that connected them to my wrist. "The foot bone's connected to the leg bone ..." I giggled. What were the rest of the words? What was wrong with me? At one time I could have recited the entire silly song.

"This isn't funny!" she barked.

I started to cry. "I'm sorry. Please don't be mad." I flopped over on my side. "I'm really tired," I said. All I wanted to do was stretch out right here and go to sleep. My eyes felt leaden with drowsiness.

"I've got to get help. Stay in these weeds and don't make any noise. I'll be back as soon as I can." She winced in sympathy when I laid my swollen hand on my thigh.

"Why can't I make any noise?" I asked, wondering why she would say such a thing. Who did she think I was going to talk to?

"Whoever left that body might still be hanging around." She pulled the tall grass up around me, in an attempt, I assumed, to disguise my hiding place.

"Don't worry. I'll stay right here," I said, patting the warm, damp ground next to me. Even if I had wanted to, I didn't have the energy to crawl anywhere.

"Lay back, so you can't be seen." She pushed me down.

"Who died and made you God?" Her bossiness was getting on my nerves.

"Will you please keep quiet? And for once, don't argue."

I giggled. "Look, Denise," I said, holding up my hand, "My hand is as big as Jack's. In fact, I think it's even bigger." For some odd reason, I found this funny. "I'm going to take a nap now," I told her.

"No!" She slapped me.

My first instinct was to slap her back, but couldn't muster the energy. My arms and legs felt heavy. *Just what business was it of hers if I took a nap?* She could be so annoying at times.

It got harder to keep my eyes open. They hovered half-closed, and my line of vision narrowed to a slit, until I could no longer fight it. I could feel myself drifting off to sleep. I was lying on a riverbank, looking up at the sky. The sun felt warm on my face. A dragonfly flitted above me, his silvery iridescent blue and green wings changing colors as he dipped and rose. There was the sound of footsteps, not ordinary footsteps, but like those of elephants, heavy thuds that shook the ground. When I opened my eyes, dust hung thick in the air. I was in the shade, propped against a tree. The noise went on. A thud, a scrape, a thud, a scrape.

Perry came up over the hill, his boots kicking up dust in the trail. Behind him he dragged something by a rope, but I couldn't tell what it was. I called weakly to him, the sound of my own voice reverberating in my head. "Perry?"

Parting the orange hawkweed that tickled my nose, I said, "Over here," but it came out as little more than a croak.

My temples throbbed as waves of pain washed over me. But now Perry was here and I could sleep. Notwithstanding his strange behavior of late, I knew he would take care of everything. After all, I'd known him for twenty years. The nausea subsided somewhat when I laid my head back down and closed my eyes. When I opened them again, Perry took a coil of binder twine from the pocket of his jeans. He wrapped the rough cord around my good wrist. "You would have to get in the way, wouldn't you?" he mumbled, pulling the rope tight and roughly jerking it behind my body.

In confusion, I asked, "What are you doing?" When he touched my other hand I screamed. Then he was gone, as if I had screamed him away, and I told myself, it was all a dream and I heard Denise's voice.

"Perry," Denise said, "You startled me. What are you doing out here?"

"Nice day. Thought I'd go up to the overlook and have a couple beers, just take in the view. I thought I heard something, so I came over to investigate and it turned out to be Carol. What happened? All I've gotten from her is gibberish."

"Echo dumped her and took off, so we doubled up on Chevron. We had trouble crossing the creek and she got dumped again. Her helmet flew off and she hit her head on a rock. Then he stepped on her hand and ankle. Guess I didn't hide her as well as I thought."

"What're you hiding her from?" Perry asked.

"We found a body on the north side of the Pinnacle. Some weirdo hung toys and odds and ends in a tree next to the body. It's really strange," she said. "Sheriff Morton's on his way."

Perry pointed to the marks in the dirt, leading from the trail into the chicory, goldenrod and Queen Anne's Lace where I lay. "Next time you hide someone, cover your tracks," he said.

"What's the matter with me?" I asked no one in particular. Baling twine held branches, each about a foot long and pale green where the bark had been freshly whittled away, to my swollen wrist. Fragments of dream mixed with fragments of reality in a cauldron of confusion. How long had I lain here?

"Your wrist may be broken," Perry answered. "I've made a splint to brace it, just in case. The swelling doesn't seem to have gotten worse." He brushed the damp hair from my forehead.

Had I imagined him roughly tying my hands? Had that been a dream? Had I mistaken him tying my hands for him having made the makeshift splint? I looked at my other wrist, the one Chevron had not stepped on, and there were red marks on the flesh.

"Looks like you've got a nasty bump on the head, too," he said.

"I'm so sleepy," I said, wilting back against the tree again.

"You might have a concussion," Denise said.

"I can't have a broken hand now." I was thinking of my eighty-three-year-old neighbor. "Who'll bring Marge's groceries?" Then I remembered Saint and the promise I'd made. "And what about Saint?"

"Don't worry about Saint or Marge right now." Denise folded a bandanna into a triangle and knotted it. "Do you think you can make it to the trailhead? I left the truck there. Otherwise, we have to get an ambulance."

"No! No ambulances." I was adamant, assuming our insurance did not cover the cost.

"I can carry her," Perry said.

Being carried by him, or anyone else for that matter, did not sound appealing. I stood up to demonstrate that it wouldn't be necessary. My ankle hurt, but if I didn't put my full weight on it, I thought I could make it the mile back to the truck. Worse than anything else was my throbbing head.

Denise slipped the bandanna around my neck. "Slide your arm in here."

"Why'd you hit me?" I asked her.

"I don't know what you're talking about."

"Back there, before you left. You hit me." Was I wrong? Had I imagined her slapping me the same way I'd mistaken Perry's making a splint for tying me up?

She looked away and I knew she remembered. "When a person has a concussion, you shouldn't let them sleep. I was just trying to keep you awake. It was for your own good."

I wondered about that, but kept quiet.

Chapter Seven

"It's only a concussion, a bruised ankle, and sprained wrist. I'm not terminal." The well-wishers around my bedside had worn my patience thin. Denise stood at the foot of the bed, chain-smoking her horrid brown cigarettes and staring as if I were a magician about to perform a disappearing act. The drapes would need airing after she left. If she stayed much longer, I'd have to wash the walls, too.

Richard wasn't any better, hovering near the window like a silent sentinel. His face was tight, the skin taut over high cheekbones, his icy blue eyes unwavering. He'd been out by the road clearing brush when Echo had come clattering at a full gallop into my drive. He caught the frightened horse, unsaddled him and put him away, then called the police.

Perry had stayed until Denise and I made it back to her truck. Then he left, saying he had to get home. I ran my fingers over the red marks on my wrist, still confused and wondering if he'd some-how caused them.

"Marge is here, the horses are fed and stalls cleaned, everything's shipshape," I said. All that mattered was that my animals were taken care of. And though I was truly grateful for the help, I needed some privacy, too. "Denise and Richard, you should go home. You've both got work in the morning," I said, trying to sound as if it were for their own good that they leave.

Marge, my elderly neighbor, who normally accepted my help, sat in the gold wing chair next to the window, flipping through *House Beautiful*. She looked up and said, "She's right. I'll stay until at least tomorrow."

We'd already been through this. "Marge, you don't have to spend the night. I have a telephone and one good hand." Truth was, I protested only half-heartedly when it came to Marge. It was nice having her here, she was quiet, minded her own business, and we got along. And her cooking was fabulous. The aroma of her handiwork wafted in from the kitchen and with any luck it would soon mask the cigarette smoke. My head ached, I was hungry, and in a black mood. Maybe if I feigned sleepiness, they'd all go away except Marge. "Really, you guys should go."

"Carol, where are your manners?" Marge admonished. "Denise and Richard, would you stay for dinner? It'll be ready soon."

"What are we having?" I asked. The accident had not diminished my voracious appetite. I was hoping it was her paprika chicken and those dreamy mashed potatoes with roasted garlic.

"Lasagna," she answered.

Just as good. "Excellent," I said. My mood instantly elevated several notches.

"She's back to normal in one respect, anyway," Denise said. "Thanks, Marge, but I threw a beef stew into the slow cooker this morning. Should be done by now. But call if you need anything," she said. "Anything." She picked up her keys and purse from the night stand. Because I had no ashtrays, she stubbed out her cigarette in the waste basket. The silver-hinged fish she wore on a chain around her neck dangled in my face when she leaned over to hug me.

"What about you, Richard?" Marge asked.

"I'm not sure of what Louis has in mind for dinner," he said, not taking his eyes off me. Something was unsettling in the way he stared.

"There's plenty for one more, if he'd like to join us."

I threw Marge an incinerating glance. "I'm sure Louis is far too busy to bother with us," I said. "Tomorrow is a work day and he's probably ironing his outfit or something. By the way ..." I directed my question to Richard, "What *does* Louis do for a job? You said he painted."

"He's curator at an art gallery in downtown Birmingham. One of those snobby places where everyone discusses over wine the *true meaning* of the artist's work."

His comment reminded me of an interview I'd heard. "Kind of like when they asked Hemingway to explain *The Old Man and the Sea*. He told them there wasn't any symbolism, that the sea is the sea, the old man is an old man, the boy is a boy and the fish is a fish, or something to that effect. All the symbolism is just shit."

"Now that's a guy I can relate to. Don't say in four words what you can say in two," Richard said.

"Or, in Jack's case, zero," I said. The only time Jack was anywhere near this side of garrulous was when he'd had a few too many beers.

Richard shrugged. "It's all a load of bullshit if you ask me, but Louis thinks it's a wonderful job and he's happy, so who am I to question that?"

*   *   *   *

After dinner, Marge and I sipped Darjeeling and looked out over the back pasture. The valleys were filling with twilight mist. My horses pulled hay from a bunk feeder that Richard had filled with the instructed amounts of first and second cutting hay. "So why didn't Richard and Louis show up for dinner?" I asked. My foot stretched out on a kitchen chair, I shifted the ice bag from the left side of my ankle to the right.

"Louis had a headache," Marge said. She shot me a sideways glance, checking to see that I hadn't let the ice slide too low.

"Lucky us. Did you know he was wearing a woman's robe this morning? Bright yellow."

Marge laughed. "The other one's got his eye on you," she said.

"The other one? Richard?" I thought of Richard telling me of Louis's jealousy. "Don't be crazy," I said.

Marge folded her napkin into a neat little square and pressed it under her saucer. "Just telling you what I see," she said, matter of factly.

"For heaven's sake, that's ridiculous. A, I'm older than he is; B, he's gay; and C, a man that handsome could certainly find a woman more attractive than me, that is, if he was even inclined to want a woman, which I don't think he is." *What would Richard want with me, dumpy and middle-aged?*

"In the eighty-three years I've been on this earth, I've learned a few things and one of them is that I know when a man's got his eye on a certain woman."

"Your barometer is off this time." I poured myself another cup of tea. Marge held her hand over her cup. "Besides, he's gay," I said again.

"I'm not so sure of that," Marge said. "Louis might be, but what do we know about Richard?"

"For that matter, what do we really know about either of them?" I asked. "They just appeared one day after Rene moved out." Steam spiraled and rose from my cup.

"Speaking of Rene," Marge said, "With all the excitement, I forgot to tell you that I'd gotten a letter from her last week. They've put Ron's house up for sale. He thought it would be better to find someplace new to both of them, so it wasn't like she'd moved into his house. Such a nice man." She smoothed an imaginary wrinkle from her blouse. "A real sweetheart."

"Isn't it just insane? They get married and have a daughter, then get divorced. The daughter is murdered, and by dealing with her death, she brings her parents back together and they remarry. People are amazing. I wonder why they ever split up? They seem so meant for each other."

"Who knows?" Marge shrugged. "They'd already gotten divorced before she came into the neighborhood, so none of us even knew him. Rene's going to be teaching in the Sonoma School District. Subbing for now, but she's sure it'll turn into full time."

"After what they've been through, losing a daughter, they deserve some happiness," I said.

"And now, here *we* are with another murder," Marge said.

"What's going on, anyway? Has everyone gone completely and totally berserk? There was a time when nothing newsworthy ever happened, and then, within six months, we've had two murders." In my mind's eye, I saw the hand poking up from the shallow grave again. "Touching that hand was awful, Marge. The skin was gray and the flesh was cold and hard."

"Put it out of your mind."

Easier said than done. "When Denise went for help, I had a dream. I don't know if I was unconscious or hallucinating or what, but Perry was in it and then I woke up and Perry really was there and I wasn't quite so sure it had been a dream."

"Your mind plays tricks on you when you've had a shock," she said, real concern in her blue eyes.

She was a pure treasure of a friend. Denise was too, when we weren't butting heads. Maybe that was the biggest treasure of all in a friend, to just be yourself and for that to be enough. "But what was really odd, Marge, was that he was tying my hands together with binder twine. I screamed because he was hurting me."

"That had to be a dream. He would never do anything like that."

"Then where did these come from?" I showed her the angry red marks on my wrist.

She shook her head. "I don't know. But he would no sooner hurt you than he'd hurt his own mother. He's just not like that. A bit quiet, maybe, but when has that ever been a bad thing in a man? When Roy was still alive, we used to play poker with Perry and Lida. We had a great time." For a moment, her eyes seemed to drift off and I knew she was thinking about her deceased husband.

"I suppose you're right," I said, running my fingers over the welts.

She put her teacup in the sink. "But be careful with Richard. Now that Jack's gone, if you aren't careful, there's going to be talk." She looked at her watch and, before I got a word in, said, "Time to get the muffins out of the oven. Hope you like blueberry."

*   *   *   *

Sheriff Morton leaned on my doorbell, juggling a nearly eaten ice cream cone in one hand and his Stetson in the other.

"Those waffle cones they have in town sure are good, aren't they?" Marge asked, holding the door open. "Handmade too, baked right there."

"My wife says I've got to lose thirty pounds before our daughter's wedding in November." He crunched on the last of the waffle cone. "I figure I got, what, a good six weeks? Plenty of time," he said.

My eyes inadvertently stopped at the paunch protruding over his belt. For one awkward moment, no one said anything while we stood in the doorway. "Come on in," I finally said.

"They get you all fixed up there at the hospital?" he asked me.

"A concussion, banged-up ankle, and sprained wrist," I said, summing it up. "Three days' bed rest, wear the wrist brace, and don't lift anything heavy. Then come back in for a recheck."

"I see you're following orders, especially the one about the bed rest. How long you going to be off work?" he asked.

Was he worried I might have enough time to get underfoot? "This week, at least." Not wanting the contentious nature of our relationship to continue, I decided I would do everything possible to steer it in another direction. "Has the body been identified?" I asked, diverting the conversation.

He took a photo from his inside jacket pocket and passed it to Marge, who glanced at it and gave it to me. The woman in the photo was slim and attractive, wavy red hair cascading over her shoulders. Not at all like the corpse. "Who is she?" I asked.

"Alice McGowen. Ran the hair salon in town."

"I know the one," Marge said, "Over on Main Street. What's the name of it?" She tapped her forehead, trying to remember.

"The Mane Thing," I said and gave the photo back to the sheriff.

"Yeah, that's it," Sheriff Morton said. "Thirty-five, single mom."

"How'd she die?" I asked.

He looked down, brushing lint from the brim of his hat.

"We could have seen for ourselves this afternoon, if we'd been so inclined," I reminded him.

"It appears she was tied to a tree and her wrists were cut." He said it fast, as if he wanted to rid himself of the words. "Bled to death."

A sacrificial lamb. Marge gasped and held her hand to her mouth. I remained unemotional, not letting my shock show. I wanted him to believe I could handle anything he threw my way. "How do you know she was tied to a tree?" I asked.

"There were marks on the tree and blood in the soil at the base."

"Is the murder linked to the others?" I asked.

He stayed noncommittal. "Might be."

"I need one of my pain pills," I said, my head pounding. I limped into the kitchen for a glass of water, waving away Marge's offer of help. Her muffins, cooling on the counter, stirred a thought. "Can I get you something, Sheriff? Blueberry muffin? Fresh out of the oven."

"Yeah, maybe," he said.

It would be easy to suck information from him. "A couple of them?" I asked.

"Sounds good."

"So, you were saying ... it's linked to the others?" I asked.

"Well, now, I didn't exactly say that." His testy nature was never far from the surface.

Marge sat quietly, her hands folded in her lap. She seemed to have recovered. "Butter on those muffins?" I asked.

"Okay."

I arranged the muffins on a stoneware plate, then put the plate, along with butter, a knife and napkins, on a tray. My wrist screamed when I tried to pick up the snack tray. Quickly I let go of it and it banged down on the counter.

Marge hopped up. "Let me help you with that, dear." She carried it into the living room.

I felt like such an invalid, needing an eighty-three-year-old woman to carry things for me. "Seems all the murders have been after a rainstorm," I said. The sheriff appeared to be mesmerized, watching the tray. Steam rose as Marge cut each muffin in half. She spread a generous dollop of butter over each half, the butter slowly melting over the succulent berries. "Surely that's not by chance?" I asked.

"There's got to be a significance in it. We're just not exactly sure what it is." He eyed the plate hungrily. Dieting, for this man, must be sheer hell.

"Let's see, if memory serves me, they've all been very attractive, mid-thirties, and single. You know what would go really good with these muffins?" I asked.

"They look just fine the way they are, Miss Carol." He reached for a muffin but I slid the tray away.

"Some of Marge's killer coffee, with real half-and-half, not that fake substitute stuff. Might as well splurge before your diet starts." Everyone has their own form of Achilles' heel. His was obviously the inability to restrain what went into his stomach.

Marge, taking the cue, said, "Only take a minute or two to make." She hurried into the kitchen, taking the muffins with her.

There was a lot of rattling and banging, cupboard doors opening and closing, water running. Good ol' Marge, fast on the uptake. I had a feeling the coffee was going to take more than a minute or two. "Okay, so we know it has something to do with good-looking, young, single women and rain," I said. He was going to earn those muffins. I had a stake in this now. The killer was in my territory. Who would be next if he wasn't stopped?

"And what about those trinkets in the tree?" Marge called from the kitchen.

"Yeah, how do they fit in?" I asked. Another score for Marge. "You don't hang weird stuff like that in a tree for no reason." If only he weren't so close-mouthed. He had to know more than he was letting on, even if it was speculative.

"We're investigating that right now." He had taken a seat on the couch and Camille, a self-proclaimed one-cat welcoming committee, had wedged herself between his belly and his knees, onto his lap. His sparse salt and pepper hair was damp and beads of perspiration dotted his hairline. "Seems there's a custom in certain Indian tribes that settled in the Pacific Northwest and up into Alaska. When a member of the tribe died by violent means, objects that belonged to the victim were hung on a tree. This thing, this 'victim tree,' if you will, was a sort of tribute."

I tapped my chin, thinking. "By violent means, do you mean in a scuffle with another tribe?"

"Any death other than by natural causes or from disease. Something like a hunting accident. Or yes, if there had been trouble with a nearby tribe, I suppose that, too."

"But not necessarily murder victims only?" *Give me something significant to go on. Some modus operandi that links the killings so I've got somewhere to start.*

"We don't know yet," he said. "Were the ornaments things the person would need in the afterlife, or were they simply things the person treasured? Lots of unanswered questions." Camille, unable to get comfortable on his nonexistent lap, sat vertically inclined, on his chest, her claws embedded in his shirt. I wished she would give it up. Her stubbornness was embarrassing.

"But it proves the killer knew this, what was her name, this Alice McGowen, doesn't it?" I asked. "Otherwise how would he have gotten the stuff?"

He gently released Camille's nails from his shirt, depositing her on the floor with a pat to her head. She sauntered past, giving me a look of disgust. "*Proves* is a bit cocky. What it is, is an indication the victim was acquainted with the killer."

"So you may be looking for a murderer with a Native American background? From a tribe in the northwest?"

"Could be it's the victims that had Native American ties," he said. "We're checking that out. It's just too early to tell."

There was a lot we didn't know. I looked up at the ceiling, at the cobwebs hanging from the barn beams, and made a mental note to knock them down the next time I cleaned. "That is a problem, isn't it?" I said. "I mean, it could go either way."

"Those are questions for the anthropologist—the same guy doing the report on the bones the coyotes dug up. But we do know those bones aren't linked to these recent murders. Those are old bones. He told me as much before he even started his study." He eyed me over the tops of his wire-rimmed glasses. "Off the record, of course."

"Of course," I said, nodding in agreement. It seemed like an eon ago that Denise and I had found the bones and with everything else, I'd forgotten them. The aroma of fresh coffee escaped the kitchen and wafted into the living room. "How long until we find out?"

"He'll have the report in another week or so," Sheriff Morton said. "He's running tests."

"Were there victim trees in the other murders?"

"Yes."

Pay dirt! The link, the killer's method of operation. I wondered if he had let it slip, or if he'd actually meant to tell me. Either way, I got what I wanted, a link with which I could begin to piece together how this killer reasoned. I called to Marge in the kitchen, "Hey, Marge, is that coffee ready?" I had a feeling it was. "And bring the muffins back."

"Don't take this lightly," Sheriff Morton said. His gray eyes bored into mine and he pointed a stubby finger. "This person has killed more than once and there's no reason to believe he won't kill again. Leave this alone. Let us do our jobs."

I held up my braced wrist. "How on earth could I do otherwise?"

*   *   *   *

It was late when Denise called. "What're you going to do about work?"

"Work" was a law firm thirty miles south, in a suburb of Detroit. "I'll call in the morning." I turned a corner on the page of the veterinary report I'd printed off the Internet. "I'm supposed to be on total bed rest until Wednesday, when I get the wrist x-rayed again to see if there's tendon damage. No typing until then." *Wasn't that just too bad?*

"Is Jack coming home?"

"What for? So we can sit and stare at each other? Besides, Marge is here." It was the same old problem with Jack. If he came home now, he'd just have to make up the time later.

"It doesn't seem right not to tell him."

"What good would it do?" I didn't want to get into it with her. I was tired of justifying him being gone. "Besides, I've got a bigger problem. Like how I tell him we're taking in a starved horse."

"True. That's part of the reason I'm calling. I talked to Sue about Saint."

Soon my poor Saint would be with me. "When can we take him?" I asked. My blood pressure must have soared because my head started pounding again.

"You can't do anything in the condition you're in," she said.

"We told her we'd take him as soon as he could travel. If I go back on that, he might end up with someone else," I said.

"I know. But you've got to admit, this isn't the greatest time for you to start a rehabilitation project. So here's the plan: I'll drive over on Tuesday, pick him up and bring him to your place. Then I'll help you out, just until your wrist is healed."

"Can I at least ride over there with you to get him?" I could feel my project, the one I'd taken on so I could feel I'd finally done something worthwhile and noble, slipping through my fingers.

"What happened to the three days' bed rest?"

"So I'm shaving off one day. Big deal." Denise's precision was occasionally annoying. "Besides, there's lots we need to do. I've been reading up—it's recommended to start an underweight horse slowly, on a very plain diet of alfalfa hay, free choice salt, and water. Six pounds of hay per day at first, broken up into six feedings. Then slowly increase the amount per feeding, while cutting down on the frequency of the feedings."

"Alfalfa?" she asked incredulously. "That's surprising. I would have thought you'd want to stick with timothy," she said.

"I thought so, too. But not according to these guidelines I printed off the Internet." I flipped back to the first page and recited the title. "*Care Guidelines for Equine Rescue and Retirement Facilities* by the American Association of Equine Practitioners. Echo and Feather are on an alfalfa and timothy mix, so I'll need to get some straight alfalfa." I made a mental note to call my hay dealer, realizing that because of this damn fool wrist of mine, and Jack being gone, I'd have to pay him extra to stack the hay in my barn. One more argument for the fact that, though Jack's job paid well, his being away sometimes ended up costing more.

"What about grain?" she asked.

"No grain or supplements at first. I guess these horses are really prone to not only colic, but major organ failure if you overload them too quickly." An overwhelming feeling that maybe I'd taken on more than I should have sent a shudder through me. "Sounds like we'll have to watch him day and night," I said.

Chapter Eight

Monday morning. Marge's quilted polyester housecoat, vintage 1966, rustled when her arm moved back and forth, filling in the squares of her crossword puzzle. "What'd your office manager say?" she asked.

"Don't worry about a thing," I said, my voice taking on an affected tone, "You poor dear, after your three days of bed rest are done, we'll find you a non-typing job until your wrist is healed. And don't be concerned about missing one single day of pay."

Marge laughed. "Bed rest, malarkey." She rolled her eyes. "You haven't been in bed for five minutes."

"I most certainly have," I said, irate. "Last night, after Sheriff Morton left and you went to check on your kittens, I laid down the entire time." Hannibal purred and rubbed against my leg. I reciprocated by tickling his back. "They'll put me in the receptionist job, I just know it."

My toast popped up and flew out of the toaster, one piece landing on the kitchen counter, the other on the floor. "Why the hell can't somebody in this country make a toaster that works right?" I brushed off the piece that fell on the floor, then held it up to the light, checking for cat hair.

With her pencil, Marge scratched letters into the boxes, then stopped. "For starters, that toaster most likely wasn't made in this country. What small appliance is anymore? China or Korea, more likely."

"Don't get me started," I said. It was entirely too early for politics and, unfortunately, I had a strong opinion on just about everything.

"What's a seven-letter word for 'without protestation?' Approve doesn't work." She erased the letters she'd just penciled in. "Then what will the receptionist do?"

"Huh?" I'd totally lost the trail of the conversation.

Marge saw my confused look. "The receptionist."

"Oh, her," I said, finally comprehending. "God only knows. Condone," I said.

Marge took a sip of coffee. "C-o-n-d-o-n-e. Yep, that works. I ought to rat on you. Tell them you're not following doctor's orders anyway and they might just as well reassign your job today. Pay you back for ratting on me last spring."

It now occurred to me that Marge had a slightly vindictive side. "I did *not* rat on you!"

Last spring Marge had gotten herself mixed up in some trouble, and although she hadn't really done anything wrong, she hadn't told the entire truth either, about the death of an old friend.

"In fact, if I remember correctly, I saved your butt from federal prison, withholding evidence like you did," I said. "If it hadn't been for me, going to the sheriff with the evidence you should have gone to him with, you might have been arrested." It was obvious by her smug look that Marge wasn't the least bit grateful. "Besides, Jack was the one who insisted I tell Morton everything."

"Poor Jack. He gets blamed for everything," Marge said.

A change of subject was in order. "Want to make jelly today? The grapes are ready." I loved grape jelly day. Snipping the grapes from the vines, washing, boiling and straining them, drinking a little of the hot fragrant juice before pouring it into the jars. Then nervously checking the jars until I was sure each one had properly sealed. For just one day, the world was perfect. I could pretend I was June Cleaver or Donna Reed, though I'm not sure I ever saw an episode where either of them made grape jelly. It just seemed like something they would do.

"They're past ready, the birds are starting to get them," she said.

Richard slid the glass patio door open. He brushed sawdust from his boots and after unlacing them, pulled them off and left them on the welcome mat.

"Everything all right down at the barn?" I asked. Whenever someone else fed my horses I suffered anxiety pangs. "Is Echo stiff from the fall?"

"He's fine, don't worry," he said, pulling out a chair.

"Coffee, Richard?" Marge asked. She was taking a cup from its peg. "Cream? Sugar?"

"Black is good, Marge."

He sat at the table with us, Marge's crossword puzzle half done, me having tea and dressed in the sweat suit I'd slept in. His hair was the color of wheat, when the pale golden heads, with just a hint of ochre beginning to show, were ready for harvest. It was tousled with a mind of its own. The disheveled look fit him. "Thanks for feeding, Richard, but I should be able to manage tonight on my own."

"No, you won't." He smiled but had a "don't mess with me" look on his face. "And don't clean stalls, either. I can do them. I've got a short day today, just some detailing on a Firebird."

It was the first time Richard mentioned what he did for a living. "Detailing?" I asked. "Do you paint cars?"

He nodded. "Custom pin-striping and painting on vintage models, things like flames shooting across the hood of a Camaro, or a lightning bolt on a Mustang."

"So you and Louis are both painters, only you paint on metal and he on paper?" I asked.

"Something like that."

"There goes the mail truck," Marge said, peeking out the window. "I'll run home, take care of my kittens, and bring in my mail." She put her cup in the sink. "See you in an hour or so."

Richard lingered over one cup of coffee, then another. When I told him Marge and I were planning to make grape jelly, he offered to pick the grapes. He seemed like the kind of man that wanted to be included in every mundane family-oriented aspect of life. It seemed perfect that he was here.

The snippers and purple-stained basket were down in the basement. I got them while Richard fetched the ladder down from the hayloft. He carried it across the lawn and set it up next to the arbor, checking to make sure all four legs were steady. Then he climbed to the top step. Standing under the arbor, I snipped the grapes with my good hand, letting them fall into the basket on the ground.

"Careful of your jacket," I said, "Grape stains are impossible to get out. Wouldn't Louis really have a fit then?"

"Holy Moses, I'd never hear the end of it."

I wondered about his work, if a "short day" meant he could go in at any time he chose. "What's the name of your paint shop?" I asked, watching a cluster of grapes fall into the basket.

He lowered a handful down to me. In the crystal morning light, his azure eyes were endless. I saw into them and never saw out again, like the sea. "Nothing very imaginative, I'm afraid."

"Come on," I teased. "I won't laugh, I promise." I lifted the basket. He dropped the grapes into it, his long fingers already stained purple. A hornet buzzed by my head, weaving in and out through the vines, then stopping to light on a curled brown leaf. "Well, come on … Let's have it," I said.

"Superior Paint."

"Superior Paint?" I *did* want to laugh. It was so old-fashioned, so stogy. "That's it? Hardly does justice to what you described, flames and lightning bolts."

"I wasn't in one of my most creative moods when I thought of it, and now it's too much trouble to change. All the paperwork. But then, working for a law firm, I guess I don't have to tell you about paperwork, do I?"

"It's just a matter of redrafting your incorporation documents. Not a lot of trouble." The basket was nearly full, plenty enough for a dozen jelly jars and some leftover for juice. "The attorneys I work for can take care of it. That is, if you want to." Realizing how pushy I must have sounded, I was embarrassed. "I'm sorry, I didn't mean to take over; here I am, changing the name of your business, and you not even sure of what you want."

"No, don't be sorry. It's nice," he said.

"What's nice?" I asked, wondering what he meant.

"Having someone who cares." He dropped another cluster into the basket.

"But you've got Louis," I said. What was lacking in his relationship with Louis? What did he want that wasn't there?

"It's not the same." I wondered if he wished he'd been married, had a wife and children.

"But Richard, you can do whatever you want, can't you? Have whatever you want? If you don't like something, change it."

"If only it were that simple, Carol." A pigeon hawk circled above us, then flew across the road and over Richard's property on the other side of the evergreens. "We're nearly done here," he said.

I wanted to ask him why it wasn't that simple, what stopped him. But instead, I held the ladder steady with my good hand while he climbed down. "We'll have to separate these from the stems and sort them," I said. I heard the thump of a mailbox door and Marge came out from behind the pines, ambling down the driveway, her pink jogging suit clashing with the orange, yellow, and red oak trees.

"Post card from Jack," she said, waving the mail.

She traded me the stack of mail for the snippers. "Geez," I said, "he must have mailed it the instant he got into town; he hasn't even been gone a whole forty-eight hours." The front of the postcard showed the empty dining room of the Red Ledge Motel. Tables and chairs in an Early American light maple. Awful red carpeting. The photo appeared to be pre-1970. *Right up Jack's alley.* He probably wiped the dust from the postcard before he paid a nickel for it. I read the message aloud:

Dear Carol:

Ian and I are rooming together to save money. Cut my finger opening a can of beans.

Love, Jack.

P.S. Please forward my October issue of Guns & Ammo.

"Poor dear," Marge said.

"He's accident-prone," I said, flipping through the mail.

"Not his finger. Eating canned beans."

Jack had that effect on people, always evoking feelings of sympathy without trying. It was a special gift he had. "Poor dear," I mocked, separating junk mail from bills. "Since I'm not there, he'll need to dispose of the tin can himself. How are the kittens?"

"Hardly kittens anymore. More like teenagers."

"Just think, Marge, you're raising teenagers again. You going to keep all three?"

"I guess so. At this point I'd feel awful separating them. They'd be lonely without each other. They're family."

"Isn't it funny how when you come from a big family and people are always around, you get so you crave solitude, yet kids that were raised as the only child are just the opposite."

"How about you, Richard?" Marge asked. "Did you come from a large family?"

"No," he said. He picked up his jacket from the lawn and shook the grass from it. "Just one brother. Half brother, actually."

"Were you raised around here?" I asked, my curiosity raised.

"No, out of state."

"Oh really, where?"

"New Mexico, Alaska, Washington, you name it, we were there." He quickly turned away, making it obvious he did not want to talk about his family.

"Well, ladies, I'll leave you to the magic that turns this ..." he motioned to the basket of grapes, "into jam."

"Jelly," I corrected.

"There's a difference?" He rolled a grape between his fingers, then popped it into his mouth. I watched, knowing how sour the grapes were, anticipating, but his face didn't change.

"Jam has pieces of fruit in it, jelly is only the juice. Right, Marge?"

"Basically," she answered. "Dinner tonight, Richard? What would you think of quiche and Caesar salad?"

"I'd say it sounds great, but I think Louis is working on a new recipe. There's a white rubbery lump in our refrigerator."

"A white lump? What on earth could that be?" Marge asked. "What does it smell like?"

Richard thought for a moment. "Didn't really smell like anything."

The pine trees behind Richard swayed. I squinted in the sun. "Probably tofu," I said.

"What's tofu?" Marge asked, wrinkling her nose.

"Soybean curd." Surprised that I was the only one who knew what it was, and hardly a gourmet, I said, "It's quite healthy."

Marge made a face. "All this new fangled stuff they're coming up with. Pretty soon they'll have us eating plastic. How do you cook it?"

New fangled or not, she seemed interested. "It's good in stir fry. And I've got a delicious recipe for tofu pumpkin pie."

The wind blew Richard's fair hair forward, covering part of his face. "I don't really care what I eat, as long as Louis is happy." He picked up the overloaded basket. "Where do you want these?"

"On the patio table, please," I said. The sun was now very warm, so I cranked the umbrella open. He set the basket on the table.

"At any rate, I'll be coming by later to clean the stalls."

I started to protest, but he shook his head. "And I do *not* want to hear about how you can do them yourself. Your hand is never going to get better if you don't give it a couple days to heal. End of discussion."

"Oz has spoken," I mimicked. Watching him walk down my driveway, it was like a Ralph Lauren advertisement had come to life. Most appealing was his apparent lack of vanity.

"You've got that look on your face again," I said to Marge.

"What look?" she asked innocently.

"You know. The one that says, 'You'd better watch out. The neighbors will talk.' Might I remind you it was *you* who asked him to dinner, not me? Besides, which neighbors? There's only you and Richard and Louis and a few people farther down the road I don't even know. Just who is it you're afraid will gossip?"

"The ones you think least likely, that's who."

Her look of seriousness made me feel she had lots more to say on this subject. Maybe I should take heed. She *did* have the wisdom that hopefully comes with age. But what of my own feelings? A friendship with Richard was enticing. I liked Richard, he liked me, and I saw nothing wrong with that. Was it only because he was a man, and I was a married woman, that a friendship shouldn't blossom? And I wondered who she meant by least likely. "Like Denise?" I asked.

"Like nobody in particular, I'm just saying you never know, that's all. Believe me, Carol, I'm only looking out for you."

"I know you are, Marge," I said, giving her hand a little squeeze, her skin papery and delicate. I wished the rest of my life could be just like this—spending time with a good friend in the October sun, instead of sitting at a desk in some high-rise, artificially lit office complex. "Did I thank you for all you've done? The cooking and the cleaning? For dropping everything and coming here?"

She waved me off with a flick of her wrist. "Glad to help. You'd do the same for me, I know you would."

Though flattered she thought that well of me, the truth was that never in a million years would I ever be as good of a person as Marge was, as unselfish and caring. I just didn't have it in me. "Might just as well start on these now," I said, plopping into a chair, and taking a cluster of grapes from the basket. "No sense making a mess in the house. Besides, on a gorgeous day like this, I don't want to miss a single minute of being outside." Curled brown leaves blew across the deck. "Soon enough it'll be snowing and we'll all be housebound."

*   *   *   *

Marge's Caesar salad was excellent; the lettuce crisp, the dressing not too tangy. Everywhere were signs of her handiwork, from the freshly laundered kitchen towels hanging from the oven door to the spotless stove and countertops. It was better than having a maid, a butler, and a cook—she was all of them rolled into one.

It was late by the time Richard showed up, sans Louis. He dropped off two bottles of Merlot at the house, then headed down to clean stalls. A half hour later, we sat at the kitchen table talking. The wine was cold, and my fingertips melted translucent ovals onto my glass. We talked about gardening and how the blooms on Marge's Rose of Sharon were the prettiest and most profuse of any we'd seen. The second bottle was nearly dry when Marge looked at her watch and announced it was time for *Snakes Alive*.

I shivered. "I hate snakes, even on television."

"They're God's creatures, just like everything else on this earth," Marge said, padding into the kitchen wearing pink fuzzy slippers. She rinsed her teacup and put it on the drain board. "Don't worry, I'll watch it in the bedroom. I can't miss tonight's episode—pit vipers."

It was just like her to find something good to say, even about a snake. "If I ever touched a snake, I believe I'd need psychiatric counseling," I said. Everyone laughed except me.

"See you in the morning," Marge said. She went into the bedroom at the end of the hall and closed the door.

"I can't believe she watches a program about snakes just before going to bed," I shivered. "I'd have nightmares."

He shrugged. "Some people just aren't afraid of them." We picked up our glasses and moved into the living room. I lit the candles on the mantle, then sank into Jack's leather easy chair. The leather smelled faintly of his after shave. When would I see him next? He had not set an actual date, but only said it "would depend on how the job went." Richard stretched his lanky frame out on the sofa.

"I've got to find a way to tell Jack I'm getting a starved and probably foundered horse."

Candlelight flickered on Richard's face. "One of the horses from the newspaper?"

I nodded.

"What's 'foundered?'" Richard asked.

"It's a crippling disease of the hooves." How did I simplify such a complex condition to a non-horseman? "There's a bone inside the hoof called a coffin bone. Laminae, or tissue, hold the bone in place. But sometimes, certain things can cause swelling inside the hoof, and the laminae let loose of the coffin bone. It begins to rotate, or tip, pointing downward out of the sole of the foot." The explanation, though not in perfect veterinary terms, was close enough to suffice.

"And that process begins with starvation?"

"Not the starvation itself. More likely, it starts when you put them back on feed. It's touch-and-go for a while. He's a beautiful dappled gray, with big, kind eyes. I'm going to call him Saint," I rambled. "Jack will wonder if I've lost my mind."

"He's a lucky man," Richard said.

I felt heat rising in my face. "Lucky?" I asked, embarrassed.

"To have such an honest woman. You're so simple." He set his goblet on the glass-topped collection table.

"Thanks very much," I said, not entirely happy with his choice of words.

"I don't mean simple as in 'simple-minded.' I mean simple in the way—"

"What you see is what you get? Transparent?" I quipped. Somehow I knew that wasn't what he meant, but said it anyway, trying to be difficult.

"No, not transparent, either. I mean good. And true. True like a best friend or a close brother or sister." He topped off my wine, upending the second bottle.

I'd already had too much. "*Merci*," I raised my glass. "It's very good. Sweet and spicy."

"Like the company," he said, raising his glass to meet mine.

Warmth crept up my neck and into my face, making me glad the lighting was low. Then he favored me with his beguiling crooked smile. When I quickly turned my head, Richard was a blur; the wine playing games with my eyes and when they focused again, I saw a shadow in his eyes that hadn't been there earlier. "What's the matter?" I asked. He didn't answer right away and I wondered if he'd heard.

"Louis," he finally said.

I did not want to be privy to the details of Richard and Louis's lovers' relationship. The clock on the mantle chimed. "The witching hour. Whatever is that supposed to mean, anyway?"

"Between midnight and one o'clock is the hour when men are bewitched by their lovers," Richard said.

"Is that the problem you're having with Louis?" I asked.

"What?" He seemed confused.

"Louis has bewitched you?"

He threw his head back and laughed and I thought how different he looked, wondering if he was younger than the give-or-take thirty-nine years I thought him to be. "Is that what you think? That Louis is my lover?"

"We all thought it. Marge, Denise, and I. The other day, when you said he was jealous, I thought you meant ... were we wrong?" I pulled my knee up under me, sitting cross-legged, the ice broken on the subject I'd wondered about.

"I guess I was fair game. New to the neighborhood and living with a man who occasionally wears women's clothes, what would you expect?"

"But you never answered. Were we wrong?"

"By a long shot." He smiled crookedly.

"If he's not your lover, then what is he?" I asked, embarrassed. Now it was my turn to be confused.

"Louis is my half-brother."

I couldn't conceal my surprise. "The half-brother you didn't want to talk about earlier?" I asked, remembering how strangely he'd acted this afternoon when Marge and I had asked him about family.

"I doubt you're interested in our family's skeletons."

I tried not to appear too eager. I wanted him to believe that I cared, and if he needed or wanted someone to talk to, then I was there. The wine had me feeling sappy and emotional. "Yes, I really am."

"I don't know …" He avoided my eyes.

"Try me. I'm a good listener."

He looked at his empty glass. "We might need something a little stronger for this."

"I've got just the thing." Might as well do it up good. Neither of us was driving anywhere tonight. I took our wine glasses into the kitchen and rinsed them in the sink. Dragging over a kitchen chair to climb on, I stretched my hand far to the back of the liquor cupboard for Jack's Crown Royal. "He saves this for special occasions. But what the hell, I figure, he's not here, is he?" My hand touched the soft velvet pouch. Suddenly I swayed, feeling a little woozy.

"You okay?" Richard asked. Like a cat, he'd come up behind me without a sound. I let out a surprised yelp as the purple pouch slipped through my fingers. He caught it by the gold draw cord.

"Sorry, I scared you." He reached his other arm around me and slid two shot glasses from the shelf. "You shouldn't be climbing on chairs. What if you fell?" He helped me down. A full head taller than me, I fit exactly underneath the crook of his chin.

Agent Orange, an overweight and lazy male cat I'd inherited when my neighbor moved away, had commandeered the easy chair in my absence, so Richard and I both sat on the sofa. Whiskers twitching, the cat lifted his head, sniffed the air, and having decided that our drinks didn't interest him, went back to sleep.

The whiskey slipped down my throat, leaving my arms heavy, as if they weighed a hundred pounds each. With hard work, my lips carefully enunciating each word, I prodded him. "So tell me about Louis."

"You're positive about this? You really want to know?"

He seemed reluctant, like he was half wishing I'd say no. "Positively, absolutely," I said. "Shoot."

"Louis was the product of an affair my father had. He came to live with us when he was seven, after his mother died. I was nine. We moved around a lot because my father was a geologist for an oil exploration company. We went wherever there was the promise of oil: Texas, New Mexico, Alaska. It seemed we'd just get settled, and he'd be sent off to look for oil somewhere else. He'd go ahead of us to find somewhere to live, then he'd send for us. Sometimes we didn't see him for a month or more. At first, everything seemed fine. I honestly don't remember anything unusual until we moved to New Mexico, which for me, at ten years old, was my fourth move. She always made sure nothing showed by the time he got home."

"She? Showed?" I asked, wondering who and what he meant.

"My mother. She must have hated Louis," Richard explained. "She didn't want to be saddled with raising him. Of course, Dad had no idea. He thought everything was fine. She had us both so terrified, she knew we wouldn't tell." He swirled the whiskey in his glass.

"What did she do to Louis?" Did I really want to know?

He looked up at the ceiling. "Things you wouldn't believe."

I touched the back of his hand softly and noticed yellow paint on his knuckles and remembered the Firebird he painted this morning. The back of his hand was rough, but his fingers were long and refined. I intertwined mine through his and steeled myself for the worst. *What had happened?* A dull throb in my temples promised a full-blown headache by morning. "What things?"

"She burned him."

"No!" I sucked in my breath. Had I heard him right? "How?"

"With cigarettes. I should have stopped her. If only I'd told my father."

Anger welled up inside me. How could someone do such a thing to a child? "But you were only ten!" A child himself, Richard had not been able to help his brother. Now I understood Louis's huge canvases of black flowers in their home across the road.

"I was afraid of what she would do to me if I told."

No words of sympathy or comfort seemed appropriate as I tried to comprehend the hellish childhood Louis and Richard had endured.

He threw back the shot of whiskey and poured another. "Because of me, Louis suffered."

"It wasn't because of you! What about your father? Shouldn't he accept some blame here? Men are all too quick to assume everything on the home front is fine. Instead of being afraid of disrupting status quo, check into what's happening to your children. Take an interest."

"I could have stopped it, but I didn't."

I thought of my life at ten years old, and how my biggest problem had been managing to get my clothes up off the bedroom floor and into the hamper on laundry day. Catching turtles with my sister. Riding my bike for miles. "No, you couldn't have stopped it. What would you have done?"

"Something. Anything." His jaw was stubbornly set, fighting for control. "If anyone ever hurts him again, I'll kill them. I owe him that much." He finished his whiskey and set the glass down on the end table.

"I'm so sorry," was all I could say.

"I shouldn't have told you." He took my face in his hands, softly framing it. "You really do care, don't you? I can see it in your eyes." He pulled me to him, and for a moment everything was jumbled up and there was no right or wrong or thoughts of where this would lead. There was only his warm touch and the closeness I craved.

Then the light over the sink flashed on, hot and bright and water spat from the tap. Marge. For only a second, our eyes met. She didn't say a word, but drank her water, then turned and marched back to bed.

*   *   *   *

"It wasn't what you thought!"

Marge resolutely plopped her overnight bag on a chair. "So now you know what I'm thinking?"

"I mean you didn't see what you thought you saw," I said. My head ached. Mixing wine and whiskey had been a bad idea. What had possessed me to do such a thing? The morning sunlight wreaked havoc on my eyes. Two doves fluttered at the bird feeder. "What I mean is, what it looked like isn't what you saw."

Marge threw me a look of disgust. "Oh, for heaven's sake, Carol, would you please make some sense?"

"You've been harping on it for days now. 'Be careful, people will talk, Carol.' Who is it that will talk, Marge? There was only you and me and Richard."

"It's just not right." She straightened a picture frame hanging askew in the hallway.

"What's not right? *Nothing* happened."

"Not for any lack of interest on your part."

Her words hit me like a blow to the stomach. Instantly I retaliated. "I'm surprised at your lack of charity, Miss Never-Misses-Church-on-Sunday. If you are so concerned that Richard and I are having an affair, then just leave. I wouldn't want you to tarnish your path to the pearly gates by associating with an adulteress." I was sorry the instant the words were out. *Why couldn't I keep my big mouth shut?*

"Well! I never took you for the type to run around on her husband. I'll not be part of it!"

"Part of what?" I demanded, hot tears stinging my cheeks. "There's nothing to be a part of! I am *not* running around on my husband!"

"And Jack gone barely three days," she added, her opinion clearly unchanged.

"So call him up and tell him. Tell him his wife's having an affair. He probably wouldn't even care! And while you're at it, do me a favor and tell him to get his ass home where it belongs."

Marge stood open-mouthed. The lack of a quick come-back on her part only served to fuel my rampage. And even though I knew, as sure as I knew the sun was going to rise tomorrow morning, that I was saying things I'd be apologizing for later, I didn't stop. "I'm so sick of you and everybody else thinking that we have the perfect marriage! That Jack is such a pillar of salt." Pillar of salt? That wasn't right. That was Lot's wife. "Pillar of stone, or whatever the hell he is." I couldn't even argue without making myself look like an idiot.

"I believe the expression is pillar of the community."

"Whatever." My head throbbed. I went to the bathroom for my pain pills. That was when I saw the mirror. The same grotesquely childish scrawl, the same red lipstick. "No!" I screamed, backing out of the bathroom and nearly slamming into Marge, who had dropped her bag and came running. My shaky hand pointed to the mirror.

Chapter Nine

"Drop dead," Sheriff Morton repeated, more to himself than Marge or I. "All right ladies, now let's get this straight—you both used the bathroom off the master bedroom this morning and not the one off the hallway?" Marge brought a tray with coffee, cream and sugar to the dining room table.

"Not exactly. Marge has been staying in my bedroom, the master, so she's been using that one," I said.

"And which one did you use?" he asked me, his felt-tip pen hovering over his notepad.

Just how much was one expected to reveal in this type of interrogation? "I didn't," I said. "It seemed late when I woke up and I didn't want to bother anyone, so I hurried down to feed the horses, and I … um, I … went down at the barn."

"Then you've got a bathroom in the barn?" He looked up from his scribbling.

"Not exactly," I said, avoiding his eyes. With my fingernail, I traced the pattern on the place mat.

Marge stopped with a teaspoon of sugar midway to her cup. "Oh, Carol, you can't mean ... I hope you're not serious!"

"Everyone does it. It's not a big deal," I said.

"Everyone does what?" Sheriff Morton asked, looking first at me, then at Marge, his eyebrows raised questioningly.

It *was* rather embarrassing to have to admit, especially to a policeman, and I wondered if there was some sort of health code or law or something that prohibited it, and now I'd gone and blown the whistle on everyone else, too. "Pees in their barn," I said.

Marge reacted first. "That's disgusting! Is it any wonder our wells are poisoned with things like this going on right on our own door-steps." She got up and unceremoniously dumped her coffee down the kitchen sink.

"I did *not* pee on your doorstep! And my barn is 200 feet from my well!"

"I don't care—"

"Ladies, ladies, ladies!" Sheriff Morton boomed, clearly not amused. "I haven't got all day."

"Sorry," I mumbled.

Marge sat down.

"Okay, so when was the last time either of you used the bath-room off the hallway? You first," he said, pointing to me.

"Last night, after Marge had gone back to bed," I said. "A little after midnight, I guess. Richard had just left." Marge's face tight-ened at the mention of Richard's name. She just wouldn't give the poor guy a chance.

Sheriff Morton scribbled on his notepad. "Did Richard use that bathroom?"

"Not that I remember," I said.

"And you?" Sheriff Morton asked Marge, "When did you last use the bathroom off the hallway?"

"I didn't. I'd unpacked some toiletries, things I use everyday and just left them out on the countertop in the master bath, so I've been using that bathroom only. That is, since Sunday, when I moved in to help Carol."

Marge, ever practical. Her small yellow case, monogrammed in block letters, each item in a special compartment, had been on the countertop Sunday night when I'd brought a stack of fresh towels. Maybe when I was eighty-three, I'd be as organized.

If I lived to see eighty-three, that is, and things weren't looking good in that department. The worst part, the part that really made me shiver, was thinking how close this madman had been to us. Literally feet away, the door to the master bedroom just down the hall and the guest bedroom right across the way. Maybe he'd even stood next to our beds while we slept.

"Did you lock the door after Richard left?" the sheriff asked.

"Yes," I answered.

Marge set a plate of shortbread cookies next to him. His hand came up but seemed to hesitate. "No, thanks," he said. "The powers that be have informed me that I absolutely, positively must start that God-awful diet today."

"Oh, dear," Marge said, nonplused. She whisked the plate off the table.

"Are you sure you locked it? No question about that?"

"None." I shook my head resolutely.

"No windows broken, jimmied sills, anything like that?"

"Everything looks fine," I said. Marge nodded her head.

"What about the possibility it was one of you three?" He threw this out, seemingly for its effect.

"Why on earth would I scribble on my own mirror and scare Marge half to death? That's just plain absurd! And as for her," I said, pointing to Marge, "she's incapable of making a mess like that. And I told you, I used the bathroom after Richard left. I certainly would have noticed something on the mirror when I brushed my teeth. I may have been a little tipsy, but I wasn't *that* drunk."

"Tipsy?" Marge asked. "That's what you call it?"

I ignored her.

"A break-in with no obvious signs of damage doesn't warrant fingerprinting," the sheriff said. "Don't touch anything in that room, and I'll send the photographer over. Your statements will be transcribed, and we'll leave it at that for now."

"When he comes back and murders one of us, will that warrant fingerprinting?" I asked, "Or will we be waiting for something else then?"

"Carol," Marge said, "Simmer down. And be polite—"

"No, dammit, I won't. All polite gets you around here is dead. What do they know about the hairdresser—what's her name—Alice somebody? What are we paying you guys for, anyway?"

"There were no messages on the mirrors of the murdered women," Sheriff Morton said. "I really don't see anything linking this to the murders. Tell you what, though, I'll send a drive-by a couple times a night to check things out, for the next day or two.

"What good will that do? All he's going to see is what's going on at the front of the house. Somebody could be crawling in my dining room window and your patrol officer wouldn't know a thing about it."

"I know you're concerned, and I don't blame you, but I really don't see what else I can do at this point."

Bureaucracy! I got up and threw my coffee down the sink, too.

*   *   *   *

Another post card arrived Tuesday afternoon. I read it aloud to Marge.

Dear Carol:

Started work on the warehouse. The other company left a real mess. Sprained my wrist lifting some boards, but Ian took me to the hospital, where they wrapped it up. Doing fine now.

Love you, Jack.

P.S. Ian and I are thinking of hiring a cleaning lady. What should we pay her?

"Pity the sucker who ends up with that job," I said. Jack was no Mr. Clean. Marge had been reading the newspaper while her chicken stew cooled. "I don't mind telling you, Marge, I'm scared. This weirdo leaving mirror messages knows me, and knows I'm here alone."

"You're not alone," Marge said, bending back one corner of the paper. "I'm here."

Thank God for that. "What I meant was, they knew when Jack left."

"Maybe not," she said, folding the newspaper and setting it aside. She plucked a dumpling from the thick chicken gravy and let it cool for a moment on her spoon.

"How do you figure? A random break-in the first night Jack was gone? Too coincidental," I said. Was someone mad at me for something so trivial I failed to even remember what it was? What else could it be? I sampled a fluffy dumpling from my bowl, along with a bit of carrot. "Marge, Marge, Marge ... I do believe you've outdone yourself."

She shrugged, deflecting the compliment. "Who knows Jack is gone? Think back. Who did you tell?"

"Well, you, of course. I may have told Perry, I'm not sure." I tried to remember my conversation with him. "Yes, I think I did. And Denise, which means Todd knows. Where does it stop? If I tell Denise and Denise tells Todd and Todd tells someone, the possibilities are endless."

"You're right," she said.

"You know, Marge, I've been thinking … when Denise gets off work, we're supposed to bring Saint home, and if we do, you'll be here alone. Even with the new door locks, I'm not sure that's a good idea."

After the sheriff left, the first thing I did was call a locksmith. Marge had delayed her leaving, and truth be known, I would have paid her to stay if I had to. I was afraid, and not too proud to admit it. "Lida should be back from her sister's by now and I'd feel better if she came over while we're gone."

But when I rang Lida's number, Perry answered and said Lida still wasn't back, that her sister had gotten sick, so Lida put off her return. "When do you expect her?" I asked.

"In another day or two." There was silence on the other end of the line. Perry wasn't normally garrulous, but twice in a row now he'd been unusually short, as if he were in a hurry or for whatever reason, he didn't want to talk to me. Probably nothing more than being caught up in one of his many projects, I thought, shrugging it off.

"All right, then," I said, and with one last attempt at conversation, added, "Denise and I are bringing my new horse home today."

"Oh?" came his vague response. His voice had an unfriendly tone to it, not at all like him. What was going on?

"Have her call me when she gets home, okay?" I nervously curled the telephone cord around my forefinger.

"Will do," he said, and then hung up.

Bizarre, I thought, replacing the phone. "Seems Lida still isn't home," I told Marge. "Kind of a strange conversation."

"Strange in what way?" She buttered a slice of bread.

"Vague about when Lida's coming back. Seems funny, like he's hiding something." I went back to my stew, which had cooled off considerably. That was fine with me, as I disliked very hot food.

"Have you done anything to make him mad lately?"

A fat dumpling was poised on my spoon. "Of course not! What kind of a question is that?" I said, indignantly.

"Just wondering, that's all. It's a gift you have, you know." She shrugged it off. "No matter, I need to check my answering machine and spend some time with the kittens anyway, so I'll go home while you're with Denise. Swing by and pick me up on your way back."

*   *   *   *

"Denise, it was weird," I said, "Like he didn't want to talk to me." I related the conversation I'd had with Perry. Bumping along the interstate in Denise's truck, the horse trailer rattled behind us. We started out as soon as Denise got off work, making use of what little daylight was left.

We were heading south, where much of the state's corn crop grew. Combines were coming in from the fields with the day's haul. Wagons loaded with tons of the yellow grain were ready to ship to county elevators, where it was mixed into special blends to be sold as horse and cattle feed.

"I could have saved you the call," she said. "I stopped by Lida's on the way home from work. I thought maybe she'd go with us, being as how you're sort of a semi-invalid." She grinned.

Not thrilled at being termed a "semi-invalid," I smiled weakly and said nothing. Hopefully, my invalid status would end tomorrow with my follow-up doctor visit, but then, so too would my life of leisure. *C'est la vie.*

"Funny thing is," Denise went on, "when I pulled into the yard, I parked under the apple trees by the side of the driveway."

"And?" I asked, wondering what she was getting at.

"Perry came from the house with a plate of food and it looked like he was headed down the fruit cellar with it."

"Huh? The fruit cellar?"

"And guess what else he had? This is really weird."

"What?" I asked, wishing she would hurry up and get to the point.

"A wig!"

"A wig? You've got to be joking." What on earth would Perry be doing with a wig?

She flipped her blinker on and swerved to avoid a line of construction barrels blocking the slow lane ahead. "No, I'm not kidding. A black wig, about shoulder length. So he sets the plate and the wig down on the door to the fruit cellar and comes over. But he kept watching it, and when one of the cats moseyed over there, he swept it up. Trying to break the ice, I made a joke about him eating leftovers while Lida was gone, but he didn't seem amused. I didn't dare ask about the wig."

"Did you ask him where Lida was?"

"Sure—and I got the same answer you did. I wanted to look around, make sure her horses were being taken care of, but I felt sort of strange having to drag conversation out of him, so I just said goodbye and left. It looked like he had the horses locked up in the barn, which I doubt Lida would be very happy about. You know how freaked out she is about making sure they get their fresh air and sunshine. It's like she runs a Swiss health spa for horses."

"You think something's up?" I asked.

"Like what?"

"Like I don't know ... like maybe he's done something with Lida," I said, suddenly suspicious. "First, you witness them having a fight. Then she suddenly decides to visit her sister in South Carolina, which we both know just isn't like Lida. She always plans her trips out to the tiniest detail as far as animal care goes. And she never even mentioned that she was planning to go out of town. Then, she doesn't come home when Perry originally says she's coming home. Are you thinking what I'm thinking?"

"Don't be silly. Lida and Perry have been married fifty years. Seems to me that if he wanted to get rid of her, he would have done it long ago."

"Maybe not. Maybe something new came up. Maybe there's an insurance policy about to expire or maybe she finally pushed him over the limit." Something worried me about Lida's absence, something I just couldn't put on the back burner. "I'd hate to think we sat idly by while she was tortured, chained to a wall in a dark, dank fruit cellar."

"Talk about an overactive imagination!" She pulled off the interstate and coasted to a stop on the exit ramp. "Do we take a left or a right here?"

The map was in the bucket with the carrots, on the floor between my feet. I switched the overhead light on and my finger traced the pink fluorescent line marking our route. "Left," I said, switching off the light. "I admit it sounds farfetched, but did you ever think we'd find bones, or a body, or that I'd have death threats scrawled across my bathroom mirror? Somebody knows how to get into my house without breaking in. No windows are broken and no locks are disturbed." She inched out onto the patched asphalt road, the horse trailer rattling in protest. "Maybe we should call missing persons."

"How can we report her missing when her husband says she's visiting her sister? You can't just walk into the police station and accuse Perry of ... what is it we're accusing him of, anyway?" Denise asked.

"Seems to me it wouldn't take that much time for Sheriff Morton to check up, call the sister, to just see if she's there. Trouble is, the minute he sees me, he'll immediately get defensive and difficult, just because it was me calling it to his attention. Even more so now, after this morning's blowup."

"Have you got the sister's phone number?"

"No," I said, realizing dismally that I didn't even have her name. "All I know is that she lives in South Carolina."

"Oh, that narrows our search," Denise said sarcastically.

"I know it sounds like a long shot, but I've just got a feeling, a nagging suspicion." Something wouldn't let go of me. There had been so much happening lately, how could I not worry? Part of me said Lida was fine, but another part said maybe she *wasn't*. Maybe it wasn't too late to do something about it.

"So call Perry and ask for the sister's phone number. Say you want to ask Lida something, anything, just to get the number. Then give her a call. It's as simple as that."

"Except then he's alerted to the fact that I'm suspicious. I've got to find a way to get the sister's phone number or the address without Perry knowing. If we could—"

"Not a chance! After last week with the coyotes, you're not dragging me into another one of your hare-brained escapades!" She looked straight ahead, both hands on the steering wheel. "Subject closed. *Finis.*"

Admittedly, Denise had gone on a few capers that, although I wouldn't exactly call them "hare-brained," hadn't exactly been Einstein-level, either, so I had no rebuttal. We rounded a curve in the road and I saw the farm's lights.

"There it is," I said.

She flicked on her turn signal. "Not to change the subject, but I've been meaning to ask—have you seen my Celtic cross? I wore it last weekend and I can't find it."

Rarely was Denise without either her cross or another favorite necklace, a silver-hinged fish. "You wore the fish Sunday; I remember it dangling in my face when you bent over," I recalled.

"I've looked everywhere for the cross, but it's disappeared."

"I haven't seen it. Marge vacuumed on Monday. She probably would have noticed if she'd sucked up a good-sized cross like that, but I'll ask her anyway."

I rolled my window down when we pulled into the stable yard. The night air was cool and damp. Fireflies flitted in the grass at the edge of the drive, their bellies blinking. Clouds covered part of the moon and I wondered if lunar phases had played a part in any of the murders, like the rain had. "It's gonna' rain," I said. "The bodies have always been found after it rains, which means he either kills them just before or during the rain."

"It's not going to rain," Denise said, unconcerned, but I noticed she punched down the lock on the driver side door before slamming it shut.

"Feels like rain to me." I grabbed the bucket, carrots, halter, and lead rope from the truck. "I wasn't sure if we'd get to keep the nice leather halter he was wearing on Saturday, so I brought one, just in case."

"They had money for expensive leather halters with gold name plates, but none for feed," Denise said. "It's just so damned ironic, isn't it?"

"Pretty screwed-up." We trudged through the mud into the barn, and peering down the long aisle, saw a woman sweeping the floor. "Hello," I called to her. "We're here to pick up the gray horse."

She leaned her push broom against a stall door and walked toward us. "Name's Carlitta," she said, sticking out her hand. "Sue ran home to take care of her own horses, but she left papers for you to sign in the tack room."

"Papers?" I asked. I hadn't stopped to think there would be paperwork, but why not? In our litigious society, everything depends on a paper trail.

"Routine stuff. All the rehabilitators sign them. Until the judge gives the order, the horses are still the property of the owners. So right now, it's like you're a foster home and the animal is under the protection of Horse Heaven. Sue's got it all written down for you."

Carlitta pulled her thick black hair into a pony tail and twisted an elastic band around it. "He was a tad bit colicky on Sunday; the vet gave him more oil and said it wasn't anything serious."

Denise leaned against the stall door, her thumbs caught in the pockets of her jeans. "Looks like you've got your work cut out for you, Carol, bad hand and all."

"Yeah." Corn oil, a necessary evil, helped move along any gut blockages, but was a mess to clean up.

"You won't believe the change in him since the weekend. He's been up and eating and doing great. Come into the tack room and I'll get those papers," Carlitta said.

We followed her down the shed row, past a row of empty stalls. The stall floors had been stripped, the dung and fetid sawdust hauled away. A tremendous amount of work had been done in the three days since we'd first been there. "Most of the other horses have gone to their foster homes," she said.

I wondered what the final count was on the animals that hadn't made it. "Place sure smells better."

Carlitta flipped a switch and light flooded another section of the barn. "We moved everybody that was left to this wing." Horses poked their heads over the Dutch doors. Above the cacophony of rattling feed buckets, the thud of a well-placed hoof on a stall wall, and the stamping and pawing at doors, a shrill whinny rose. "Most of them are feeling better," Carlitta said. "Raising a ruckus when it's feeding time."

"It's a shame what happened here," Denise said.

"Sure is." Carlitta held the door to the tack room open. Denise and I sat at a small wooden table while Carlitta flipped through a notebook and pulled out four documents, each a different color. Yellow, blue, green, pink … she picked up the yellow one.

"This says you took possession of the horse," Carlitta said. "The vet already filled out his description. You sign here." A grubby finger with a bitten-down nail pointed to the section completed by the veterinarian. Next was a blue paper. "This one lists the food he's supposed to get, what kind, the amount, stuff like that. You sign it, agreeing to care for the horse as prescribed."

"I figured there would be a special diet. I've been studying feeding guidelines for rescued horses."

Carlitta's face showed acknowledgment. "The ones on the Internet that were just recently published by the AAEP?"

I nodded, signing the document.

She laid the blue page, face down, on the yellow sheet. "There's controversy surrounding them."

"Let me guess, the alfalfa? We were wondering about it too," I said.

"I suppose they know what they're talking about, weren't the researchers from University of Cal-Davis? But still, some vets don't agree with the straight alfalfa diet. They think timothy would be better or a mixture of the two. The jury is still out."

Denise said, "Maybe the alfalfa in Southern California is different. Ours is too rich to feed straight."

"Do they even have alfalfa in Southern California?" I asked. "Isn't it a desert?"

Carlitta shrugged. "You'll see from our feeding schedule that our vet is on the fence. He prefers a mixed hay and a teeny bit of plain oats. Sue said to take a bale of our hay to start, then slowly transfer him over to your hay a little at a time."

There was an electric kettle on the counter. She flipped a red switch at the base. "Hot chocolate?"

I shook my head.

Denise was probably hoping for a beer. "None for me, thanks."

"The first inclination is to start pouring feed into them, but that's the absolutely worst thing. Start slowly, otherwise you'll have founder, kidney failure, you name it. Bad news."

She picked up the green sheet. "This says you agree that after the horse is rehabilitated, you'll return him to either Horse Heaven or the original owners, if the original owners are ever found, whichever the judge decides."

"Give him back to the people that nearly starved him to death?" Denise said, her face showing shock.

Carlitta's thick black hair worked its way out of the elastic band with each turn of her head. "It's disgusting and it doesn't seem right, but unfortunately, that's the way it works."

I shifted in my chair. "That's a load of bullshit."

She smiled resignedly. "I know that and you know that, but we've got to play these games with the lawyers. In this case, I can tell you, these people aren't coming back, so I wouldn't worry about it. If they do, they've got a lot bigger problems than getting their horses back. The whole farm is in foreclosure and they skipped out on everybody, from feed dealers to blacksmiths."

The kettle kicked off and she poured powdered chocolate into a cup. "Don't do anything with the pink sheet right now. That's for later, if the judge awards ownership to Horse Heaven and you decide you'd like to buy the horse."

It was entitled "Final Ownership." I read the section that had been handwritten, signed, and dated by the attending veterinarian. It gave Saint's vital statistics, gray Thoroughbred gelding, three years old, and showed left- and right-side drawing profiles of the horse. My eyes, snagged by the dollar sign at the bottom of the page, fell to the valuation. Stunned, I elbowed Denise, my finger pointing to the staggering amount. With a sinking heart, I knew I could never come up with that amount. Not in this lifetime.

What was the sense of taking Saint, of rehabilitating him, if only to give him back, possibly to the original owner? Maybe I shouldn't take him at all. "I've forgotten my glasses in the truck," I said, eyes pleading with Denise.

Denise and I had known each other for so long that we communicated in facial expressions as much as words. "I'll help you," she said, and explained to Carlitta, "My truck's got these funny locks—takes a knack to get them open. We'll be right back."

"What do I do?" I asked as soon as we were out of earshot. "If I take him and rehabilitate him, I'll never be able to buy him; I don't have that kind of money."

We were back at the truck now, the grass at the edge of the drive alive with crickets and fireflies. "Look, you're doing this for the horse, right? What does money have to do with it?"

"I thought I'd be able to keep him. I thought they *gave* the horse to you in exchange for nursing it back to health."

She opened the door and sat on the seat of the old truck, her arms cradled around her knees. She thought for a moment, then looked up. "You never answered me, Carol. Are you doing this for the horse or because you thought you got something for free?"

"Dammit!" I pushed the toe of my boot into the mud, then kicked a clod off into the grass, silencing the crickets. "The way I see it, either I take the horse and save him, but don't get to keep him, or I let him die."

"That's it in a nutshell. You'll spend your time and money and you'll work your tail off. And maybe you'll end up with a broken heart."

We went back in and I signed Carlitta's yellow, blue and green papers. The ominous pink sheet I simply took, a reminder of what was to come, the decisions that would have to be made later.

We were amazed at how much Saint had improved. He loaded without incident, stepping into Denise's trailer and standing quietly. The ropes we brought and the elaborate plans for supporting him on the way home were unnecessary. We picked Marge up on the way back, and with the three of us crammed on the bench seat of the pickup, Denise and I filled her in, both of us talking at once.

"How on earth did they come up with that amount? That's more than I paid for my house," Marge said, when told of the price tag Saint carried.

Denise dodged potholes in the dirt road. "It was a racing stable. Some of those bloodlines are mighty expensive."

Wedged in the middle, I was getting jostled from both sides. "Maybe it's based on what *they* paid for him."

"If they were worth that much, why didn't they sell them, instead of abandoning them?" Marge asked. "Even sold by the pound to the meat packers, they'd have gotten something. This way, they've got nothing."

"Maybe they do," I said, and told her how sometimes the judge awards the animals back to the original owners.

"Chances are that isn't going to happen in this case. Those horses were in bad shape; anyone would agree that was gross animal cruelty," Denise said.

We dropped Marge at my front door before driving the trailer down to the barn. There was a box on the front porch. "Looks like the UPS man was here," I said.

I gave Marge the keys to the front door. "What do you want me to do with it?" she asked.

"Just bring it in, I'll open it after we get Saint settled in." I didn't remember sending for any mail orders.

We bumped across the lawn and down to the stable, then Denise backed the trailer up to the gate. "I'd better put Echo and Feather in their stalls before we unload him." Horses, when meeting for the first time, sometimes had sniffing sessions that quickly deteriorated. Other times they became instant buddies. It was always a toss-up as to which it would be, so it was better to play safe. "Feather's steel shoes walloping Saint's bony ribcage is the last thing that poor horse needs," I said.

I enticed Feather and Echo into their stalls with a scoop of sweet feed, then opened the gate. Denise carefully backed the trailer into the paddock. When it was positioned, she shut off the truck and pulled the parking brake. I undid the butt rope, let the ramp down and inched Saint slowly out of the trailer. He whinnied nervously. Feather and Echo stretched their heads over their Dutch doors, trying to touch noses with Saint. Feather called loudly to him. "I'll put him in the stall across the aisle, so they can see him but not touch him."

Even though he couldn't reach him, Echo tried to appear ferocious, snapping at Saint when we walked past. "My, what big teeth you have," Denise teased, giving his blaze face a good rubbing, which sent white hairs swirling.

"He's such a big baby, he never thinks he gets enough attention."

We bedded all three stalls with fresh sawdust and filled water buckets. Denise took Sue's hay from the trailer and set it outside Saint's stall. With my hay knife, I slashed the binder twine and pulled a flake off. Bright green and leafy, it smelled like a summer meadow. "Nice stuff. I wonder what she pays for it," I said.

"Plenty, I'll bet."

Denise finished sweeping out her trailer and together we lifted and latched the heavy ramp. We leaned against the stall door, watching Saint. Done in from the trip, he munched his meager serving of hay, then contentedly settled into the fluffy sawdust.

"I'll check back later, before I go to bed," I said. "Let's shut off the lights and go up. I'm beat."

We trudged up to the house, tired and dirty, and plopped down onto the sofa. Every bone in my body ached. "Who's the package from?"

Marge shrugged. "No name, just a street address in Indiana."

The contents slid loosely back and forth when I shook it. The computer-printed address and return labels gave no clue as to the sender. "I guess we won't know until we open it, will we?"

"Probably from Jack. He bought a gift and had it wrapped and sent. So thoughtful," Marge said.

"It's that fancy teddy she's been wanting," Denise said sardonically.

"Yeah, that must be it." I got a knife from the kitchen to cut the box open. "The red one with the black lace." I detested red.

"It has an odd smell," Marge said.

"More likely it's his dirty laundry," I said. I sliced along one edge, careful not to push the blade in too far, then reached my fingers into the box to tear apart the packing tape holding the ends together. Something inside the box, cool and dry, brushed against my thumb. *Flowers*? Maybe he *did* miss me after all. And he knows I love yellow roses. But the box wasn't long and narrow like flower boxes usually were. Marge and Denise watched raptly.

"Well, come on already, tear it!" Denise said.

I pulled up and tore the lid from the box with such force that the contents flew through the air and seemed to twist and wriggle. Denise screamed, spun around and body slammed me, knocking me to the floor. Confused, I lay there with my eyes closed. A tickling sensation, like someone lightly running their fingers along my skin, traveled up my body, first over my wrist, then up my arm and across my neck. I tried to think of what it could be when Denise yelled, "Snake!"

I opened my eyes as it slithered in soft curving waves toward my face.

Chapter Ten

"That old lady's got guts!" Denise exclaimed, after checking to make sure Marge was still in the bathroom. "Picked that snake right up and threw it out the door, like nobody's business."

"I hope the stupid thing freezes to death," I said, holding an ice bag on the painful knot on my forehead. "What moron wraps up a snake in a box like a gift? That's really sick." My skin still crawled with the feel of the reptile slithering across it, a sensation I strongly doubted I would forget. "I say we leave Sheriff Morton out of this one. Let's find who sent it ourselves. We'll get more accomplished without him."

"I don't like that idea one bit," Marge said, coming out of the bathroom, her perfect white curls freshly lacquered, catching the tail-end of my suggestion. "Taking the law into your own hands will get you nothing but trouble."

"It's just that he doesn't *do* anything. He's bound by so many legalities and so much red tape, he gets nothing accomplished."

"Vigilante law is not the answer."

"I'm with Marge on this one," Denise added. She turned the torn brown packaging paper over in her hands. "Besides, what have we got to go on? No doubt this is a phony return address."

"Sent by someone who knew Jack went to Indiana and assumed you would open it, thinking that's who it was from," Marge said. "Which is exactly what you did."

I moved the ice bag to my swollen cheek. "Have you ever considered professional football?"

Denise reached for her cigarettes on the glass-topped coffee table. "I'm sorry for the body slam; it was reflex."

"Yeah, right. Well, anyway, why can't we go to UPS and ask them who paid to ship it? They must keep track of that sort of thing."

"I don't need UPS to figure out who this points to," Marge said. "Or the messages on the mirror either." She shifted in her chair, smoothing her skirt. "You realize it too, don't you, Carolyn?" Marge's adamant eyes locked onto mine.

"Huh?" I asked, totally befuddled.

"Why, Richard, of course."

"I just don't believe you, Marge. You've got it in for that poor guy. Did you hear any of what he told me the other night about his childhood? It was a living hell! Give him a break."

"Think about it. He had access to the bathroom mirror and you told him yourself of your snake phobia."

"And what's his motive?"

"To terrorize you. He knows your husband is gone and that you're living here alone. He's attracted to you—"

"Attracted to me! What on earth does that have to do with anything?"

"It's simple. If he scares you badly enough, you'll fall for it when he offers to temporarily move in with you—as your protector—and wheedles his way into your bedroom."

"That is absolutely crazy, Marge, just plain crazy!" I rolled my eyes. How dumb did she think I was? Did she really think I'd fall for a stupid tactic like that? Insulted that she thought I could be so easily led, I said, "I may have been born at night, but it wasn't last night."

"Maybe it's not so crazy," Denise said.

Now it was two against one. Was I blind to something others saw? I didn't think so. "You've both lost your minds."

"It would be easy enough to prove," Denise added. "Tell Richard about the second mirror message and tonight's incident and play the damsel in distress, which shouldn't be hard to do, considering the snake-in-a-box routine someone just pulled. Then wait and see if he offers to move in with you until Jack gets back. If he does … *voila*!"

"That's not fair. In fact, I believe it's called entrapment."

Denise shrugged. "Let him prove us wrong."

"Or dig his own grave, as the case may be," Marge said.

"Come on, it'll be fun, a chance to do your very best Scarlett O'Hara. What do you think, Marge? I say she bats those beautiful dark lashes and it's a cinch he falls for it."

"Hook, line and sinker, without a doubt." The oven timer buzzed, signaling Marge's brownies were done.

"I'll do it … on one condition," I said.

"Which is?" Denise asked, wary when she wasn't setting the terms.

"You come with me to Lida's," I said. "We find out what the hell's in that fruit cellar."

Denise extended her hand. "You've got yourself a deal. Five bucks says Richard's our mirror writer *and* snake sender. And that's five on top of the other five you already owe me."

Kneeling before the hearth, I stirred the burning logs in the fire-place until they snapped and glowed orange. "How soon do we go to Lida's?"

"No time like the present, but let's run the horse trailer home first," Denise replied. "No sense in hauling it around if we don't have to."

"Marge, what about you?" I asked. "You'll be here alone."

"If it's who we think it is, he's got no interest in me. I'm going to take a bath, have a cup of tea, and hit the sack."

All three of those things sounded really good. "You're not afraid?"

She scoffed at the suggestion with a flip of her hand. "Not in the least. But you two dress warm. Supposed to be a cold front moving in tonight."

*   *   *   *

Denise backed the trailer slowly, the red taillights bouncing off the metal pole barn. "A little farther," I said, leaning out the passenger door. The tire bumped up against the rock Denise used for a park-ing block and I jumped out, pushing a paver brick in front of the tire. The wind whipped my hair into my face and caught on my lips as I undid the safety chains.

Denise left the truck idling, got out, and slid the sleeve on the hitch forward, releasing it, then wound the wheel down to the cement block. "Do you see a plastic horse head hitch cover any-where? I always leave it next to the cement block." She felt around in the grass.

The beam from my flashlight crossed back and forth, over the ground near the cement block. Shadows from the swaying trees passed in and out of my line of vision. "The wind is really kicking up, maybe it blew away," I said. "Marge was right. It *is* turning colder."

"I put it right up tight against the block for just that reason. It's got to be here somewhere. It keeps the rain from running down inside the crank."

"I'll keep looking for it while you explain to Todd that we're going to Lida's. And remember, he doesn't need all the details. Marge knows where we are if we're not back in a couple of hours. The fewer in on this, the better." It was nearly midnight already, and a jittery feeling I couldn't shake had me anxious to get going.

I looked for the hitch cover while Denise ran up to the house, shining Jack's camp light underneath the trailer and in the tall grass growing at the edge of the pole barn. When my hands began to ache from the cold, I got inside the truck and turned the heater blower on high, warming my fingers above the vent on the dash. I anxiously thought of Lida. Something didn't sit right about her being gone longer than expected, and the fact that she was gone at all without telling us just wasn't like her.

Denise came out of the house with her black winter jacket on. "It was like the Spanish Inquisition," she said, pulling herself up into the big diesel.

"What'd you tell him?"

"That we had to go to Lida's to look for something."

"Little does he know it's Lida herself we're looking for." I wondered if part of me was afraid of what we might find.

"Did you find the hitch cover?" she asked.

"No, but I wouldn't worry about it. It'll turn up in the morning, when you can see better."

Ten minutes later, Denise pulled onto the grass at the edge of Lida's property and killed the headlights. We got our flashlights and started down the driveway on foot. The chalet stood far back from the road, the warm glow of its lights barely visible.

Crouching low, we crossed the wooden bridge over the creek, which cut Lida's acreage in half, separating front orchards from fenced pasture, then stayed close to the massive weeping willows that lined the drive. Tucking my arms around myself, I pulled my fleece jacket tight against the quickly growing cold.

The horses, put up for the night in the front paddock and curious about nighttime visitors, walked the fence line alongside us. A dog barked somewhere far off. It belonged to a neighbor, because Lida didn't have a dog. Cats and horses and chickens, but thankfully no dog to announce our arrival.

The fruit cellar, between the house and the fence, was probably less than twenty feet away from a window, through which I saw Perry staring at the soft white glow of a television on the opposite wall. I was quickly losing what little nerve I had, and I wasn't sure if it was fear of being caught or fear of something else, but knew I couldn't back out now—not after dragging Denise along.

Before there was more time to think, I grabbed the handles that opened the doors to the cellar, each opening outward, like an armoire, and finding the doors heavier than expected, I lurched forward under their weight. Denise saw me falling and caught one of the handles before it fell back. I silently mouthed "thank you" to her.

Shining the light at my feet, we started down the uneven wooden steps that ended at a dirt floor. The air in the cellar was cave-like, dank, and smelling of moist earth and mold. My light scanned the walls. The cellar seemed to be a catch-all, with stacks of boxes lining one wall. Some of the boxes I recognized as having been at Lida's last garage sale. A wig lay on top of one. I picked it up, letting the hair hang down. Shoulder length, dark brown, loosely curled at the ends, just as Denise had described. Underneath it was a white sweater and navy blue pleated skirt. These things could not have belonged to Lida. Not only were they ultra-conservative, contrary to Lida's flamboyance, but they weren't her size. We replaced the clothes and I laid the wig on top, careful to put everything back just as we had found it. If they weren't Lida's, whose were they?

With only small circles of light to guide us, we tentatively explored the interior of the cellar. With Denise in front, I realized how steady she was. I would have turned and ran. She twisted around, tapped my arm, then pointed to the far corner, where a wheelbarrow and shovel stood leaning against the wall. My light, aimed lower than Denise's, fell to a square wooden frame on the floor. The soil inside the structure had been dug away so the boards were now flush with the floor. A bag of concrete lay within the framework.

I sucked in my breath, stifling a scream. I stood rooted, unable to put a priority on what I should do, my thoughts scattered like derailed train cars.

"He's killed her and now he's covering over her grave with cement!" Denise hissed. She grabbed the shovel and started digging, pitching the shovelfuls of dirt out of the frame. "Start digging!" she whispered, her voice low and dictatorial.

Frantically, I searched for something—anything—to dig with, clawing through layers of ancient National Geographics and old clothing in the boxes along the wall. I found a coffee can filled with rusty nails. I dumped the nails and began scooping the dirt Denise had loosened with the spade, adding my meager offering to her quickly growing pile. After a while, the hook and loop fasteners on my wrist brace loosened, and my wrist started to ache. I stopped to pull them taut.

We worked with concentration and soon we knew each other's movements, how many seconds it took Denise to loosen a shovelful and how long it took me to fill my can and pitch it over my shoulder. Because the dirt had been recently disturbed, it wasn't packed tightly. For Denise, this was good; but for me, with only a coffee can, it was still slow-going. The back of my cotton turtleneck quickly became soaked with sweat.

Suddenly, the basement flooded with light. Blinking against the glare, we saw an illuminated second staircase in the opposite corner. Perry stood at the top. My eyes traveled to the shiny object in his right hand. A pistol.

*   *   *   *

"Whatever gets into that head of yours, you trespass without a second thought for anyone else's property," Sheriff Morton barked. "Digging up a man's basement in the middle of the night!" At the police station, they separated Denise and me, like common criminals on television cop shows, hoping one would squeal on the other. In this case, there was no doubt who was fully to blame.

That Lida had been in danger and Perry was somehow responsible had seemed so plausible earlier. But Sheriff Morton refused to believe Perry was guilty of anything. He also made it clear that if a missing persons report was to be filed, it would be filed by Perry, not by Denise or I.

As for the wooden frame, concrete, and wheelbarrow, Perry planned on surprising Lida by pouring a concrete base for a new water softener before her return. Now he wasn't sure he could fix it before she got home. He also explained to Sheriff Morton, with considerable disgust, how he'd spent painstaking hours leveling the dirt within the wooden frame.

Personally, I thought the whole water softener thing sounded like a cover-up for something else. But if it was true, I'd ruined his surprise for Lida and made a complete mess of things. I'd turned Perry against me and would be lucky if either he or Lida ever spoke to me again. I had succeeded only in making myself into a fool.

"You really ought to stop meddling in the affairs of others," Sheriff Morton said. "You'll be lucky if Perry doesn't press charges."

Apparently, he'd swallowed Perry's entire story. "What kind of charges?" I barely croaked the words. Hopefully nothing involving money. Or jail time. Community service, maybe?

"Monetary damages."

"Can't I just fix the dirt? I'll make it level, I swear, it'll be absolutely flat, perfect." *Just give me a chance to go back there.* I saw myself on my knees, working on leveling Lida's cellar floor for days, in-between investigating the piles and boxes around the perimeter.

"It's up to Perry. He might consider breaking and entering."

Not likely he'd want me to come back. "We didn't break into anything, at least not the way we came in. That cellar door was unlocked. I didn't know there was an entrance into the house through the cellar."

"Like I said, I'll discuss it with Perry and decide. For now, you can go. Denise is waiting to drive you home."

If he was letting me go, there was a good chance Perry had already decided not to press charges. He was playing my bluff. With relief, I decided to broach another subject. "I was wondering if you've heard anything about the skull the coyotes found in the woods. Off the record, of course."

"No, and if I did," he shook his finger at me, "I certainly wouldn't tell *you*. By the way, when are you going back to work? You're a real nuisance when you've got extra time on your hands."

And you're a pain in the butt when you're dieting. "Actually," I said, looking at my watch, and just now realizing that on a normal day I'd be getting up to go to work in a couple of hours, "I've got a doctor's appointment this morning. Don't worry, my life of leisure will soon be over."

Sheriff Morton left the room and I was alone and utterly desolate. My best friends were angry, and my husband was gone. Was "busybody" the word others used to describe me? At what point does caring become meddling? Was I off-base in thinking something was up with Lida's absence?

I pulled on my jacket, struggling to get the sleeve over the bulky wrist brace, and left the room. Denise sat on a bench in the lobby, reading a magazine, the smoke from her cigarette curling softly.

"I guess we can go," I said.

"Yeah."

She looked at her watch. "Not much sense in going home to bed now, is there? Almost time to go to work." She ground her cigarette out in the ashtray.

"My follow-up appointment for my wrist is today. I'll probably have to go back tomorrow." At some point, my wrist had stopped hurting, though I wasn't sure when, exactly.

"Oh, yeah, I forgot."

"Denise, I'm really sorry. For all of this," I said.

"Hey, don't worry about it. I was the one who started digging. Did they give you the song and dance about having to pay to fix the basement?"

I felt stupid and close to tears. "Sort of. I offered to fix it myself. He knows I don't have the money to hire anyone." I brushed the corner of my eye.

The doors of the police station banged shut behind us. The air was cool and damp, and clouds had moved in during the night. Her truck was parked a couple spaces down, at the curb.

"Do you believe that crap about a cement base for the water softener?" she asked.

Surprised, I gave her a quick sideways glance. Maybe I wasn't the only one with suspicions. "What do you mean?"

"He's lying. That's a lame excuse he pulled out of a hat. Water softener, my ass."

"What can we do about it?" I felt defeated, only slightly buoyed up by the fact that Denise didn't believe Perry, either.

"I don't know. Morton seems to believe him. 'Course I guess he would, being they're old buddies." She dug in her purse for her keys.

"They are?" This was news to me.

"Hell, yeah, they're in the same bowling league. Have been for years. Todd and I were on it, too, at one time. World's most boring sport." She got in and reached across the seat to unlock the passenger door. "Let's put our heads together over breakfast. We'll think of something."

"You've got to go to work. I don't want to keep you from what little sleep you might get."

"I couldn't sleep now anyway. Besides, it'll be like old times, like working at Fox Valley again. How many times did we spend the night with a sick horse, then went scouting out a greasy spoon open at four in the morning? Or one of us went for carry out, while the other stayed on watch."

If she was trying to make me feel better, it was working. I laughed. "Remember the horse shows? We'd braid horses all night for the early classes and then order breakfast from the guy with the portable kitchen. The one who parked his rig out by the polo field."

"How could I forget? Weak coffee in a styrofoam cup, a hard-fried egg slapped between two slices of bread. We'd eat leaning on the sand ring rail, watching riders warm up."

"It sure tasted good, though, didn't it?" I asked.

"If you like gritty eggs and cold toast."

I winced at the truth. "What happened to us?" I asked, unable to shake this melancholy feeling that somehow my life was in shambles, even though, when I analyzed it, I had all the things I'd ever wanted: a house with enough land to stable my horses, a career, and a husband who, though gone most of the time, said he loved me. Something was still missing and I couldn't quite put my finger on it.

"Time is what happened," she said. In the dim light from the overhead lamp, I saw the creases at the corners of her eyes. "Jobs and families and bills and years. We just plain *got older*." She slammed her door. "Let's get some chow. You're weird and morose when you haven't eaten."

Chapter Eleven

By the time I left Dr. Walsh's office, it was late afternoon. He'd sent me to the radiologist in the next medical building. Dr. Hsu took X-rays and directed me to deliver both the films and myself back to Dr. Walsh. I felt like a ping-pong ball, bouncing between the two buildings, though my bounce was decreasing.

The doctors suggested that I return to work on Monday wearing the steel-plated wrist brace to prevent overflexion. My ankle was badly bruised and shouldn't cause problems, provided I didn't take up hiking.

The rain still held off, but seemed inevitable. When I got home I thought about taking Feather out for a quick ride before the storm. "Just my luck, there'll be a downpour the instant I mount up," I gloomily told Marge, after explaining the circumstances of Denise's and my arrest and the declaration that I was fit to return to work next week. I removed the wrist brace and laid it on the dining room table.

"Go, it'll do you good," she said absently. She got two eggs out of the refrigerator and cracked them into the big mixing bowl.

"What are you making?"

She measured a cup of flour and dumped that in too. "An experiment."

"Need any help?"

"Nope."

"Guess I will go for a ride, then." She smiled but I knew she wasn't really paying attention, preoccupied with her recipe.

I brought Feather in from the pasture and put her in her stall. She wore a layer of dried mud like a suit of armor. Saint snuffled through his sawdust bed, searching for leftover bits of hay. My fingers ached to dump a heaping scoop of sweet feed into his manger and watch him gulp it in one greedy, slobbering frenzy. *And several hours later, I'll be begging a veterinarian to attend a sick horse, emergency call extra.* Instead I gave them carrots.

These were not your ordinary carrots. They were mammoth. Purchased in bulk at the farmer's market, these carrots were of such enormous and unwieldy sizes as to be unrecognizable to their cousins, the dainty inhabitants of grocery produce aisles. All three horses crunched with delight.

While Feather snacked, I groomed quickly, hoping to ride out and return before the rain. Riding in the rain is not fun. Not that I can't take a little drizzle in stride, but a cold, soaking, dripping-from-the-eyelashes rain imparts a special form of misery. I'd done it for years, exercise riding for Fox Valley, and later, when showing my own horses. But after I traded my stable hand position for a career that, though not as enjoyable, was less strenuous and far better paying, I vowed to myself, *no more riding in the rain.* I'd become the fair-weather rider I'd previously regarded with disdain—lazy, overweight and, God forbid, *middle-aged.*

We trotted down the gravel road, passing shuttered houses where no one seemed to be at home. Eerily quiet, even the birds seemed to have closed themselves away today. Feather's ears moved forward and back, like radar, catching every movement, every sign of life.

We stepped off the road and down onto the soft dirt trail, littered by the season's first damp fallen leaves. Barely more than a deer track, by late autumn leaves would obliterate the path. Feather left silent hoofprints in the sandy loam.

Enter these enchanted woods, you who dare. I tried to remember where the words came from. A long-ago English literature class? John Donne? No. George Meredith. The forest a shrouded gray blanket of sky and fog, it was not clear where either began or ended. The air was thick and heavy. Ominous thunder rumbled from beyond the western ridge. One horrendous, loud crack came, sharp and splitting, like a rifle shot. Rain lightly tapped the leaves of the ancient oaks, then began to drip from leaf to leaf. Soon it streamed from the tips of the branches in tiny waterfalls.

This would have to happen now, just as I'd predicted. I cursed silently. We could wait out the storm, in a valley, nestled under a stand of huge tamarack pines, safe from lightning and dry, at least for a short while. I rode there. The needles underneath the trees were still bone dry. I got off Feather and pulled her in, my saddle brushing the undersides of the lowest boughs. The rain became heavier. One loud crack of thunder after another obliterated any other sounds. The rain fell in sheets all around us, while the wind blew a spray under the limbs where I shivered. Rain dripped from Feather's nose. It ran inside the ventilation holes in my helmet, down my hair, and underneath the collar of my jacket. Miserable, I looked out over the pewter landscape, furious with myself for having tried to squeeze a ride in before the storm.

Then I saw something halfway up the hill to my left. It moved like a specter through the low rolling fog. At first, I thought it was vapor rising from the wet earth, since except for last night, it had been warm these last days and this was a cold, terrible, hard-driving rain. What was it? I held my hand over my eyes to shield them from the rain. Barely discernible between the torrents, it appeared human, head bent low against the wind and rain, hurriedly descending the hill.

A quick-falling twilight deepened the shadows. Moving quickly, the figure was closer now. Whoever it was wore a full-length waxed Australian coat, made for horsemen. I owned one just like it. The tails of the coat wrapped around the legs and closed with snaps to form a waterproof trouser cover, useful when riding in the rain and permitting easier walking while on the ground. I called out, to share our shelter, for what little refuge it offered. But with the rain, thunder, and rivers falling from the branches, I couldn't hear the words from my own lips. They melded into the cacophony of the storm's fury.

A jagged streak of light ran down a tall pine's trunk at the hill's crest. This same tree was struck by lightning last year. Withered and grayed, its branches were brittle. The tree split, one-half still anchored, the other half rolling down the hill. The log gained speed and crashed over brush and saplings. I screamed a futile warning to the stranger, but he was intent only on the ground in front of him. I don't know what suddenly made me think it was a man, I was not close enough to know for certain. I struggled to move Feather out from under the tamaracks, so I could wave my arms at him. Feather spooked, threw her head up and sharply jerked on the bridle, wrenching my shoulder backward. The log bearing down on the stranger crushed a path through the fern and bracken.

Frantic, I tied Feather's reins to a branch, close to the bit. The rain beat my back, mattering little now, as every inch of me was drenched. The log only feet away from the stranger now, I screamed repeatedly, running at him with flailing arms. He looked up, but when his eyes followed my pointing finger up the hill, it was too late. The end of the log grazed the outside of his right leg, just below the knee, and sent him sprawling. It knocked him clear of the log's path, which descended to the valley floor.

I ran toward him, preparing myself for the worst and gathering options. If he was hurt, I'd have to use Feather to carry him. But before I could get to him, he was already limping up the hill, away from me.

Gasping with the exertion of the climb, I stopped, confused. Even injured, he was well ahead of me. I collapsed into a bed of crushed fern and watched the twilight and swirling fog swallow him.

A shiny red object was on the ground next to my hand. I picked it up and turned it over in my hands, examining it. It was a plastic horse head hitch cover, like Denise's. Had he dropped it? Then I knew. The victim tree! The jewelry, knickknacks and articles of clothing. He had taken Denise's hitch cover and he probably had her lost silver cross, too. No one yet understood victim trees or how the killer chose and acquired the victim's objects. What I *did* know now was that my discovery indicated Denise was a target.

Rain figured into his ritualistic killings. Did he perceive the rain as cleansing? Was he preparing the sacrificial site, placing the ornaments on the tree during a rainstorm? How far in advance of the murder did he do this? How much time did we have to warn Denise? I was shivering, and not entirely from the cold rain.

Sliding downhill on wet cinnamon fern, grabbing saplings and branches to steady myself, I worked my way to the bottom of the hill. Though I knew I was not his prey, that provided little reassurance. I nervously kept checking behind me, expecting a shadow to emerge from the curtain of rain.

Feather, though frenzied, was still tied where I'd left her. We galloped out of the valley, taking the main trail that connected to the gravel road. Without the trees as shelter, cold needles of rain stung my face. Drenched, my thin windbreaker clung like a wet T-shirt and provided no warmth. Feather's long, ground-covering canter was effortless, and ten miserable minutes later we galloped across my lawn, clumps of wet grass flying from Feather's hooves. Dismounting at the gate, I pulled her into the barn, out of the rain. I slipped her leather halter over her head and snapped the cross ties to the halter's brass rings, then threw a wool cooler over her steaming back. "Sorry, Feather, I'll be right back."

I ran up to the house. "Marge!" I called from just inside the patio's sliding glass door. On the mat with my soggy boots and dripping hair, I detected the faint musty smell of the furnace kicking on for the first time in the fall. I yelled again. "Marge!"

"All right, all right, I'm coming. Hold your horses." She appeared in the hallway. "Guess you didn't make it home before the rain."

"Marge, this is important. Call Denise right away. Tell her to lock all her doors and windows and stay in the house. Don't answer the phone or the door. Don't talk to anyone."

Her eyes were wide. "Huh?"

"There's no time to explain. I'll put Feather up, and then we'll go."

"Go where?"

"To Denise's. I've found her trailer hitch cover."

"You're not making a bit of sense." She pulled her pink sweater around her. "Get into some dry clothes, before you catch pneumonia. You're shivering."

If only she knew what I knew, she'd shiver too. I'd been so close to him. So close to seeing his face! "Not now, Marge—I'll be back in five minutes, ten tops." I turned and ran back to the stable before the warmth of the house lured me into dawdling.

What linked the murdered women? And what ultimately linked them to Denise? There was a common denominator—I just hadn't found it yet. All female, aged mid-thirties to mid-forties. Not all from the same town. Same county? I tried keeping my thoughts abstract. Hair color, height, build? But those were physical traits. Maybe the link was less obvious, like education, religious beliefs, or ethnic background.

Steam rose from under the old German saddle when I lifted it from Feather's back. I rubbed her down with a thick towel and put her in her stall. Pulling her blanket over her, I packed tufts of straw up under the fleecy lining, to form a layer of air between the blanket and her sweat-soaked coat. Saint nickered when I doled out a thin flake of second-cutting alfalfa hay to Feather and Echo each. "It's the special stuff for you." I tossed him a flake of Sue's hay. "Only one flake each. I don't want anybody getting sick on me."

A strong wind whipped the barn door from my hands, throwing it against its hinges. I slammed the door shut and bolted it, then hurried across the waterlogged lawn, up to the house. Water squished between my frozen toes with each step.

Marge was on the phone. "Here she is." She cupped her hand over the mouthpiece. "Todd's gone to the hardware store ... she's alone, but she's fine. What's this all about?"

"Thank you, dear Lord, thank you," I mouthed the words, looking up, and took the phone.

"Denise, Marge and I are on our way. I'll explain things later. Lock all your doors and windows, if you haven't already. Don't let anyone in."

"Is this something we should notify Sheriff Morton about?" Marge called from my closet, where she was pulling clothes off hangers.

"Hang on a second, Denise." I covered the phone. "We're the last people on earth he wants to hear from right now. And trust me, the feeling is mutual."

Marge gave me jeans, my wool fisherman's sweater, and a pair of warm, thick socks. "Go change," she ordered. "I'll keep her on the line until we leave."

*   *   *   *

"Is it yours?" I asked.

Denise turned the plastic hitch cover over. "Maybe ... I'm not sure. Where was it?"

"On the trail that goes down into the valley where the trilliums bloom. We were waiting out the rain under the tamaracks. Do you remember the tree at the top of the hill, the tallest one that was struck by lightning last year?" I didn't wait for her answer. "It got hit again, and this time half of it toppled and rolled down the hill. There was someone coming down the hill, but it was raining so hard and thundering, he didn't hear me when I yelled. The log knocked him down. He wasn't badly hurt; he couldn't have been, because when he saw me, he ran the other way. Anyway, I found it where he fell."

Denise appeared confused. "I still don't understand why he'd want it. They're a dime a dozen."

"Stop. Think. The trees with the ornaments—the victim trees."

Her face blanched white. "No!"

"Bingo."

Her eyes widened. "The silver-hinged fish necklace—it's gone, too! I wanted to wear it today, but I looked for it this morning and it wasn't where I usually leave it. I forgot all about it until just now."

She ran to her bedroom—Marge and I following—and flung open her small wooden jewelry box, slapping the lid against the dresser mirror. Denise pulled out a jumble of tangled necklaces, which she attempted to unsnarl with shaking fingers. She threw the whole balled-up mess down on the dresser and wilted onto the bed.

"It's gone," she said, visibly shaken.

Marge sat next to her and softly put her arms around her. "I think we should call the sheriff," she said, looking up at me, where I stood carefully plucking the chains, one by one, from the tangle.

Denise brushed her hair from her face. "What does he want with *me?*"

In a frustrated mental soliloquy, I asked myself the same question. How did he choose his victims? Physical similarities? Age? What was it? There were a thousand things it could be.

I gave up on the tangled necklaces. "She's right, it's not here."

"This is dangerous. It isn't a game." Marge's voice was small and scared. And Marge did not scare easily.

"Wait a minute." Denise sat up and wiped her eyes. "This is all just speculation. We don't know anything for sure. Maybe it was someone else's hitch cover. There have got to be dozens of people that have them. And the fish ... oh, hell, I don't know ... possibly it means nothing at all."

Possibly it does.

"And right now I'm fed up to *here*"—she made a gesture with her leveled hand across her eyes—"with Morton treating us like ignorant schoolgirls."

"He's a pompous ass," I agreed.

"And he's got a devil of a temper," Denise said. "After this morning, I'm not looking for a second helping."

"But if we don't call the police, what *do* we do?" Marge asked.

"First of all," I said, pointing my finger at Denise, "you are not to be alone at any time until this guy is caught. Which brings us to another problem: what do we tell Todd?"

"Nothing," Denise said. "He'd insist on notifying Morton, who will place me under house arrest. Forget it." Diablo, Denise's Doberman pinscher, sidled up to lick her hand. "Reining finals are this weekend and Todd will make a big fuss about my going." The muscles in her jaw tensed. "I haven't worked all year to quit now."

This was probably the real reason behind her reluctance to call the sheriff. Denise had two strong qualities: one, she was fiercely competitive where her reining horses were concerned, and two, she could be infuriatingly stubborn. Last summer, on a ninety-degree day, she single-handedly unloaded an entire semi-trailer of hay, when help was only a phone call away. Stubbornness was one thing. Stupidity was another.

"Yeah, you're right, he would want you to cancel." In the scheme of the universe, I wasn't sure Todd thought reining competitions were all that necessary. Trying to visualize what was scribbled on my calendar for Saturday, I was thinking maybe I could go with her.

"The way I see it, I'd be better off in a crowd anyway," Denise said.

"But you'd be traveling to and from the show alone, and what if you break down on the highway?" *Or what if the breakdown was arranged?* "I might be able to go along," I said, not fully committing myself, in case she decided to cancel of her own accord before Saturday. Playing horse show lackey and indentured servant to Denise was not my idea of a perfect Saturday. On the other hand, nothing was more important than her life. If she insisted on going, I would tag along.

"Wait a minute," Marge blurted out suddenly. "Fingerprints on the plastic horse head!"

"But then we have to spill the beans to Morton," Denise said.

"Not necessarily." I plopped next to Denise on the bed, bracing my elbows on my knees. Diablo, all friendliness even though he must have smelled cat on me, moved over to my side. Wrinkling my nose, I pushed him away as diplomatically as possible, as he smelled, well, *doggy*. "We call Morton, just to speculate, of course—"

"Of course," Marge reiterated.

"We ask what would be the possibility of getting a fingerprint from an object. An object that I, hypothetically speaking, of course, found in the woods."

"Hypothetically, of course," Marge said, absent-mindedly, absorbed in thought.

"I'll ask about the differences in porous and nonporous surfaces and what the chances are of lifting a fingerprint, and how the weather might affect the quality of the print. If he says the chances are good, we give him the hitch cover, merely stating the general location of where we found it."

Denise flopped backward on the bed, studying the ceiling. "But how do we make him understand its importance, without mentioning the circumstances?"

"Yeah, you're right. To him it's just a hunk of plastic."

"Maybe he won't need an explanation," Marge mumbled, chewing a fingernail.

"Don't bank on that," I said, not keen on Morton's powers of deduction. "There's another downside," I said sheepishly. Since the killer had last handled the hitch cover, it had fallen in the mud, been picked up and carried in my pocket for several hours and, most recently, had been displayed to both Marge and Denise, all without the benefit of my having worn gloves. "If it ever had any prints, I've probably obliterated them."

"It's still worth a try," Marge said, ever hopeful.

Denise spoke candidly. "The person with the best chance of having a decent conversation with Morton is you, Marge. Quite frankly, I'm not even sure he'd take a call from either Carol or I."

"He's such an ass," I said.

Marge scowled. "That's the second time you've called him that. I wish you'd stop swearing."

"Ass is not swearing," I corrected her. "Swearing is when you use God's name in anger, which I never do." They both stared at me, speechless, Marge with a look of disbelief. "Well, rarely," I corrected. "Look, don't we have more important things to discuss here?" I asked, attempting to redirect the conversation's focus. "Denise is right, Marge. At least he'll talk to you."

"Use the phone in the living room," Denise said. "The number for the police is taped to the back of the handset."

Marge was back almost instantly. "He's in a meeting. I didn't want to say it was an emergency, so I left my number, well, actually, I left *your* number, Carol, and they said he'd call in the morning."

"There's something else we need: information on victim trees," I said, thinking aloud. "What the cultural significance is, when it began, that sort of thing. It might give us an idea of what makes this guy tick. Denise, can your computer access the Internet?"

She rolled her eyes. "Yeah, sure, except it's so slow, we'll be here all night. Santa needs to bring us a new one."

Denise's kitchen wall clock showed seven o'clock, straight up. "Marge, you stay with Denise while I go to the library. It'll take less time in the long run to use their Internet connection." Fifteen minutes' drive time each way, I calculated, and half an hour at the computer. "I should be back in an hour," I told them, grabbing my jacket.

It was already black out, darkness coming early with approaching winter, and in a few weeks, when we set our clocks back an hour at the end of Daylight Savings Time, it would come even earlier. The rain had stopped. If the cloud cover moved off, we'd get a heavy frost tonight. I turned my truck's heater up a notch.

Only one woman was working at the center island, another at the main entrance desk of the library. The smell of old books beckoned, a void a computer would never fill. After signing the Internet user's log, I sat down at a terminal and, speeding through warnings and security advice, entered my search criteria. All sorts of things about victims and trees popped up on the screen, but very little about victim trees. I scrolled down and read, clicking the small hand icon on items that seemed promising, then printing the pages out.

In Washington State, trees had been set up in communities wishing to commemorate deceased victims of crime. One star was hung on the tree for each life lost. Nothing, however, was mentioned about personal items which had belonged to the victims becoming part of the display. In Nepal, only two years ago, a newspaper article told of how trees were decorated with the decapitated heads of rivals of the Maoist rebellion, making Nepal a serious contender for anyone's list of worst vacation destinations.

Then I searched for trees as cultural symbols, and learned that trees figured prominently in many ethnic and tribal customs. There was evidence of North American Indians who believed that anything casting a shadow possessed a spirit. The larger the shadow, the more intelligent the spirit. The massive cottonwood trees of the upper Missouri Valley, having expansive shadows, were considered highly intelligent.

The Ojebway Indians of North America seldom cut down living trees, their medicine men professing they had heard the wailing of trees under the axe.

A globally shared belief was that spirits of deceased relatives inhabited trees, in various forms.

Still another source told of how each year, until the late nineteenth century in the Kangra Mountains of the Punjab, a maiden was sacrificed to an old cedar tree. The families of the village took turns in supplying a victim, who was either fastened to the trunk of the tree or laid at the base. The article didn't tell in what way the victim was sacrificed, nor was it clear as to whether she was fastened to the tree before or after death.

I wondered the same about our victims. If they had been killed before, it almost certainly pointed to the killer being a man. What woman had the strength to carry another woman's dead weight a mile into the woods, over terrain so rough and hilly it was impassable without a four-wheel-drive vehicle? Then I wondered about our killer and what significance trees held for him. Was it a worship ritual? Didn't Druids worship trees? Was he a Druid?

Sure, it was possible he was a Druid. Or a member of a ritualistic cult. But my research showed he could be almost any nationality, race or religion, and at some point in time that culture had used a tree in some symbolic nature. Like a Christmas tree.

The front-desk librarian came over to my work station. She wore a beautiful silk paisley skirt in earth tones and an orange sweater. "Fifteen minutes until we close, ma'am," she said pleasantly. The name on her badge said, "Nora."

I smiled. "I'm about done here anyway." Deflated, I had found no answers, only more conjecture. I sent the pages I wanted to the printer, shut down the computer and went up to the reception desk. The log book for Internet users to sign in and out of lay on the countertop.

"How many sheets did you print?" Nora asked. Her pretty auburn hair was cut short and curled softly around her face.

Her question caught me by surprise. I don't know why it should have, since it wasn't the first time I'd used their printer. My mind was off in another direction. "I'm sorry, I forgot to count them." Laying the pages on the desk, I leafed through them, counting. The article about the cottonwoods and the Indians of the upper Missouri Valley happened to be on top.

"Wow, everybody's interested in Indians today," Nora said.

I glanced up quizzically, trying not to lose count. Multitasking has never been my forte. "How so?" I asked.

"There was a guy in here earlier asking for plat books. Said he's looking for an Indian burial ground." She took off her brown frame glasses, folded them up and put them in the top drawer of the desk.

"Oh, really?" She had my full attention now. "What did he look like?"

"Obviously Indian. Very classic. Long black hair, dark-skinned. And the nose, you know, a very prominent nose."

Roman-nosed, I thought, though for some reason she must not want to say it. Everyone worried about being politically correct these days.

"He was wearing one of those long canvas coats."

"An Australian coat?" I asked. "Dark green, waxy fabric. Sort of a cape across the shoulders?" What were the chances?

She nodded. "I remember because the stiff fabric rustled when he moved. And he was soaking wet. Of course, there's nothing unusual about that today, is there?"

An Aussie coat. Soaking wet. He sounded like our man in the woods. The one who'd dropped Denise's hitch cover. How long had he been in this area? "Did you know him?"

"Not much chance of that, I'm afraid. Said he was from Virginia, up looking for his great grandmother's grave. I guess she lived in the old farmhouse that used to be up there on what's state land now. Isn't it a horse park or bridle paths or something?"

She seemed talkative and not in a hurry to close the library. "Yeah, it's an equestrian campground and trails," I said. Why on earth would a total stranger single Denise out and start collecting objects that belonged to her, presumably for a victim tree? I wondered if the murders had begun when he arrived in town. "Did you have the plat books he wanted?" I asked.

"Nope. Have to go to the county seat for those. And that's not Oakland County up there, I don't think. I wasn't sure which county it was. Living right around here, where all three counties meet, I get confused. Did you know the drug store is built right on the county line? The liquor counter is in a different county than the pharmacy."

"Imagine that," I said. I vaguely remembered seeing a sign that said liquor could only be purchased at a certain counter. Now I knew why. "It's Lapeer County up there where that old farmhouse used to be."

"See, wouldn't you know it, I gave him a bum steer. Told him I thought it was Genesee."

"Did he say where he was staying? Are his relatives still in the area?" Did this stranger have knowledge of the bones the coyotes had found? Hadn't the professor said they were old bones and not related to the recent murders?

"Didn't ask. To tell you the truth, I wanted to get rid of him. He was dripping water all over the floor. Gave me a creepy feeling, too, I don't know why. It was after school and we had kids running all over the place, tearing everything up. I didn't have time to deal with him."

Jack had mentioned a recent newspaper article saying the library was swamped with kids every day after school. But right now, I wanted to know more about the stranger. "So what about him made you feel uneasy?" I asked Nora.

"Well, for one thing, he was really big, you know, not big like *fat*, just … big. Tall. Had to be at least six-four." She looked up, as if he were standing in front of her.

The guy I'd seen in the woods was tall, possibly six foot or taller. I wondered if it could be him. "Why do you think he wants to find his great grandmother's grave? Did he say?"

She shrugged her shoulders. "Lots of people are into researching family trees nowadays. Or maybe he just wanted to know where she's buried, to put up a marker or something. Who knows?"

Trying not to appear overly nosy, I asked, "Do you remember anything more about him?"

She thought for a moment, looking beyond me, her finger on her chin. "No, not really. Like I said, the kids were driving us crazy. Why do you ask?" A hint of suspicion had crept into her voice.

"Oh, I just thought I might be able to help him, that's all. I ride up there and could show him where the foundation of the old house is." Her smile was restored, all suspicion gone. I had finished counting the sheets. "I've got fifty-two pages here," I said, hoping I had counted accurately. It seemed the payment for pages was more or less on the honor system.

"That'll be $5.20, please."

I gave her a $10 bill. "Keep the change for the new book fund."

"Why, thank you." She unlocked a drawer and threw the money in a jar. "Need a receipt?"

I shook my head. A gust of wind rattled the window behind the desk. "That wind is getting nasty."

"Winter's coming. Before you know it, there'll be snow," she said.

Driving home, my mind was anywhere but on the road. Should I tell Morton someone had turned up and was looking for Indian graves? How could I? I didn't know anything about him, except what I'd heard through the librarian. Morton would only accuse me of meddling again.

The bodies had all been found after a rainstorm. Was that random luck, or did it have an important meaning? It had to be more than coincidence. If it was significant, we had just bought some time, because after the storm of this afternoon moved off, the forecast was for clear and cold. Temperatures were supposed to dip below freezing, so any precipitation would more likely be snow, not rain. For the first time, I looked forward to winter, if it meant an end to the killing.

Break a conundrum into its smallest pieces ... wasn't that always best? *Think.* Two natural elements figured into the equation: rain and trees. What was rain? Water. Without it, there was no life, plant or otherwise. We drink it, we cook with it, we play in it, and—I reveled suddenly—*we clean with it*! A cleansing ritual?

But if the killer was an obsessive neatnik, he would not kill by slashing his victims' wrists. That was far too messy. What about a religious symbolism in the mixing of blood and rain, something that alluded to the mixing of wine and water into Christ's blood? Unanswered questions began piling up.

Todd's car still wasn't in Denise's driveway. I went up to the door, rang the bell and waited. Denise had hung a miniature scarecrow on her front door. He wore denim bib overalls and had a teeny pitchfork glued to his hand. She always went in for the countryish seasonal decorations the little store in town hawked.

Marge answered the door. "Thank God you're back. I was beginning to worry." She closed the door behind me, pressing the button in on the lock. "What'd you find?"

"Lots of stuff involving trees. It seems every culture has different rituals. But not anything really concrete that points to our guy. But something really interesting happened." I gave Marge the pages I'd printed out.

Denise sat on the sofa with a knitted orange afghan around her shoulders. Diablo lay on the floor, his head across her feet. "What?"

"Just by pure chance, I got to talking with the librarian, Nora, about a guy who'd come in earlier today looking for county plat books. Says he's looking for Indian burial grounds. Claims his great grandmother is buried up there where the old farmhouse burned down. Near the bones the coyotes dug up."

Marge sat down on the sofa, carefully stepping over Diablo. Wheels were spinning in that fine-tuned brain of hers. She started to say something.

"Wait, it gets better," I said. "So Nora says this guy was dripping wet and wore a long green Australian coat!"

"So?" Denise asked. They both stared at me blankly.

"The coat! I forgot to tell you about the coat! The guy in the woods this afternoon wore a long dark green Aussie coat, the waxed canvas kind."

"And this person that came into the library had the same coat?" Denise asked.

"Yes, indeed!" I said triumphantly. "Nora said she'd never seen him before."

"So what you're saying is that this total stranger, who nobody's ever seen before, just fell out of the sky, is killing women from this area and I'm next? In a nutshell?" Denise asked sarcastically. "So how do you propose we go about finding him?"

It seemed she had boiled my theory right down to nothing. "That's what I don't have worked out yet."

"What about the research?" Denise asked.

"Not sure any of it means anything to us. Marge has the printouts. When's Todd coming home?"

She looked at her watch nervously. "Should have been here by now. He must have stopped off for a beer."

Hopefully it wouldn't turn into a six-pack. "Okay if Marge stays until he gets here? Feather was soaking wet when I put her away. I left a blanket on her, and you know how I hate blanketing horses. It's past feeding, too. Make up some excuse, whatever, then call me when he gets home. I'll come back for Marge."

Denise reached down to pat Diablo's head. "I'm not helpless, you know."

I understood how she felt, being treated as if she were a child. "The point is for you not to be alone."

"How long can we keep that up?" A gust of wind rattled the big sliding window.

"As long as it takes," I said.

*   *   *   *

Pulling into my drive, I realized that, once again I had forgotten to leave my porch light on. While I fumbled with my keys in the dark, Hannibal kneaded his paws on the door mat, impatient to be let into the warm house. "I know, I know you want in," I told him. He answered with chirps and purrs.

One by one, I held each key up, to discern in the scanty moonlight which was the house key. The hooting of an owl came from the back pasture. Hannibal sniffed my pant leg. "I don't even use half the keys on this ring," I grumbled to myself. There was a movement in the pine trees. A raccoon or an opossum? Hannibal meowed and continued his parade through and around my legs. A long shadow fell upon my lawn. What was it? With shaking hands, the keys rattled in my fingers as I tried each one, making it a game, telling myself to calm down, to carefully try each key, that the next one would surely be the right one. I wanted to pray, but the words wouldn't come in any order, they jumbled erratically in my brain and flashed like neon signs. The shadow loomed larger.

The rhythmic crunch of shoes on the gravel drive paralleled my worst fears and drove away any hope that the shadow had been that of an animal, the neighbor's dog or one of the many deer that came to pilfer from my garden at night. In a loud voice, I spoke gibberish to Hannibal in a last attempt to conceal my fear, all the while thinking, should I try to run? Too late. At this point I wouldn't be able to put enough distance between us. A trickle of cold sweat inched its way down my back.

The last key slid home. I pushed the door open, Hannibal rushing ahead, weaving through the sliver of opening, into the house. A hand gripped my sleeve.

Chapter Twelve

The scent of Richard's cologne filled my nostrils. He said my name, over the ringing in my ears. Relief surged through me. Giddy, I wanted to both cry and laugh.

"What's wrong?" he asked.

Stepping back, I saw his face. My hands shook. "You startled me. I thought you were …" I stopped. *A murderer?* "Someone else." My heart raced and thudded. "You shouldn't sneak up on people like that."

"Sorry. In the moonlight, I figured you saw me. You're shivering."

"It's cold," I lied. It seemed silly, to have been afraid. His presence made me feel safe and calmed me. Wobbly, I leaned against him.

"Where's Marge?" He peered over my shoulder, into the dark house.

"With Denise. We're worried about leaving Denise alone. It may sound crazy, but we think this madman killer is after her." My eyes lingered on his face, tracing the angular lines of his jaw. "Richard, there's something else." Was I a traitor? I had to keep up my end of Denise's challenge. "Someone sent me a snake, wrapped like a gift, yesterday." There. It was done. Was he going to fall for it, just like Marge and Denise said he would? And if he offered to stay with me so I wasn't alone, did it have to be for Marge and Denise's reasons? Was it because he truly cared about me, or because he had another agenda?

"What the hell …?"

"It's all right," I said. "Marge threw it outside. It's probably made its way to the pond by now. In this weather, maybe the damned thing froze to death. No one was bitten."

He put his hands on my shoulders, making it impossible for me to look away. "I'm worried about your safety. Will you please call your husband and ask him to come home?"

"No," I said flatly. Let him stay and finish his damned warehouse. Otherwise, only half of him was really home anyway.

"Didn't think so," he said. He shook my shoulders lightly. "Your stubbornness is exasperating. Maddening."

"I refuse to go running to Jack for protection."

"He would want to know what's going on here. He deserves to know."

I scoffed at the suggestion. "He knew we had a murderer on the loose before he left. Do you think that stopped him from going? Hell, no. The only thing that's important to Jack is his job. I'm expected to fend for myself. And I don't want him to come home because he thinks I *need* him. Then I'm just an impediment to him doing what he wants."

"Either he's crazy or you're reading him wrong. You've got to remember, the murders didn't hit so close to home until *after* he left. He would not have left you alone if he knew you were in danger."

Richard didn't know my husband the way I knew him. Many years ago, I'd learned not to stand in Jack's way when it came to his job. I would lose against that opponent every time. "I've got Marge."

"Marge?" he asked incredulously. "Marge needs someone to look after *her*." He let go of me and walked a few steps off, turned around and came back. "Are you absolutely sure you won't call Jack?"

"Yes, I'm sure," I said, adamant that I would not allow my mind to be changed.

"I'll talk to him if you don't want to."

That was the absolutely last thing I wanted. "No," I said.

"Then what would you think of me staying here? Just at night?"

My heart sank. Was Richard using me? Was it just as Denise suggested, that he'd sent the snake? She would gloat. *I told you so*, she would say. He seemed so sincere in his shock; I found that hard to believe. And what about his pressing me to tell Jack? Would a man interested in ulterior motives offer to talk to the woman's husband? "Jack being gone is exactly why I *don't* think you should move in here." If only the man knew how easily I could have been swayed, against my better judgment, to let him stay.

It didn't matter why he wanted to stay—I only knew I didn't want him to leave. I thought of Jack. How would I explain it to him? "What makes you think I'm in danger?" I asked.

"A snake in a box? That's not enough warning? I can't believe you're taking this so casually."

Maybe I wasn't terribly worried because somewhere, deep inside me, I feared Denise was right. "Denise and Marge think *you* sent the snake."

"Me? Why the hell would I do that?" he looked at me as if I'd lost my mind.

"As a ploy. Damsel in distress and all that hogwash." I studied my feet, embarrassed. How desperately I wanted to believe he had nothing to do with my ominous package.

"You know what? I don't give a damn what they think!" He took my face in his hands and tipping my chin up, met my eyes. "What do *you* think?"

Good question. What *did* I think? Richard was kind and compassionate. Wasn't his sensibility to Louis a testimony? He let people think he was living with a gay man when in reality he was taking care of his brother. Half brother.

He pulled me closer, the sleeve of his thick corduroy shirt touching my face. In the warmth of his body and his scent, a dreamy veil settled lightly over me. If there were a place where only today mattered and no one worried about tomorrow, a place that knew no guilt or shame, succumbing would have been easy. "I don't know what I think. One part of me was hoping it *was* you, because then I didn't have to think about it being anything more sinister. But another part of me was rooting for you, to be able to go to Marge and Denise and say, 'See, I told you it wasn't him. I knew he was kind, good and honorable.'"

He ran his hand over my hair, tucking a piece behind my ear. "Why couldn't I be all those things and still want to stay with you? Why does it have to be a bad thing for me to want to help you? As a neighbor? As a friend? Why do people have to read all these other things into something that's really very innocent? I know you're married. I'm aware of that. And I'm not trying to change that. Honestly, I'm not. It doesn't have to mean anything more than me wanting to make sure you're safe. Let them think what they will, we know the truth. Don't shut me out because of what others might think."

I pulled back, away from his hold. "Richard, don't justify it." It was the wrong thing to say. The words were a heavy door slamming shut between us.

His eyes glazed over, not looking at me, but through me. Then he took my house keys from where they hung in the door's lock and pressed them into my hand. "Whether or not you want to be with me is your decision," he said in a carefully controlled voice that seethed with anger. "But I won't leave you alone, even if you haven't got enough sense to take care of yourself. You're coming with me."

"Where to?"

"The police station. I'll prove I didn't send that snake by helping you file the report," he took my hand and pulled me out of the doorway. "I can't believe you think I'd do something as sick as that."

"I didn't say *I* believed it," I protested. We crossed the road in silence after that, until he thrust open the door of his pickup truck and literally pushed me onto the seat. "It was Denise and Marge," I said, feeling childish and stupid.

"Save it," he said abruptly. He slammed the door, went around to the driver's side and started the truck.

The miles to the police station were spent in awkward silence. I'd insulted him with the accusation, and I wanted to tell him I was sorry, but didn't know where to begin, so I said nothing.

For the second time that day, I waited in the police station, while Sheriff Morton finished a meeting. The sound of clicking keyboards came from behind cubicle walls. A narrow hallway led to doorways of private offices. Sheriff Morton's nameplate hung on the first door to the left. Affixed to the wall outside his office was a row of coat hooks. All were empty except one. On it hung a forest green Aussie coat, identical to the one worn by the man in the woods. That made three—the man in the woods, Nora's stranger and whoever owned this one! Was it Morton's?

I stared. My fingers ached to touch it, to know if it was wet. Could it be the coat I'd seen worn in a horrible rainstorm in the woods only hours ago? It *looked* wet, but was it? I desperately hoped it was. Could I convince myself that it was, without actually feeling the cloth? I had to know.

I left Richard waiting on the bench. When I ran the waxy fabric under my fingers, it felt cool and wet. There was a large mud stain on the right side. But was it the same coat? I sized it up. The person in the woods hadn't been small, and neither was this coat. But then, hadn't Nora said the stranger was over six feet tall?

Richard came over. "What are you doing?" he whispered.

"I've got to know whose coat this is."

He nervously looked around the station. "Why?"

I quickly told him about the storm, the person wearing the coat who dropped Denise's hitch cover, and how that related to the victim trees. "If this coat is Morton's, he could be the man I saw in the woods this afternoon. Who else could get away with it? That's why it seems no progress is being made on the case. That's exactly how he wants it. And he wants me to mind my own business, so he figures he'll scare me by sending me a snake in a box."

"He should know better. You don't scare that easily. Come to think of it, you're not that great at minding your own business, either."

I rolled my eyes and scowled. "Very funny."

"But even if he did do it, how does that keep you out of his hair? I don't understand your logic," Richard said.

"He wants me so worried about what's going on in my own life that I don't have time to worry about anything else. He wants to steer me off the track."

"Don't you think that's a bit far-fetched? I know you've had your differences, but what you're accusing him of is really serious."

"What about the coat? I'll bet it's his. And if it is, is it just a coincidence that it's the same coat as the person who dropped the hitch cover wore? The person who was on his way to setting up another victim tree? The person who went to great lengths to assure I didn't see his face? Whoever was in the woods fell on his right side. The right side of this coat has mud on it. I'm trying to tell you, Richard, it all fits."

The only thing that didn't fit was Nora's stranger. Where did that leave him?

Sheriff Morton's door squeaked open. He frowned. "Oh, please, tell me it's not you again."

"In the flesh." I smiled sheepishly. "We were just admiring this coat. Richard wants one. Do you know who it belongs to and where they bought it?"

"Of course I know whose it is," the sheriff said. "It's mine. I got it the last time I went home to visit my sister."

I lifted the coat from the hook and held it out. It was surprisingly heavy. "Home? Where's that?"

He snatched it from me and hung it back up. "Ketchikan. You think *our* weather is bad? It rains every five minutes there."

*   *   *   *

"How do you even know it was Denise's hitch cover? Maybe it's his and it just happened to fall out of his pocket when he slipped," Richard said as he unlocked the passenger-side door.

I got in and stretched over to unlock his side. "Then why'd he run off like a scared jackrabbit when all I wanted to do was help? What's he hiding?"

"Lots of people have coats like that. And anyone who wore theirs today would have gotten it wet, and, yes, probably muddy, too. You

KAREN R. WILSON 151

can't go to the police saying the sheriff is a murderer based on the coat he wears."

"You're right about that. I'd be laughed out of there in an instant. We've got to think of another way."

He started the truck and pulled out onto the highway. "You're making too much out of this. I think you should drop it."

He seemed to have forgotten about my accusation that he'd sent the snake and I was more than happy to return to status quo, though I was confused as to exactly what status quo was.

However ambivalent I was in my feelings for Richard, I wasn't unsure regarding Sheriff Morton. The person I now believed sent the reptile sat opposite me, took notes and feigned concern. Morton deserved an Academy Award for his performance tonight. He'd played me for a fool, but I'd kept my mouth shut.

"Hungry? Richard asked. We were approaching the only restaurant within ten miles that was open this late on a weeknight: McDonald's.

Between riding in the thunderstorm, the trip to Denise's, the library, and then another meeting with Sheriff Morton, I hadn't gotten around to lunch or dinner. "Now that you mention it, yes. Drive-through is fine."

By now I was anxious to get home. It was long past feeding. "Get something for Marge, too," I said, getting my wallet out. "Todd is probably home by now, so we can pick her up." As long as Marge stayed with me, we could sidestep the subject of my being alone and Richard's offer to stay.

At the drive-through window Richard waved away my offer of money and then passed the warm sacks to me. "Hope you don't mind," I said, tearing into one of the bags. He was polite enough to not appear shocked or disgusted at my inhalation of a handful of fries. I was suddenly ravenous.

"You can't go around accusing people of things," he said.

Richard declined my offer of a french fry. "I was coerced into blaming you for the snake incident. It wasn't my idea." I never remembered a fish sandwich having tasted quite this delicious before.

"Not me. Morton. For one thing, no one's going to take you seriously. What you need is a plan." Richard gunned the big truck and pulled back into the sparse traffic. The truck reminded me of my mother's 1960 Dodge; the interior's faded blue upholstery smelled old and dusty.

"Funny you should say that because I *do* have a plan. I'll patrol the park daily and search for places he's likely to use as the sacrificial sites. Every time I find a tree that appears unusual in any way, or if I find anything hanging in it, I take everything down and dispose of it myself. If the site isn't properly prepared, he won't be able to go through with the murder."

"That would be an impossible task. It would take way more time than you've got, and how could you be sure you'd covered every area? Maybe that's something the park ranger could do."

"What park ranger? Thanks to salary cuts, we no longer have one. Someone comes in once a week to empty trash bins and collect the money from the fee box. His time is divvied up between six state parks that cover three counties. The man basically drives around and empties trash cans, and that's about it." What would happen to our parks as land became more and more valuable and the costs to maintain it rose higher and higher?

"Okay, then, that won't work." He stopped for a light, then turned left onto the gravel road.

A fragment of an idea came to me. "Richard, what if we formed a group, a sort of concerned citizens group? Seven of us could each patrol one day a week, check out anything that seems suspicious or remove anything odd we see in the trees—anything that doesn't seem to belong there."

"That's great, except what if Morton decides to go somewhere else, like a different park? What's to stop him?"

"Yeah, you're right." We were back where we began. At least he hadn't laughed at me or told me I was an idiot. "Maybe it boils down to me having to blow the whistle on him."

"Look at the deer, in that hayfield," he said, pointing his finger. He slowed the truck and we watched three deer grazing on alfalfa. The hay had been taken off in early September. "With what for evidence? All you've got is a lot of guesswork."

"How can I not do *something*? I'll feel responsible if there's another murder."

"You're blaming yourself for something that hasn't even happened yet."

"Okay, what's your solution?" I balled up the paper sandwich wrapper and threw it inside one of the bags. Pointing to the street ahead, I said, "Take a left on Washburn."

"I don't have a solution. All I know is that I'm worried about you."

I groaned, hoping we weren't headed in that direction again. His hand closed over mine. "I won't lecture and I won't bring it up again, if you promise that you'll be careful."

"Of course, I'll be careful."

"Seriously. Lock your doors. Don't go into the woods alone. Don't ride alone."

"I can take care of myself." I wiped my fingers on a paper napkin.

"It's that streak of independence that bothers me most."

"Denise's place is the second one on the right," I said, pointing ahead.

Her horses stood like two dark sentinels in the paddock that ran alongside her driveway and down to the road. They raced the truck, bucking and kicking up the hill, their breath frosty in the night air.

"Her foster horse must be in the barn," I said. We parked next to Todd's blue Yukon.

"Geez, is it ever cold!" I said, getting out of the warm truck. "I think it's dropped twenty degrees since this afternoon." I pulled my coat tight around me and hunkered down.

"Carol, you go on in and gather up Marge. I'll see if I can settle the horses down. Ask Denise if she'd like them brought in, will you? With the weather changing like this, they should probably be stalled up tonight." He took off his jacket and put it around my shoulders, adding a layer of warmth over me.

Marge held the door open, Diablo by her side. The Doberman's figure silhouetted the doorway. Not everyone knew the dog was a complete pushover, more likely to lick an intruder than bite him. Still, his appearance was intimidating.

"Ready to go?" I asked.

"What's *he* doing here?" she whispered, her disapproval evident.

"*He* is here because, when I went home to feed my horses—which by the way, I still haven't done—he came over and after I accused him of sending the snake, he insisted that we file a police report."

"That's the first good idea he's had yet." Marge pushed the door closed behind me. I slipped my shoes off and left them on the braided rug near the door. "This is one time I agree with him."

The Doberman slid his black head under my hand. "I found something very interesting hanging on a peg at the police station—an Australian coat, full length, dark green, soaking wet, and muddy on the right side. It practically walked right up and introduced itself."

Marge's mouth fell open in disbelief. "Whose was it?"

"That's the kicker—Sheriff Morton's."

"You're saying you think it was him you saw in the woods?" She scoffed. "I find that really hard to believe."

"I'm not saying for sure it was him, but I can't say it wasn't, either." Marge's skepticism didn't surprise me. Morton was in a position of authority. I, on the other hand, had no preconceived ideas regarding authoritative figures. There were good and bad cops, just like any other field. "Where's Denise?" I asked.

"Taking a shower." She lowered her voice. "Todd's in the living room. She's adamant about Todd not knowing anything, at least for right now. She's still set on making it to the reining finals, and doesn't want anything to get in her way."

The reining finals did pose a problem. They were in Lansing and would involve a trip of a couple hours of driving each way. I resigned myself to the fact that I would be going. It would be a Saturday of watching innumerable horses canter patterns and perform sliding stops. "We've got to make sure she doesn't call Morton. We obviously can't expect any help from him."

"Good heavens, no," Marge said. "Even if he *is* innocent, we just can't take that chance, now can we?"

"Sometimes people and situations aren't always what they seem to be," I said, thinking this was my opportunity to clear myself. I looked Marge square in the face and said, "I couldn't have an affair with Richard, even if it was what I wanted most in the whole world, which it isn't. Don't you see that about me, Marge?"

"It's not you I don't trust. He might take advantage of the situation, Jack being gone and all."

"It's not what he wants either. He told me so tonight. Even though it's only been a short time, I really feel I've gotten to know him."

"Then what's in it for him? Why is he being so helpful?"

"Why does there have to be something in it for him? Maybe he's just the typical all-American nice guy, looking out for a neighbor." Were there still people around like that, people who weren't self-serving? I wanted to believe there were.

"Yeah, and I'm the pope," Marge said, still skeptical. She gathered up her jacket and scarf from the back of a kitchen chair.

"I want to talk to Denise before we leave," I said. "I'll only be a minute."

From the bathroom came the sound of running water. I knocked on the door, then went in. The lavender-scented room was warm and steamy, the outline of Denise's body visible behind the translucent shower doors. I yelled to be heard above the water. "We're going back to my place now."

The faucet squeaked when she turned off the water. "Sure. Todd's home," she answered. "He doesn't know and I want it to stay that way. I'll be all right."

"How do you know that?"

"Don't worry. I've got Diablo. He'll take care of me."

"I wouldn't rely on him. It's easy to knock off a dog." Perching on the vanity, I told her about Richard taking me to the police station and the coat. "That son of a bitch Morton," I said, "Stringing us along all the time, acting like he was concerned about finding the killer."

The bathroom mirror was covered with steam; I wiped it away with my sleeve. The messages written in lipstick came to mind and I wondered if Morton was responsible for those, too. *Drop dead* and *mind your own business*. The man had a lot of nerve.

"How does someone like that live with themselves?" Denise asked. She stepped out of the shower, a huge pink towel covering most of her.

I could not recall one single thing I owned that was pink, dismissing it as too feminine. "Maybe he's got that disease, I forget the name now—it starts with an "S"—the one where you're more than one person."

She stepped on the bathroom scale, looked down, grimaced, and stepped off. "Yeah, but doesn't the first person know what the second person did, in which case, you'd still have to live with your-selves?"

"Hell, I think there've been people who had tons of personalities, like twelve or fifteen or more," I said. "Anyway, I think it's called multiple personality disorder or something like that."

"Schizophrenia," Denise said, opening a drawer that contained what had to be every beauty product known.

"I thought that was what you got when you took too much Vitamin B-6."

"That's hives. I believe Vitamin B-6 is what is used to cure it."

"Cure what?"

"Schizophrenia." She sprinkled bath power between her toes and I marveled at how, unlike myself, both she and Marge paid attention to the most minute of details. Who had time for primping?

"Marge would love your towel. Everything the woman owns is pink."

"Pink goes good with white hair." She held her head upside-down and sprayed styling lotion on her wet hair. "Can you get me the Velcro curlers, second drawer under where your sitting?"

The yellow curlers were stuck together in a lump nearly the size of a basketball. I squeezed them out of the vanity drawer and gave them to her. "By the way, Richard wants to know if you want your horses brought in. The weather's changing and it's getting nasty cold."

"Yeah. Stalls are cleaned and there's hay already in the mangers. What's up with you and him, anyway?" Denise asked matter of factly, as if she were my mother.

"*Nothing's up* with us. He's just a friend, that's all. I've gotten to know him and he's a really nice guy. But just when I get to thinking our friendship is fine, Marge comes along and makes me feel like I did something wrong. Like I should be ashamed of myself. And now you're doing the same thing."

She shrugged. "She just doesn't want either you or Jack to get hurt. She cares for both of you."

"Well, there you go, there's one of the problems to begin with. Everybody has this image of Jack being the most wonderful husband. Everybody thinks, 'Poor Jack, he has such a loud and overbearing wife.' There's a lot you don't know."

"There is in any marriage, Todd's and mine included."

"It's just that, no matter what he does, he comes out smelling like a rose. Like this job out of state. Some warehouse in Indiana is more important than leaving your wife alone with a madman on the loose."

"Carol, Richard is ready to go," Marge called up the stairs. Since when did she care about what Richard wanted? More likely, Marge was ready to go.

Denise poked her head out of the door. "Tell him I'll take him up on his offer to bring my horses in."

"I gotta' go," I said. "Sorry for the husband-related tirade. This isn't exactly a good time for Jack and me." That was an understatement. "I owe you."

"No sweat. You've listened to plenty of mine, so I guess we're even. Tell Richard thanks for putting my horses in."

✳   ✳   ✳   ✳

Richard stuck his head inside the feed room door, his hand resting on the handle. "There's something wrong with Saint." After leaving Denise's, we came straight down to my barn to feed and water. I was in the feed room measuring oats and alfalfa pellets into buckets, while Richard picked stalls one last time before tucking the horses in.

"Wrong in what way?" I dropped the feed scoop, suddenly scared. He should have been fed hours ago. Mostly I had worried about Feather, not Saint. She'd been ridden hard and put away wet. And then to feed late, a good two to three hours later than normal, was unforgivable.

"He's laying down and won't get up." His eyes were wide with alarm.

Chapter Thirteen

Feather and Echo raised their heads and stopped chewing when I ran past. Hay dangled from their mouths. *Please, God, make him be fine*, I prayed. *Make it something minor that Richard, not being a horseman, didn't understand. Make it nothing at all.*

There was no gray nose over his half door nor inquisitive ears working back and forth. Horses are curious creatures. Unless something was wrong.

I shouldn't have left him, shouldn't have gone to the library or the police station or any of the other places I'd been. I should have stayed home and kept an eye on this horse. He had only just come from the throes of death days ago and he'd been entrusted to my care.

The bolt on the stall door wasn't latched. I wondered if Richard left it open or if I'd forgotten it this afternoon. Saint was flat out on his side, not a good sign. Horses sometimes laid flat out in the warm spring sun, turned out on pasture, but rarely in their stalls. There simply wasn't the room in the average ten-by-ten stall for a full-sized horse to spread out. He groaned. Maybe he laid down and found himself too close to the stall walls to get up? That was called being "cast," and usually wasn't a big deal, most of the time they found their own way out of the predicament. Sometimes with the help of ropes they had to be rolled over, so they could get a leg underneath their body. On rare occasions the situation turned disastrous, but overall, a horse being cast was not the worst thing that could happen. Colic or founder—those were the words no one ever wanted to hear.

A horse could founder for a million different reasons or for no apparent reason at all. A condition that affected the tissue inside the hooves, it brought unbearable pain. When forced to move, the animal walked in a stiff, legs-out-in-front kind of a gait, trying to keep the weight on the hind legs.

Colic, or gastric upset, had some of the same causes as founder—overeating, spring grass, or other changes in diet. It could be deadly.

I knelt by Saint's side and stroked his neck. "What's wrong fella?" I whispered. He didn't raise his head from the sawdust, but his big dark eyes slowly opened and closed when my hand slid over his nose. I felt his hooves; they were cool to the touch. I moved my hand up, and pushed my finger into his coronary band, the place where the hard hoof wall turned fleshy. It seemed normal. I put my head to Saint's side.

"What are you doing?" Richard asked.

"Listening for gut sounds. No gut sounds is supposed to be an indication of colic, though I've known colicked horses that had them. It's probably just another old wives' tale. Anyway, I can hear gurgling. Let's put his halter on and see if we can get him to stand up."

Richard got a leather halter and lead from the hook on the back of the stall door. I lifted Saint's head and instructed Richard on how to slip the halter on. "Ready?" I asked, getting up. My knees had already stiffened up from crouching.

Richard nodded and leaned back, all his weight against the lead rope. I took hold of the halter's cheek strap and pulled until the muscles in my arms burned. My sprained wrist ached. Saint groaned and pulled back. "Get up, Saint," I pleaded. We were holding his head taut, trying to keep him from flopping back down, but we weren't gaining any ground at all. Saint made no effort to get his forelegs out in front to push himself up. "Let him back down for a minute," I said, out of breath. "He's not cast. There's plenty of room for him to get his hind legs up under him."

"Then what's wrong?" Richard asked.

"His hooves feel cool, but if it is founder, sometimes their feet hurt so bad, they refuse to stand. Only I can't tell if that's what it is until he gets up." I looked around the stall, to see if he'd eaten this afternoon's hay. I'd been really careful to make sure he got only the hay from Sue. Hay was trampled into his bedding. In the corners and against the walls, sawdust lay in heaps. "It looks like he's been thrashing in the stall."

"What does that mean?" Richard was puzzled.

"Usually colic. A stomachache. Horses can't throw up, so if they eat something bad, there isn't any way for them to get rid of it. Sometimes the vet will give them oil through a stomach tube and try to push everything out. They roll around because they're in pain. But the rolling can cause a twisted gut, and surgery is the only thing that will fix that."

Richard looked around the stall, at the hay and sawdust that had been thrown up against the walls. "So his gut might already be twisted?"

"That's worst-case scenario." I scratched Saint behind the ears. He lay listlessly on the stall floor, neck wet with sweat. His eyes followed me. "Let's get the vet."

Richard glanced at his watch. "At 10:30 at night?"

"Vets are used to being called at night, especially horse vets. But Saint's not mine, so I have to call Sue first. Her phone number is up at the house."

Richard knelt down and laid Saint's head on his lap. He stroked the horse's gray nose. "Poor thing," he said, his voice low, calming. "He's in so much pain, you can see it in his eyes. Nothing should ever have to suffer like this, animal or human."

"Stay with him, will you?" I asked. "Just hold his head like that and keep him still. I'll be back as soon as I can."

Marge looked up from the television when I slammed the glass door. "I don't believe this rotten luck!" I said. "Saint is colicked!" In three leaps and without taking off my muddy barn shoes, I was at the kitchen drawer that held my address book. My hands shook as I flipped through the pages, trying to remember Sue's last name. "Dammit, Marge, I'm so useless! I can't remember Sue's last name! Because of the court order, I've got to call her first."

"Sue who?" Marge asked.

"If I knew her last name I could find her phone number!" I threw the book down, exasperated.

She grabbed the phone off the hook and started pressing buttons.

Somewhere on my desk in the spare bedroom were the documents Carlitta had given me the night we brought Saint home. The phone number would be on them. I rifled through a stack of papers. Where had I put them?

"Denise is getting in touch with Sue, then she'll be right over," Marge yelled from the kitchen.

"I fed him the right hay. I did everything they said. I followed their instructions to the letter on the amount and the type of food and everything else," I said. *But I'd been a couple hours late in feeding.* "Marge, this can't be happening!"

"Fretting will do no good. Remember last spring when my old Bailey got poisoned and you drove us to the dog hospital? I know you can be strong and sensible."

The phone rang and I pounced on it, thinking it was Denise, Sue, or the vet, but it was Jack and there wasn't time to talk. "Sorry, can't talk now. I've got a sick horse," I said, pinching the phone between my ear and shoulder. Where were those papers from Sue? The vet would want to see them.

"No. Not Feather. Not Echo either. Another horse is staying here." How could I explain all of this now? I hadn't told him about Saint yet; I'd been waiting for the right time and it certainly wasn't now. "It's a long story," I said, checking the clock. "I don't have time to go into it. Marge is here."

That was going to take explaining too. "I hurt my wrist on Sunday and she's been helping out." Talk about a simplified version. He hadn't even been gone a week, yet it seemed there was so much he didn't know. "Give me the number where you're staying. I'll call you back."

I scribbled it down. "He was abandoned, nearly dead from starvation. I'm just acting as a foster home." When he asked me how much this was costing, my anger flared. Why did he have to reduce everything to dollars and cents? "Don't worry about the money. I've got to get off the phone," I said tersely, hanging up.

Within thirty seconds it rang again. It was Sue. "We had a little trouble with him on Sunday, but he seemed to be doing so much better, we thought he'd be okay to ship out. Dr. Rogers is on a farm an hour south of me, which means he's two hours from your place. He's calling in a guy closer to you, a Dr. Murray from Davison. Anyway, this Dr. Murray needs directions, so call him right away."

I wrote the phone number on an orange sticky note. "He's such a sweet horse and I'm so scared. I hope he'll be okay."

"Hang in there. We do the best we can with these rescued animals, but sometimes Mother Nature takes over."

After describing Saint's symptoms and giving Dr. Murray directions, I headed back to the stable. Marge packed me off with two mugs and a Thermos of hot tea spiked with Maker's Mark whiskey. Good old Marge, always concerned with creature comforts.

Echo, resident busybody, stopped chewing hay and poked his nose over his door. "What's happening, big guy?" I said, ruffling his mane on my way past.

Richard hadn't moved, Saint's head still in his lap. "Sometimes he groans and his eyes drift away. They almost cloud over," he said.

"The vet's on his way. He's coming from Davison, so it'll be about a half hour. Marge made us some hot tea." I set the Thermos down next to Richard. "I'll get a blanket to put over him."

When I came back with Echo's winter rug, Richard helped arrange it over Saint. I sat down and he pulled a corner of the blanket up over us, too. I passed a mug of tea to Richard. My cold fingers felt good wrapped around the steaming cup. The wind whistled through the old boards of the barn. The big willow tree creaked.

"Anything we can do until he gets here?" Richard asked.

"We'd better not; might only make matters worse. Has he been quiet most of the time?"

"He moves his eyes like he's watching, begging me to end his misery." Richard stroked Saint's neck.

"Don't say that. He's going to be fine." If only I felt as positive as my words. "You okay? It's cold."

Richard shrugged. "I'm all right. The tea's good. What's in it?"

"Maker's Mark and sugar." Benny snuggled up on my lap, purring. A huge old thing, he was black as India ink.

"I could never have animals," Richard said.

My knees were starting to ache again. I shifted my weight. "What do you mean?" Sometimes he said the strangest things.

"This is awful. Watching him suffer. I keep asking myself, wouldn't it be kinder to just put a bullet through his head?"

Richard's frankness shocked me. "Well, I guess if we'd done all we could and there was no hope of him ever getting better, as a last resort, maybe. But there's a good chance he'll pull out of this. Horses colic and they recover. Horses founder and they still live. Neither one is an automatic death sentence."

His face was drawn. "But you said they can both be fatal."

"They *can* be, but they don't *have* to be." A whiskey-induced leaden feeling traveled down my limbs.

He seemed genuinely concerned and unwilling to leave it at that. "At what point do you say it's gone on long enough?"

"The vet will tell you. You've got to trust them to know what's best. It's like when a woman is having a baby. There's a lot of pain involved, but you don't say, 'Put her out of her misery.'"

"But there's a second life involved in childbirth."

"Yeah, so two people are suffering instead of one. Being born has to be an ordeal for the baby, too."

He mulled this over for a moment. "This world is a terrible place, full of anger, pain, and suffering. Sometimes it makes me sick." He reached over to pat Benny's head.

How many times had I thought the very same thing? But there was more to it than that—I'd seen the flip side. "I won't say there's no misery here. But there's beauty, too. Like snow on a mountain or the sound of my horses whinnying when they see me in the morning." Hoping I didn't sound corny, I tried to explain. "You've got to search for something. Something you can grasp and say, 'Look, this is a beautiful thing.' Take special notice of those things and thank God that you have them."

"You see the good. I see the bad." He refilled his mug, then offered me the Thermos. "I come back to the same conclusion, time after time, what kind of a God lets these things happen? An innocent child should not suffer."

Even though I hadn't known Richard long, it was long enough to understand the guilt he carried. "It's not your fault, you know. I mean, about Louis, that he was abused and you weren't. You can't beat yourself up about it for the rest of your life."

But Richard was determined. His jaw was set in the way I'd come to recognize. "I told him I would make it up to him, and I intend to."

What an impossible undertaking. He was setting himself up for failure. "How can you do that?" I asked.

"By making sure that no one will ever hurt him again." He spoke the words *no one* in a voice that held a quiet resolve that scared me just a little, though I understood sometimes sheer determination was what it took.

But as good as his intentions were, they were unrealistic. "How can you control the world and how it reacts to Louis? He's scarred forever; that's undeniable. But you have to go forward from there. Get him professional help. Just the way I trust this vet, someone I've never met, to know what will be best for Saint, you've got to trust someone else to help Louis. Let them do their job."

"Don't you think we've tried that route? Analysts, psychiatrists, you name it." Now his voice held a tone of weariness.

In the low light of the stall's single incandescent bulb, I couldn't be sure of his expression and I wondered if I'd intruded. Here were two people impaired by a horrible childhood. Did it have to ruin their adult life too? "You've got to keep trying," I said.

"Once they said he was 'cured.' In reality, Louis learned to work the system to his benefit, wrapped those shrinks around his little finger; convinced them he *was* fine for my sake. He did it because he loved me and didn't want to see me suffer. That's how Louis is, more worried about me than himself."

"You didn't buy it?"

Richard stroked Saint's nose. His long fingers lingered on the horse's velvety muzzle. "You don't fix what happened to Louis with a freaking discussion, which is what the doctors want. 'Discuss it. Get it out in the open.' What a load of bullshit. We can sit here and talk about it until hell freezes over, but that doesn't change how Louis deals with it. Or me either, for that matter."

"They're hoping that by bringing it forward, it helps the patient work through it," I said. It sounded good in theory, but did it work?

"What I told you the other night was only the tip of the iceberg. There's a lot you don't know."

Figuring now was as good a time as any to find out, I waited. He looked up at the ceiling, as if he had to pretend I wasn't there for the words to come. He spoke after a moment. "She was incredibly evil."

"Did you hate her?" It was hard to imagine a mother that was anything except loving and supportive.

Richard looked at me with disbelief. "Did I hate her? At the time, I only remembered being afraid of her. But now, sometimes the depth of my hatred scares me."

Why would someone take revenge on a child for what his parents had done? What satisfaction was gotten from hurting a child? It was so senseless. "Why didn't the teachers at school notice something was wrong with Louis? Check into the situation?"

"Back then the authorities stayed out of it. No one intervened, like they do now. And even if we *had* said something, my mother would have denied it, and they would have believed her, not us."

"Yeah, you're probably right. When we were growing up, physical punishment was condoned. Step out of line and they whacked you with a wooden paddle." Things sure had changed.

"Or worse."

"But I still don't understand what your solution is. Just how do you keep the rest of the world away from Louis?"

"I'll kill anybody that lays a hand on him."

I was about to reiterate how unrealistic that was, when the drone of a truck's engine grew. I didn't know if I was sorry or grateful that our conversation had been cut short. Possibly a little of both. Headlights bumped across the lawn, a door slammed, and we heard the creaking of the metal gate on its pins. "Anybody home?" Denise called.

"In here," I said.

She popped in. "Aren't you two cozy?" Her hair hung in damp lumps where she had pulled the curlers out.

"Sit here for very long and you'll be wearing a horse blanket, too," I said. "I hope you didn't drive over here by yourself. Not three hours ago you promised you wouldn't go anywhere alone."

"It's two measly miles!"

"I don't care. You promised." Obviously, she was not taking this threat seriously.

"Besides, it's not raining, so I figure I'm safe."

I did not find her cocky attitude amusing. "Smart ass. Just don't take any more chances."

"Yes, mother." She knelt down by Saint's side, running her hand along the crest of his neck. Her face confirmed my fear. "He looks bad."

"The vet should be here any minute," I said, checking my watch. An agonizing half hour had passed.

"Who'd you end up getting?"

"Some guy from Davison."

"Murray?" Denise pulled her cigarettes from the pocket of her denim jacket, saw my expression, and wordlessly put them back.

"You know him?" I asked.

"Sure. My neighbor uses him. He's decent," Denise said. "What're you drinking?"

"Kentucky's finest," I said, offering her my cup. "With just a hint of tea."

She declined. "Now if it was vodka—"

"We needed something to stay warm." I knew experts said alcohol had the opposite effect. Somebody's always willing to burst whatever bubble they can.

"I had a couple of ideas, but she wasn't going for them," Richard said, with a hint of playfulness that surprised me, the demeanor of just moments ago already hidden.

"That's enough out of you," I said, giving him a stern sideways glance, but trying to keep from smiling. My face felt warm and I was glad the lighting was dim.

Richard lifted Saint's head and began to slide out from under our blanket. "Actually, I'm thinking of going home for my winter coat."

"No, don't get up. I'll go," Denise quickly said. "No sense disturbing him."

Richard settled back in. "Ask Louis for the coat. Tell him it's the dark green parka in the upstairs closet. While you're there, might as well fill him in on what's happening. Tell him I don't know how late I'll be."

"Dark green parka, upstairs closet. Got it," Denise said.

"Thanks for staying with me," I told Richard after Denise had left. The discomfort of the cold and the cramped conditions were easier to bear when someone else suffered alongside.

"Sure. I'd only be thinking of you, all alone in this cold barn, anyway."

"I'm not alone. The animals are company." I scratched Benny's ears and throat. He kneaded his paws into the horse blanket.

"If Saint dies, where are you going to bury him?" Richard asked.

"He's going to be fine," I said. In my mind, there was no other outcome.

"But if he *does* die, what will you do? Will Jack come home to help you?"

I shook my head. "I'll find somebody with a back hoe and pay them a couple hundred bucks to dig a hole in the back pasture. I've got a pet cemetery back there." I held my hand over Saint's nostrils, feeling the small whoosh of his breath on my fingers. "Hold on. Just a little longer, buddy."

"You shouldn't have to do everything alone. Doesn't it bother you that he's never around?"

Benny playfully batted at a stalk of hay that was stuck to the blanket. "Yeah, a lot of the time it does, but only when I let it. I try to push it aside. It only makes for discontentment. Besides, I don't need help," I said defiantly.

"Haven't you ever wanted someone to take care of you?"

My tea was cold and I dumped the dregs. "Yeah, sure, doesn't everybody? Once I realized there was no Prince Charming to sweep me off my feet and pay all my bills, things got easier to accept."

"And you thought *I* was cynical," Richard said, smoothing the blanket over Saint's shoulder.

Maybe he was right. Was I as miserable as him?

A truck pulled up to the open gate, sending the beam of its headlights into the paddock. It was too soon for Denise to be back, so I went out, figuring it must be the vet. He was unlocking the compartment on the back of his truck that held drugs and vaccines. "Dr. Murray? I'm Carol."

"Nice to meet you," he said, as I gripped a strong, warm hand. He wore dark coveralls and Wellington boots that looked a couple sizes too big. His voice sounded younger than he looked, his hair graying around his face. He put everything in a bucket. "Lead the way," he said.

We passed Echo and Feather's stalls, Echo banging his salt block from one end of his manger to the other, his lips seeking out imaginary morsels of grain.

"What's his problem?" Dr. Murray asked, thumbing toward Echo.

"Absolutely nothing. That's normal. Resident pest."

"Every barn's got one." He stopped at Saint's stall. "This must be the fella I need to see," he said. Crouching down, Dr. Murray looked into Saint's eyes with a pen light, then checked his gums. "Sometimes the kidneys fail with these guys." He listened to the horse's heart and lungs. "How long's he been down?"

"I checked him earlier this afternoon, I guess it was about four or five o'clock. He seemed fine then, and I gave them each a flake of hay. Then we came back about an hour ago and found him like this."

"Let me see your hay."

Richard had thrown hay down from the loft yesterday and neatly stacked the bales in the feed room, the first cutting in one corner, second cutting in another. Sue's hay was by itself near the stairs. I'd given him the short course, Hay 101, instructing him on the differences between the three. "Second cutting has tiny, dark green leafs, fine stems, and a rich meadow-like smell," I explained. "And first cutting has courser stems and a lighter green color."

"This is what I fed him," I said, showing him the hay from Sue.

He peeled off a flake and looked at it closely. He held the hay up to his nose and sniffed, then put it up to the light. He shook it, watching the leafs fall to the floor. "Looks good to me."

My sigh of relief was audible. Pointing to the hay in the other corner, I said, "There's my second cutting. I give the other two horses a flake of that at each feeding. Are you ruling out colic?" I asked.

"I'd sooner guess it's a kidney problem, just because of past experience. Let's get an IV started. Has he been on any antibiotics?"

"Not that I know of." Carlitta hadn't said anything about medicine.

"Let me look at his records."

*   *   *   *

"It's going to be a long night," I said. No one knew it more than me. It was now approaching forty-eight hours since I'd last slept and a hammock in a barn aisle was starting to look like a night at the Hilton. When Denise returned with Richard's parka, she was sent back to fetch Louis and a lawn chair for Richard. Thankfully, since the vet was still there, Louis showed up wearing normal men's clothing, a turtleneck sweater and jeans, not his yellow sundress.

The vet had given Saint fluids containing electrolytes, potassium, and what seemed like a hundred other things. Then he'd separately injected the antibiotics. I only hoped there was a strong will to live somewhere in that horse's poor bony body.

Dr. Murray hung around for a while, until his wife paged him, wondering how much longer he would be. He packed up and said to give Saint an hour or two, but then he should start to perk up.

The four of us took the stall door off its hinges and put up a stall guard, a sort of criss-crossed wide webbing that was held across the opening by double-end snaps. From my hammock, which we had strung across the stable aisle and anchored by the stall door latches, I would be able to see into Saint's stall without getting up. And though I wouldn't have asked him, Richard offered to stay. I gratefully accepted. Denise left to spend the night in a warm house, snuggled in a warm bed.

For some reason, Marge wasn't upset with Richard spending the night. I guess as long as he stayed in the barn it didn't violate any neighborhood code of ethics or alert the gossip mongers. She arrived at the barn with yet a third stack of blankets.

"We've already got two sleeping bags and seven blankets. It's not like it's the dead of winter," I told her.

"The last thing you need is to get sick on top of everything else." She handed me a pair of earmuffs. "I don't see why you have to stay down here. Can't you just check on the horse every couple of hours? We could take turns waking up in the night."

"I'm not taking any chances," I said. "Besides, you don't get sick from being cold, you get sick from germs."

Marge rolled her eyes. "If the horse is meant to die, he's going to die. Being stubborn won't change it."

"Would everybody just get off the dying routine? First Richard, now you. Dr. Murray says he should take a turn for the better soon."

Louis held a carrot to Saint's nose, hoping to get the horse interested. When Saint didn't lift his head, Louis laid the carrot down. Seeing them together, I thought of how they had something in common, how they'd both been abused, and how it didn't matter that one of them was an animal and one was a human. It was tragic either way.

"Try cutting it up into small pieces and mixing it with a tiny bit of sweet feed," I told Louis. "There's a knife in the feed room on the shelf. Sweet feed's in the big steel drum."

Louis returned with the mixture. "That grain mix smells so good, almost good enough to eat myself, like granola," Louis said. "All I need is a spoon and some milk." He held the feed close to the horse's lips, but Saint still wasn't interested. "I'll put it in here, in case he wants it later," Louis said, dropping the feed into the manger. "If you don't need me for anything else, I think I'll head home. The underwashes are coming along on that new piece, and I'd like to get back to it."

"I'm all set," Richard said, arranging his sleeping bag on two lawn chairs, then putting two blankets on top of that. "Are you working on the peony?"

Louis frowned. "Something's not right with the peony, but I don't quite know what it is yet. I might just pitch it. But anyway, no, it's the delphinium."

Wishing I had the time to paint, I felt a pang of jealousy. Maybe someday I'd get back to it. Maybe when I retired, which should be in about a million years, but hopefully before I lost my eyesight from staring at a computer screen forty hours a week. "What sort of colors are you working with?" I asked Louis.

"Purples and blues right now. Very vibrant. And I'm getting the neatest iridescent effect with these subtle washes of color over color." His voice was excited, as if the colors were a beautiful and tangible thing that he could hold in his hand, yet something he was a bit afraid of and couldn't quite control.

Louis thumped his head. "I almost forgot to tell you, the woman with the Camaro left a message. She wants to know if it'll be ready for the show on Saturday."

"Oh, hell, that's right, the car show is this weekend," Richard said. "Call her first thing in the morning, will you? Tell her I'll have it done Friday afternoon."

Louis gave him a thumbs up. "Take care, brother."

Marge and Louis left and finally it was quiet except for the small sounds the other two horses made, an occasional stamping of a hoof or Echo licking his feed tub. "You sleep first," Richard said. "I'll wake you up if anything changes."

"Two hours. That's it. Then wake me."

"Sure. Two hours."

*   *   *   *

Richard was in the doorway to Saint's stall, leaning against one side. It didn't seem so cold anymore and I peeled back one of my blankets. "What time is it?"

"Almost three. Go back to sleep. He's the same. No better, no worse."

"I'm scared."

"Of what?"

"Everything. The sheriff, if he's the killer. Of Denise being the next target. Of losing Saint."

"Of Jack being gone?" he asked.

"Yes." It surprised me that he would ask me about Jack.

Richard eased himself down on the edge of my hammock. It rocked perilously for a moment. He brushed the hair back from my face, the same way Jack did on weekend mornings, when we lingered in bed longer than usual. Then I remembered I'd forgotten to return Jack's call from the night before. "Damn," I said, "I just remembered I was supposed to call him back."

"Give me the number and I'll do it. I've got a few things I'd like to tell him."

"I'll just bet you do," I said. "It would be a delightful conversation." It was too early in the morning to defend Jack, especially when Richard's feelings mirrored my own. "I don't feel like I can talk to him right now. I'm too caught up in all of this." I gestured toward Saint.

"Marge is right. What's meant to be, will be."

"No matter what I do?" I asked.

"Maybe. Go back to sleep. I'll watch Saint."

"You really care about him, don't you?"

"Yeah, sure I do. At first, I didn't have any feelings toward him one way or the other. I only cared because you cared. But tonight, watching him, it's amazing the way he communicates without words."

"I can't lose him. Not now. He's made it through the worst. The weeks of standing in that sickening stall with no food, water or sunlight. To be rescued and taken away from that and now, only to have this happen ..."

"Doesn't seem right, does it?" Richard said. Saint lay in exactly the same position as we'd left him. "His eyes seem alert, like he knows everything we're doing for him."

"Oh he does, I'm sure of that." Animals had way more feelings than we gave them credit for. "You'll make some woman a good husband," I blurted suddenly, though it had been on my mind.

Richard laughed. "Where'd *that* come from?"

"You offered to stay with me. You took the door off so I could see into Saint's stall. Jack never would have done that. He would've grumbled about having to put it back on later. And it isn't that I don't love Jack, it's just nice to have somebody around who's agreeable. Even when Jack is home, he's here, but he's not here."

Richard got up and stood in the wide doorway that opened into the paddock. He looked out, his back to me. The pale moon was shrouded by cloud cover. "I suppose I should keep my mouth shut when it concerns Jack. It's just that the man is missing so much. A great woman who loves him. This gorgeous property, the house and stable. Do you know what I'd give for those things?" He turned, so he was silhouetted in the doorway, his arm leaning against the barn door. "You deserve more. I think you've gotten so used to status quo that you just accept it as what you are due."

"This is too heavy for me right now," I said defensively. "I can't handle it."

"But, you see, that's the problem. You've put off being happy for so long that now you don't want to upset the apple cart. It's easier and more comfortable to not change."

"Are you saying I'm lazy? By not fixing what's wrong with our marriage? Sure, our marriage isn't perfect. Whose is?"

"No, I'm not saying you're lazy. Maybe afraid to make a change. By not changing, you're settling for what you get, instead of what you need. You have to decide what you want. No one can decide for you."

Suddenly, feelings of panic hit me. Like I just had too much to think about. Like I was going to melt down if I didn't back off. Maybe he was accurate, maybe I needed to think about some changes in my marriage. *Just not right now.*

"Can we talk about something else?" I asked.

"Sure. Sorry. I didn't mean to get all philosophical on you. It's really none of my business, it's just that you're a good person and I care about what happens to you."

"Thanks. Really." I *was* grateful.

"No stars tonight," he said. "Rain or snow is coming, I can smell it."

"If it rains we'll have to quarantine Denise." I sat up, bracing myself on one elbow. Problems were piling up and I was beginning to feel overwhelmed. I beat the panic down again. "How did everything get so screwed up? Denise may be on this madman's list, but there isn't anything I can do about it because the one person we're supposed to be able to trust, Sheriff Morton, is exactly who we *can't* trust. We don't know where the hell Lida is or what's happened to her. And now this horse."

"Focus on one thing. Tonight's priority is this horse. Tomorrow we worry about tomorrow."

"You make it sound easy." I guess when you're raised in the kind of environment he'd known as a child, you learned to survive one day at a time.

"You're just tired. Don't think about the other stuff. I shouldn't have brought it up. Go back to sleep. I'll wake you if anything changes with Saint."

More than happy to sink back down and let everything go, I fell asleep almost immediately. Lightness surrounded me, and I flew away, looking down at all I left behind.

Chapter Fourteen

An early low fog rolled in over the pasture, hanging thickly in the valleys. Damp and heavy, the air smelled of horses, of manure and hay and their sweet breath. It was after six o'clock. I arose and went into Saint's stall. Richard knelt beside him, his hand on his neck.

"What're you going to do about him?" he asked.

I sighed, defeated. Saint still hadn't gotten up or eaten anything. "I'll call Sue again." I pulled the crumpled orange sticky note from my jean pocket. My back ached from the army hammock and I felt incredibly tired, as if I could sleep for a year. "You need to go paint that woman's Camaro, like you promised." I didn't want him to go.

"If she wasn't taking it to a show on the weekend, I could put it off. Everything else I've got in right now can wait; most people are putting their show cars up for the winter." He seemed sad. "I'll be back as soon as I can. I'll help you bury him."

I cried then. He'd said what I couldn't bring myself to admit. That Saint wasn't going to make it.

*   *   *   *

"This is bad news," Sue said, when I got hold of her. "I thought he'd be up and around by now."

"I prayed he would be. We watched him all through the night. There's no change, either way." I leaned backward, stretching my achy joints, and noticed the rafters in the tack room needed cobwebbing.

"Usually, they improve right away after the IV fluids. I'll call Dr. Rogers and see what he wants to do, whether he's going to come out or if he wants us to call Dr. Murray again. I'll get right back to you."

While I waited, I fed Echo and Feather, who nipped at each other over their stall doors. Echo nickered when I brought his scoop of oats. "You need to slim down, young man. No molasses, no corn, just straight oats for you." He attacked them like a child given a plate of warm cookies.

Sue called back within minutes. "Dr. Rogers wants to come out. He figures he'll be there in a little over an hour. How are you doing? Did you get any sleep at all?"

"A few hours. A neighbor came in to help." Even though I'd gotten some rest, the emotional part was draining, too, with its roller coaster ups and downs and denial of what was evident.

"You sound beat. Get yourself a cup of coffee and some breakfast. There's nothing more you can do until he gets there anyway."

Through the morning fog, the lights on up at the house were faint. Marge no doubt had coffee brewing and eggs in the frying pan. She got up early even when she didn't have to. I turned Feather and Echo out and packed hay in the paddock feeder. I put a flake of hay in Saint's stall, too, just in case a miracle happened, then headed up to the house.

Marge's pink housecoat rustled as she moved between the stove and the coffeepot. "Morning. How is he?" She filled a mug with coffee.

"No change." The tone in my voice told the story. I sat down at the kitchen table. "The vet is on his way again." My hair smelled like the stable.

"Poor dear." She set the coffee in front of me. "Wash your hands and call Richard. I've made French toast with pear sauce and warm maple syrup."

How on earth had she managed pear sauce from my meager pantry? The coffee tasted strong and delicious. "Richard left around six. He's got a car to paint. It won't take him long, says he'll be back by early afternoon."

The microwave timer buzzed. She removed the maple syrup. "If I'd known, I would have started breakfast earlier. It was awfully good of him to stay."

"Yeah, it was," I agreed.

She placed a huge stack of French toast on the table. "Maybe I misjudged him."

Knowing that was as close to an apology as I was ever going to get from Marge, I sipped coffee and smiled inwardly, too tired to gloat.

*   *   *   *

"I recommend you put him down," Dr. Rogers said.

Words I did not want to hear. "What about more fluids?" I asked, searching my arsenal of remedies. "Or a stronger painkiller. Maybe we haven't given him enough time."

"More time will only prolong his suffering." The veterinarian's warm eyes met mine and I knew he was telling me the truth. "I know how you feel when it gets to this."

Did he really know? Had he ever been this frustrated? He must deal with this nearly every day, and to some extent had become hardened, in a way that I never would. I held my tears back.

"Sue needs to get the Judge's permission," he said.

For once I was thankful of our legal system's tortoise pace. It would take time to petition a judge, time in which Saint might still make a turnaround. "How long does it generally take for the judge to decide?"

"Usually a few hours. Less than a day, at any rate. In the meantime, sure, we can try more fluids, but I honestly don't think it will help."

My heart sank lower. Dr. Rogers went out to his truck for the medicine and to call Sue. I reassured Saint in a low voice, gently patting his velvet nose, struggling to accept the inevitable.

"She's on her way," he said. He unzipped his heavy jacket, reached inside and took a needle from his flannel plaid shirt. "I'll get this IV started."

"Do you see these cases often?" I asked, watching the medication drip through the plastic tubing. I poured him a cup of Marge's coffee from the Thermos.

"More often than I'd like. With the bad economy, people scrimp on feed and vet care. Most don't realize how expensive horses are. Sue was telling me she gets calls every day from people who are looking to ditch their horses because they can't afford them. Got any sugar?" he asked.

Rummaging in the paper sack, I located the box of sugar lumps. He dropped a half dozen into his hand, popped two into his coffee and ate the rest like candy. The aisle looked more like a campsite than a stable, littered with pillows, blankets, coffee cups, lawn chairs, and the cot.

"Hay is so expensive. Where does she get the money?"

"Donations mostly. The rest she gets from selling the rehabilitated horses. She's spent over $10,000 on hay this year and that's
not even enough to get her through next winter." He nodded
toward Echo and Feather in the paddock. "Better bring your other
two in, it's going to rain."

Feather pulled a mouthful of hay from the steel hay feeder. They
were nearly finished with the morning's ration. "God willing, let's
hope another woman isn't murdered tonight. Lately, every time it
rains, another body turns up."

"Wasn't the last one found near here?" he asked.

"There's state land at the end of this road." I pointed north, out
the barn door. "She was about a mile in, on one of the bridle trails."
I took lead ropes to bring Feather and Echo in from the paddock.
"The rain is symbolic in some way. Last night, when it was so cold,
I figured we're safe, it'll snow. But now it's warmed up and that
could mean trouble."

He zipped up his puffy down jacket. "Snow or rain, maybe it
doesn't matter."

That thought hadn't occurred to me. "Supposed to get cold
again tonight. Guess we'll just wait and see if it makes a difference."

*   *   *   *

Sue's red and calloused hand closed over mine. "We did everything
we could."

Her reassurance was of little comfort. "I feel awful. I can't help
but think it was because I was late in feeding last night."

"Colic and kidney failure are very common in these cases. Late
feeding probably had nothing to do with it. The people who should
feel awful are the ones who abandoned these horses, and they probably couldn't care less." She pushed back a blond curl the wind had
blown into her face.

My voice cracked when I spoke. "How can you face this day after day?"

"I can't tell you how many times I've asked myself that. But if I quit, what happens to them?"

She was right. Better to try to save the animals and fail, than to do nothing. But there had to be another way I could do my share, because I didn't think I could do this again. Too gut-wrenching.

Dr. Rogers signed the form recommending Saint be put down and Sue drove to Richard's paint shop to fax it to the Judge. Richard, nearly finished painting the Camaro, would bring it out when he received the signed form back.

Dr. Rogers was called away to stitch up a horse that had tangled with a barbed wire fence. He arranged for Dr. Murray to come as soon as we had the Judge's order.

＊   ＊   ＊   ＊

"I'll take care of it," Richard told the vet. "I know what she wants."

I walked from the barn to the house. Marge had gone home to get her mail and feed her kittens, and wouldn't return for another hour.

I felt like the day I fell from the barn roof. Like the wind had been knocked out of me and I was expecting that first painfully sharp whoosh of air into my lungs. Thunderheads were moving in, Denise was probably alone and I had a dead horse in my barn. I took the whiskey bottle down from the top shelf.

"Carol?" Richard's voice was soft behind me. "Where do you want him buried?"

"Out back." *Anywhere. I didn't care.* The house was quiet except for the wind chimes on the front porch. I felt strangely detached, not fully awake. I took a glass from the cupboard. "It's going to rain," I said. "Somebody needs to be with Denise. Can you send Louis?"

"No."

I turned around and looked at him curiously.

"His old college buddy is in town. Apparently the guy's relatives from way back were from this area and Louis and he are combing cemeteries trying to find where they're buried," he explained.

Louis's friend had to be the man the librarian spoke of. What were the odds there were two out-of-towners looking for the graves of long lost relatives? "Is he Indian?"

"Yeah, how'd you know?" Richard seemed surprised. "Full-blooded Navajo. Louis met him at the University of New Mexico."

"Yesterday, Nora, the librarian, said a guy who was, and I quote her, 'obviously Indian,' was looking for county plat books. Said he was looking for family graves." None of my research had specifically mentioned Navajo tribal customs. It might be worthwhile to check.

"Denise doesn't get off work until five, she'll be safe until then," he said.

"We should get a back hoe," I mumbled, knowing I wouldn't make the call.

Richard's voice was calm. "The two of us can manage."

He seemed like he was waiting for me to say something. "Go on ahead of me, I'll be down in a minute." I poured myself a shot, then made it a double. I offered the bottle to him, he took it, put the cap on, and slid it back onto the shelf.

The whiskey burned my throat going down, stinging every inch of the way into my stomach. Pain was better than no feeling at all. I watched as Richard crossed the lawn, trying to talk myself into going back down there. The first droplets of rain tapped the window. I dumped the ice cubes in the sink. How I was going to transport my exhausted body to the barn and dig a horse-sized grave was unclear.

My raincoat was in the foyer's walk-in closet. Jack's winter parka hung next to it. He would need to take it back with him the next time he came home. Indiana may be farther south, but their winters were just as hellish.

I smelled an unfamiliar smell. I heard the rustle of cloth. I spun around, came face to face with Perry, and screamed. More startling was the full-length Australian waxed coat he wore. Dark green, just like the sheriff's. That made four. "Just walk in, don't bother knocking," I said irritably.

His coat was unbuttoned and for the first time, I noticed he'd lost weight. The waist of his jeans was puckered where his belt cinched it in. "Figured I'd barge in unannounced, the same way you did. See how you liked it."

"I don't." *Damn him*, I thought. This was the wrong time for him to come calling. "Excuse me," I said, angrily. "I've got a horse to bury."

"I hope you've got a permit for that."

"This is Lapeer County. I don't need one." *Son of a bitch.*

"I see you got your pansy neighbor boy hanging around."

What the hell was that supposed to mean? I catalogued the smell. "You've been drinking and I'm not in the mood for your bullshit." I slammed the closet door.

He took a pouch of chewing tobacco from his inside pocket. "Still worried about Lida?"

Of course I was worried about Lida. Was that his reason for coming here? To taunt me? "Have you heard from her?" I asked.

Uninvited, he stepped from the foyer into my living room, leaving two muddy footprints. He moved stiffly, like he was sore all over. "She wanted me to let you know she'll be home soon," he said.

"You could have called to tell me that." I inched toward the glass door wall.

His mouth was contorted in an angry scowl. "But then I wouldn't have the fun of seeing you, now would I?" He moved closer.

He had an odd definition of fun. I stiffened and stepped back. "Fun? Is that what you call this?"

"As much fun as I've had leveling my basement floor where you dug it up. What were you looking for? Did you think Lida was buried there? I assure you she's not."

The patio door slid open and Richard's questioning glance went from me to Perry. "Everything okay?" he asked.

"Yeah, he was just leaving," I said, relief in my voice.

Perry hitched up his jeans. "Maybe when you're done burying your horse, you'd like to fix my floor. I've got a mind to sue you for that."

Richard moved between us. A full head taller but leaner than Perry, he possessed a rugged strength. Even so, Perry would pose a formidable adversary if it came to brute force. *Don't mess with him,* my eyes begged Richard. *Just get rid of him and let it go at that.*

"Why don't you leave her alone? If it's your basement you're worried about, I can take care of that."

Perry shoved a crooked finger in Richard's face. "I don't want your kind on my property."

Please, Richard, let it go.

"And what kind would that be?" he asked coolly, his voice calm and controlled. He spoke slowly, weighing each word.

"I think you know." The contempt in Perry's sneer was unmistakable.

Richard moved aside and slid the glass door open. "I think you'd better go."

"I'll go when I'm ready," Perry said.

"I'd say you're ready now," Richard said, pointing to the open door.

Perry stepped forward, toward the door. I held my breath, wishing this whole scene would be over. Then I saw Maximillian, my ancient Maine coon cat, on the deck. He wanted in, out of the rain, but was confused by the two men arguing in the doorway. I called to him and he darted between them, toward me. Perry saw him and viciously kicked at him as he ran past, hurling Max up against the inside of the sliding glass door. Max fell, confused. I screamed and grabbed the poor terrified cat, sheltering him in my arms.

"You bastard!" Richard yelled. He drew back his fist and hit Perry hard, sending him sprawling onto the deck. "Someone your own size might be more challenging." Perry tried to get up. Quickly, before he had a chance to retaliate, Richard hit him again. He drew back his fist a third time.

"Richard, no!" I screamed. Max struggled against me, clawing to get away, but thankfully his nails did not penetrate my heavy raincoat. I clasped him tighter.

Through surprise, Richard clearly held the upper-hand. Perry never got a punch in. As soon as he stood up, Richard knocked him flat again. "I'll kill you, you son of a bitch, if you ever bother her again," Richard spoke through gritted teeth. "Now get the hell out."

I carried Max to the back bedroom, where it was quiet, and closed the door. His eyes were wide with fear and he was trembling. I laid him on the bed and gently felt each leg and along his ribcage, checking for broken bones. I ran my hands along his coat to see if there was any bleeding. "Sweetheart," I cooed. "Everything's all right now."

Richard came in. "Is he hurt?"

"Just scared. Can you get me a towel from the bathroom to wrap him in? He's shivering." I softly tickled Max's chin.

Richard brought the towel and we gingerly swathed the thick Turkish towel around the cat, bundling him like a newborn baby, leaving just his little brown face poking out. I cradled him in my arms and soon he began to purr. "He's fine. Do you think Perry's okay?" I asked.

"I hope not. That asshole. Tomorrow he won't even remember what happened."

"You sure gave me a scare. I thought you were going to kill him."

"For a minute I wanted to. He shouldn't be driving around half drunk." Richard scratched behind Max's ears. The cat was clearly enjoying the attention and seemed to have already forgotten the incident.

"Funny, but I've never seen him drunk before," I said. "Oh, sure, I've seen him have a beer or two, but never mean and nasty like that. Something's up with him, that's for sure."

*   *   *   *

Cold rain covered us like a veil. It seeped through the double-stitched seams of my anorak, pelting my skin. With each thrust of my foot on the shovel, some of my anger and frustration dissipated, until little by little, I was too tired to be angry.

"You okay?" Richard asked.

I nodded. Tears streamed down my face. The grave we dug was quickly filling with water. Before too long we would have to climb in and pitch the dirt over our shoulders. I didn't know if I had the strength.

Pushing my hood back so I could see him, I yelled to Richard, my voice small above the rain, "We should've gotten a back hoe."

"There's not much more." His blond hair was plastered to his face in clumps.

Sweat trickled down my back. I was thoroughly soaked both inside and out. "Then how do we get him over here?" I asked.

Richard pointed to the tractor. "Drag him."

"No! I will *not* drag Saint!" I would not allow that last indignity. I threw down my shovel. "Go home, Richard," I waved him off. "This is crazy. It's filling with water as fast as we dig," I said. "I'm calling an excavator."

Chapter Fifteen

"Saw the back hoe in the paddock. Anything wrong?"

Sheriff Morton leaned on the fence post, dangling his hand dangerously close to the electric wire that ran along the inside top board. "Just buried a horse," I said, watching his hand. Apparently he hadn't seen the lightning bolt sign affixed to the corner post. He wore his standard issue jacket rather than the Aussie.

"I'm sorry to hear that. Not that pretty little mare, I hope?"

I shook my head. "He was from the farm that got raided last week. Down near the state line." I hoped he wasn't here to give me grief over burying a large animal on my property. My land was zoned agricultural.

"That's too bad. And to have your paddock all torn up like that at this time of year, too. Won't be able to plant grass until next spring."

"Jack will be thrilled about that," I said. Picking up the knife, I slashed open a bale of hay, then carried an armful past Saint's stall. Even though I'd had him only a short time, it didn't seem right that he wasn't there.

"Let me help you with that," Sheriff Morton said, opening the gate to come inside the paddock. He took two flakes of hay and dropped them into Feather's manger.

"Shake it out for her," I said irritably. I was approaching three days with little more than a couple hours of sleep, and I wondered what his real reason for being here was. "Did you want something?" I asked.

He brushed bits of hay from his shoulders. "We got the preliminary report on those bones the coyotes dug up last week."

Had it really only been last week? It seemed eons ago. I stopped doling out hay. "And?"

"Seems they're over a hundred years old. Guess there was an old farmhouse up there at one time. Used to be lots of families had their own cemeteries. There's probably some kind of markers, too. Funny thing is, there's no record of any cemetery when the land became state park, after World War II."

"Why would coyotes dig up hundred-year-old bones? Doesn't seem like they'd have much interest in them." Echo snapped at the hay in my hand, which was just out of his reach. "Bad, bad horse!" I scolded.

He pushed Echo out of the way so I could put the hay in his manger. "Beats me. At any rate, they have nothing to do with the recent murders."

I ran my hand inside Echo's water bucket, skimming for bits of hay. "Are you any closer to finding someone connected with those?"

"Afraid not." Figuring he had good reason to drag his feet with respect to the investigation, it didn't surprise me.

Was this whole conversation a charade? Could he converse so easily with someone about the very thing he'd planned and executed if, indeed, he was the killer? And why would he come here at all? To snoop?

"Have you seen anything suspicious?" he asked.

Was this his sneaky way of finding out how much I knew and therefore how dangerous I was to him? "Suspicious in what way?" I asked, playing along, pretending I knew nothing.

"Strange people hanging around. Things out of the ordinary."

"No, can't say I have. But then, because of the sick horse and the nasty weather, I haven't been off the farm much." I wasn't going to offer any more than I had to. "One odd thing, you know that Australian coat Richard and I were asking you about? Turns out Perry has one too. And apparently some guy from out of town's been in the library asking to see plat books. Looking for an old family cemetery. And the librarian says he was wearing one of those coats too."

"I had no idea they were that popular," he said. "I've had mine a few years." He fidgeted with the gate latch. "That Richard, he's different, isn't he?"

"Different?" I asked, though I knew perfectly well what he was suggesting. I wished everyone would get off Richard's case.

"You know. Funny."

"He's been a lifesaver with Jack gone," I said, not in the mood for this conversation to last much longer. It had taken the better part of the afternoon to wait for the excavator and get Saint buried. Twilight was settling in and I was dead tired. "I don't know what I would have done without him," I added.

"Why don't I find that surprising?" He closed Echo's stall door and pulled the latch.

I bristled. "What's that supposed to mean?"

"Just a friendly warning to be careful, that's all, Carol. You've got to remember, we really haven't known him all that long. Where'd he come from?"

"What difference does it make where he came from?"

"Guess it doesn't." The gate creaked as he let himself out. "Anyway, I'm going up there to look for grave markers. Want to show me exactly where you picked up that skull?"

Was he luring me into the woods? "Now?" I asked. "It's getting dark." I looked at his hands. Were these the hands that bound a young woman to a tree, slashed her wrists and left her to bleed to death? I looked closer. What was I expecting? Blood stains? He appeared so normal on the outside. What went on inside? "How about in the morning?"

The pager on his belt buzzed. He reached down and tilted the display to read it. "Got to take this one. Yeah, morning will work. I'll stop by, say, around ten o'clock?"

"Suppose it rains again?" I asked. "You still want to go?"

"Sure. Little bit of rain never hurt anybody."

No way in hell I was going into those woods alone with him. Not tonight, not tomorrow, not ever.

＊   ＊   ＊   ＊

"Denise is on the phone," Marge called from the kitchen. "Can you take it?"

Steam rose from my hot bath, where I lay steeping up to my chin. "Tell her I'll call her back." Tortoise-colored cat paws slipped under the bathroom door, tapping, as a blind person taps in front of themselves with a white cane. I'd latched the door, knowing that even if they flung themselves against it, it wouldn't push in. Too many cats in a small ranch house meant not a shred of privacy.

I soaked until my fingertips were prune-like, then dressed and met Marge for a cup of tea at the kitchen table. After explaining the purpose of Morton's latest visit, I said, "He said he wanted me to show him where the skull was, which I've already done. It was an excuse to get me into the woods."

"So how do you get out of it when he comes back tomorrow?" she asked.

"I'll think of something, don't you worry. Let me put that another way. *Tomorrow* I'll think of something. Right now, I'm going to bed."

Marge wound a finger around a perfectly lacquered white curl. "I wonder what he would do if I offered to go along," she mused.

"Don't you dare!" Some of the things she came up with lately made me wonder about her. Was she getting senile?

"All of the murdered women have been young. If it *is* him, what would he want with an old lady like me?"

"Are you willing to find out? You must be crazy!"

"No, just curious."

"Curiosity killed the cat, Marge." I put an extra tea bag in my cup, swirling it around until it sank to the bottom.

"I don't know how you can drink it like that, black like mud," she said.

"The stronger the better." What she'd said about age had gotten me wondering. "If they've all been young, I guess I'm safe too."

"You said that, not me." She yawned and stretched backward. "Remember to call Denise back, before it gets too late. I'm off to bed."

"Night," I said, wishing I was hauling my tired bones off to bed, too. I tapped Denise's number into the phone and waited. "It's me. What's up?" I asked.

"I didn't want to say anything in front of Richard or Louis, but remember when I went to get Richard's winter parka last night?" Her voice was low, conspiratorial.

A little slow in comprehending, I hesitated. "Huh?"

"When I first got to your place and Richard said he wanted his winter coat?" she said, trying to jog my memory.

"Yeah, I remember now," I said. The tea was fragrant and hot, Marge having insisted on Earl Grey, rather than our usual Darjeeling.

"Louis answered the door and when I told him what I wanted, he first looked in the downstairs closet, and I told him that Richard said the jacket was in the upstairs closet."

"Okay," I said, wondering where this was leading.

"Well, before he shut the closet door, I thought I saw something, and when he went upstairs, I peeked in and sure enough, guess what it was?"

She waited, like she was really expecting me to guess. "A pink tutu?" I asked, too tired for games.

"No, smart ass. An Australian coat, dark green."

A sense of foreboding came over me. Why hadn't Richard told me about the coat? He knew of my surprise when I'd seen the sheriff's coat on the peg at the police station and how it was the same as the man in the library and the person in the woods wore. "That makes five," I said, mentally tallying them up.

"Five?" She sounded confused.

"Yeah, Perry was here and he's got one too." I counted them off on my fingers, one at a time. "The man in the woods, the guy at the library, Perry, the sheriff and either Louis or Richard. Of course, there's really only four, since I'm figuring the guy in the woods doubles for one of the others."

"Wait, it gets better," she said. "It was damp and there was mud on the right side, near the hem."

"Dammit! Why didn't he tell me, Denise? Why?" Why would Richard not tell me that either he or Louis had one of the coats?

"Maybe he was afraid."

"Afraid of what?" I asked.

"Afraid that you'd suspect him, or Louis, like you do the sheriff and Perry. Men are cowards. Maybe he was afraid you'd think less of him."

"Well, if anything would make me think less of him, it's this. I've got a good mind to go over there right now!" Suddenly, I wasn't tired anymore.

"Don't. I just thought you'd want to know, that's the only reason I told you. Let's drop it."

Why did Richard's not telling me about the coat bother me? Maybe the fact that I thought we were friends, and friends didn't keep things from each other? Did he think I was stupid? That I wouldn't find out? Did he intentionally not tell me or was it a simple omission, something he just hadn't remembered to mention?

"Probably hundreds of people have those coats; it doesn't necessarily mean anything," Denise said.

"On the other hand, it could."

"Of course it could, but does it? It's too little to go on. We need something more concrete."

"You want concrete? Sheriff Morton stopped by tonight and tried to lure me into the woods. Now that's concrete."

"What?" Denise asked incredulously. "Did he come right out and ask, just like that?"

"Pretty much. He says the bones the coyotes dug up are over a hundred years old. Made up some story about there being an old farmhouse and a cemetery up on the hill where we found the bones. Like I was going to believe that."

There was a short silence and I knew she was taking a drag on her cigarette. She exhaled and her voice came on again, strained. "You're letting this get to you. Pretty soon you'll see a murderer behind every bush."

"Is that a polite way of saying I'm off my rocker?"

"No, nothing like that." She seemed to be flailing for words.

"Then what?" I asked, unable to keep the anger from my voice.

"I don't know. Look, you're really tired. Why don't you get a good night's rest and we'll talk again in the morning."

"Fine," I said, and hung up.

*   *   *   *

"Where's the baking powder?" Marge asked.

"In the cupboard over the stove. On the right side," I said, my mouth foaming with toothpaste. I glanced in the bathroom mirror. Maybe a little mascara would help.

"I can't make biscuits without baking powder."

She won't be happy until I weigh 300 pounds, which will be before the week is out, at this rate. Still, with all that had gone on, Marge and I were better off together, than either one of us alone. I wasn't in any hurry for Marge to leave.

The sausage smelled wonderful. "I'm sure it's up there," I yelled. A scraping sound came from the kitchen. Marge was standing on a chair, peering into the far reaches of the cupboard.

"For heaven's sake, get down from there! Do you want to fall and kill yourself?" For an eighty-three-year-old woman who was probably in the throes of osteoporosis, a fall from a chair could sound a death knell.

"You've fallen down more recently than I have. And don't try to tell me you haven't, because I saw you trip on the hose yesterday." She stepped down from the chair.

"It's in here somewhere," I said, rummaging in the cupboard. My fingers locked around a small metal can. "Here it is." The lid was a bit rusted. I triumphantly placed the can in Marge's hands.

She held it gingerly, as if it were radioactive. "What's the matter now?" I asked.

"It's so …"

"So what?"

"Well, so … old. When did you buy this?" she asked, turning the can upside-down. "Is it any good?"

"Of course it's good. Baking powder lasts forever," I said, although I had to admit the shelf life of baking powder was not within my realm of knowledge.

Holding the can at arm's length, she deciphered the tiny lettering. "I can't use this. Look right there," she pointed. "It expired in 1997."

"Don't worry. It'll be fine."

She pried the lid off with a butter knife. Peering inside, she wrinkled her nose. "Meal worms!"

I snatched the baking powder from her. "For crying out loud, Marge, there aren't any meal worms."

"There are too. Right there," she said, poking a finger into the can.

"Can we skip the biscuits?" I asked irritably.

"Everything else is in here," she said, pointing to the mixing bowl on the countertop. "And the sausage and gravy are ready. Drive me to my house; I've got some."

"Never mind, I'll just run over to Richard's. It'll be faster." They would surely have it.

"Be quick about it. This sausage won't last forever." She poked the sausages with a fork, rolling them over in the pan.

The grass on the west side of the house was still frosty where the sun hadn't warmed it yet. I blew on my fingers and started off at a jog, hoping to sprint to Richard's and back before I felt the cold. The cloudless sky was brilliant.

I knocked on Richard's door twice and waited, executing mini jumping jacks to keep warm. Neither Richard's truck nor Louis's car were in the driveway. I gently pushed on the door and finding it unlocked, stepped inside the foyer. "Richard?" I called. "Louis? Anybody home?" It felt awkward to be in someone else's home without them being there. It's only to borrow baking powder, I told myself. If I asked, I know Richard would say, sure come in any time. Isn't that what I would say to him? We're neighbors, after all.

The smell of coffee hung heavily in the air. I took off my shoes and quietly padded down the hallway, entering the kitchen. Trying several overhead cupboards, I searched, figuring he probably had his baking products, like vanilla extract, colored sprinkles, and spices, all together. But these cupboards held only dishes and glasses. Around the corner, in the hallway, a bi-fold door looked promising. I opened it to find a chef's dream. Shelves neatly stacked with every ingredient I'd ever heard of and a few I hadn't, alphabetically organized.

There it was, exactly where it should be—between bacon bits and baking soda. I turned the can upside down to check the expiration date. What were the chances that someone who alphabetized their shelves would ever allow something to expire?

"Find everything you're looking for?" Louis asked from behind me.

I jumped, dropping the baking powder. "Louis! You scared me half to death. Marge needed baking powder and the door was unlocked—I didn't think anyone would mind if I helped myself. Sorry. I called out, but you must not have heard," I said, in my defense.

"That's okay. I didn't mean to scare you," he said. His hair was wet and from his unbuttoned shirt, I gathered that he'd dressed hurriedly.

"Marge says my baking powder is expired, though I've never heard of such a thing. Have you?" I asked, nervously trying to make small talk.

"Absolutely. If it's too old, the dough won't rise." He began to button his shirt, starting with the last one. Why did women button their shirts from the top down and men from bottom up?

"News to me," I said, still feeling awkward, as if I'd been caught doing something I shouldn't, which, sort of, I had been.

I bent down to retrieve the can. Suddenly my pulse doubled. On the lowest shelf was my hay knife! The ornate handle of carved bone was unmistakable. Jack had gotten it for me on our trip to Alaska. What was it doing here? Quickly averting my eyes, I tried to cover the fact I'd seen it.

Dizziness overcame me. I swayed into the shelving.

Louis reached for my arm to steady me. "What's the matter?"

I gripped the edge of one of the shelves. "Just a sinus headache. I felt a little dizzy for a second," I mumbled. Wanting only to run, I forced myself to breathe and appear as normal as possible. "I'll bring the baking powder right back. She can't need much more than a spoonful."

How had my knife come to be here? Hadn't I used it only last night, when I opened the bale of hay? There must be a perfectly good explanation, I told myself. Denise was right. I'm letting my imagination run wild. Breathe.

Louis's face remained unchanged, devoid of emotion. He must not have noticed that I'd seen the knife. "Don't worry about it. I'll get more next time I get groceries," he said.

"Are you sure? It wouldn't be any trouble," I said.

"Nah. I think it's due to be replaced anyway." He stepped aside to let me pass. Sunlight streamed through the stained glass sidebars of the front door, into the foyer. "Sure you're okay? You don't look so good."

I willed my hands to stop trembling, but like stubborn children, they disobeyed. "I'm fine. Marge will be sending a search party out soon," I said, and giggled stupidly. My shoes lay on the rug. I jammed my feet into them. "Thanks again," I said.

When I got back, Marge immediately sensed something was wrong. "You're as white as a sheet."

Between gulping for air, I sputtered, "My knife—it's in their pantry."

Her eyes were wide. "What knife?"

"The knife I keep in the barn. It's in their pantry! That means one of them must have been here late last night. After we'd gone to bed." Why? Why would either Richard or Louis want my knife?

Her lips quivered when she spoke. "How can you be sure it's the same knife?"

"With a hand-carved bone handle, what are the chances it's not? It's not your run-of-the mill knife."

"There's one sure way to find out," she said. "Get your coat. Let's see if it's still there."

We marched over the frosty grass, into the stable. It was damned cold. "I keep it on the shelf with the vitamins and Feather's arthritis medicine." We stepped into the tack room. There was the knife, right where I'd left it. I picked it up, turned it over in my hands, wishing it could talk. "Am I losing my mind?"

"They've got one like it, that's all." Marge took the knife from me, examining it. It was about eight inches long, the rough handle etched darker where the bone had been carved away. The slightly curved blade ended in a sharp tip. "It *is* unusual," she said. "What kind of bone is it?"

"Elk or reindeer, I don't remember which. It's an Eskimo design. Jack found it at some little hole-in-the-wall shop in Anchorage. And that's what I'm trying to tell you. It's not something anyone could get from the local Sears." Benny came in through the kitty flap and sauntered over to the kibble bowl. "There is one other possibility," I said.

"Such as?" she asked, laying the knife on the shelf.

"Louis put it back before we got here."

She shook her head. "How could he? There hasn't been enough time for that."

"To slip through the pine trees alongside the house and in the back door of the barn? Plenty of time. Maybe he's here right now, listening."

"You're reading too much P.D. James lately," she scoffed.

For the second time within twenty-four hours, it was being suggested that my imagination was overly vivid. Were both Denise and Marge right? Nonetheless, I lowered my voice to a whisper. "Maybe so, but if I could just get back into Richard's pantry, I could see if the knife is still there. If it is, then they're in the clear. Only now I've got to wait for Louis to leave. If I'd known he was there, I wouldn't have gone into the house to begin with. His car must have been in the garage."

"We can watch the road from the living room, see when he heads out."

"But how do we get back into the house? I imagine he'll lock it."

"A locked door never stopped you before." She pulled her jacket tightly around her. "Let's get out of here. I'm freezing."

I wondered if, like me, her chill was caused not only by the temperature, but by the possibility that Louis was within earshot. She looked out the dusty tack room window, at the cloudless Cerulean sky. "I wonder how they think it's going to snow, when there isn't a cloud for miles," Marge said.

"You know as well as anybody how quickly that can change." I pulled the tack room door closed behind us and we headed up the hill to the house. The sun had warmed just enough to melt the heavy frost in the places that weren't in shadow. An earthy smell, like a forest after a rain, was on the wind. Maybe it would snow. "We need a plan of action," I said, tugging on the sliding glass door.

She had a quick answer. "While I finish the biscuits and salvage what's left of our breakfast, you watch the road. Then we do one-hour shifts each, until he leaves."

"Sounds fairly foolproof," I said.

Twenty minutes later I was stationed in front of the living room window, balancing my plate in one hand and a fork in the other. Camille purred on my lap, and each rhythmic swipe of her tail sent a bevy of white hairs swirling toward my food. Louis's silver sedan swung into the road. "Jackpot!" I yelled, sending Camille catapulting.

"Give him some time," Marge said calmly. "Let's make sure he's not coming back."

But springing up, I ran to the bedroom for my jacket and cell phone. "I'm heading over there. If you see either of them, call my cell. But only let it ring twice."

"Stop," she ordered. "Think out what you're going to do. Play it through in your mind." She smoothed her floral dress. "And fix your coat. You've got it on inside-out."

"Oh, for heaven's sake," I said, disgusted with myself. I took it off, turned it over and put it back on. "Remember, two rings," I said. Then I left, looking back once. The cats and Marge were in the front window, all nine pairs of eyes watching. Marge gave the thumbs up.

The west side of Richard's house would be the safest, away from the prying eyes of passersby on the road, but the door into the house off the deck was locked, as were all the windows on that side of the ground floor. I looked up, at the balcony with a door wall that opened into a second-floor bedroom, and wondered what the odds were it would be open. But since my chances of finding a ladder were probably even slimmer, I instead concentrated on the garage windows, remembering there had been a hallway off the kitchen which led to the garage.

The first window was stuck tight. Layers of old paint told me it hadn't been opened in a long time. It was just the sort of window someone might overlook checking the lock on. If I got into the garage, most likely the door into the house from there would be unlocked. With the palms of my hands, I pushed upward on its wooden frame.

Once, twice, three times I sucked in my breath and pushed, but it wouldn't budge. The window on the south side of the garage gave the same results. If I'd only brought a screwdriver along, I could use it to break the seal of old paint that cemented the sill to the frame. I scanned the ground nearby, hoping to find a sharp rock or a stick with a pointed end, but Louis's obsessive neatness had extended to the outdoors and I found nothing. Finally, I broke a short branch from one of the pine trees and pulled the smaller twigs from it, then peeled back the fibrous layers at the tip, to form a makeshift point. This I pushed into the crevice where the sill met the window pane, but it was still too blunt.

The sun sparkled on my diamond wedding ring and gave me an idea. Why hadn't I thought of it earlier? The solitaire, its sharp prongs constantly catching on my sweaters, just might cut through the tough skin of the old paint. It was worth a try.

The ring was snug. I got it off by working it back and forth, easing it over my knuckle until it finally slipped off. Pressing the diamond into the crevice between the window and the sill, I pierced the seal of paint, then worked it across the length of the sill.

This time, when I heaved upward on the window frame, I felt a slight give, as if the old wood might break free. I pushed again with all my strength. Suddenly the window moved. Not much, only about an inch. Again I heaved until my shoulders ached, and gained an opening of about five inches, still not enough for me to crawl through. Resting for a moment, I caught my breath, then pushed again until my muscles screamed. The opening slowly grew by inches, until I guessed it to be barely large enough for me to crawl through.

The patio chairs hadn't been stored for winter yet, so I dragged one over to the window, then climbed onto it. I got my knee up on the sill and pushed the upper half of my body through the opening. Twisting my leg around, I touched lightly onto the floor of the garage. The door to the house, as I'd guessed, was unlocked. I stepped into the dimly-lit narrow hallway that led to the kitchen.

Slipping off my shoes, I padded along the hall, the carpet soft under my feet. Taking the cell phone from my jacket pocket, I checked that I'd left it on and imagined what I would say, caught for a second time inside the house. If it was Richard who found me, it would be easy, the old baking powder excuse. But if it was Louis … I compulsively checked the light on the cell phone again, my fingers shaking.

Except for the ticking of the mantel clock, the house was silent. The pantry door was on my right, just around the corner from where I stood. The window over the kitchen sink was across from me. Cardinals at the bird feeder flicked seeds onto the ground.

My hands felt clammy as I pulled the pantry door open, my eyes hurriedly resting on the lower shelf. The knife was gone! So the one I'd seen earlier *had* been mine. The cell phone rang and I jumped. Then it rang once more and stopped. Louis was on his way back to the house! Instantly, I broke out in a cold sweat. First I turned to the front door, but the sound of the garage door opening cut off my escape by that route. Too easily visible by someone entering the garage. Out by way of the deck? That was in open sight of anyone coming in by either the front door or the garage.

There was only one way left. The upstairs balcony. I bolted up the stairs, taking them two at a time, and into the first door on the left, which, by placement of the balcony, I knew must be the master bedroom. Sunlight from the east-facing door wall poured in through gauzy willow-green curtains.

Then I remembered my shoes. They were on the door mat at the garage door. How could I have been so stupid? I prayed it would be

Richard and not Louis. Would he recognize my shoes? I dared hardly breathe, and waited.

"Carol?" Richard called. "Are you here?"

He'd seen the shoes! He was downstairs, and by the sound of his voice, just coming in from the garage. "I'm up here!" I called from the top of the stairs, trying to think of a reason why I'd be in his bedroom. The baking powder excuse was not going to work.

I met him on the stairs. The blue jean jacket he wore had smudges of paint on the sleeves, its collar jauntily turned up. There was paint on his hands, too, on the fine, long fingers that seemed far better suited to playing the piano than painting cars. "If you wanted to see my bedroom, you might have at least invited me," he said, ripe with innuendo.

I ignored it. Wondering where to begin and nothing coming to mind, I jumped right in. "You've got some explaining to do," I said, glaring.

"*I've* got some explaining? I'd say *you* have. For starters, what are you doing in my house?" Some of the banter was gone from his voice.

"What are *you* doing with my knife?" I crossed my arms in front of me, adamant that I would be the one asking the questions.

Was that a hint of surprise in his eyes? "What knife?" he asked.

"Don't play dumb with me," I said. My hands were shaking, though from fear or anger I could not be certain.

"Try speaking English, Carol." He stood defiantly, hands on hips, glaring right back.

"My barn knife. It was in your pantry, now it's back in my barn."

"You're not making a bit of sense, though why that should surprise me, I don't know." He jingled his keys in his hand, then put them in his jeans pocket.

"And why didn't you mention you had an Aussie coat like Sheriff Morton's? You stood there and let me make a fool of myself, asking him questions, and all the while you knew a coat just like it was hanging in your own closet." Why had he kept that little bit of knowledge from me?

"As for making a fool of you, you do quite well at that without any help from me. And I *don't* have a coat like that."

"Denise says differently."

"How the hell would she know?" he asked, obviously confused.

"The night we stayed with Saint, and she came over here for your winter coat. Louis first looked for it in the downstairs closet." I tromped down the stairs and flung the closet door open. The coat was there, just as Denise had said. "What's that?" I asked, pointing to it.

He waved it off. "Oh, that old thing. I forgot Louis even had it. And I don't think I've seen him wear it in years." He sat down at the bottom of the stairs to pull his boots off.

"Denise said it was damp and had fresh mud on it." I took the coat from its hanger to examine it. Like Sheriff Morton's coat, the waxed fabric was surprisingly heavy, but did not appear to be wet. Had there been enough time for it to dry?

"So what if he's worn it? Who cares?" He added his boots to a row of footwear in the closet.

"Stop and think about it," I said. For a smart guy, he was acting mighty dumb. Did I have to spell it out for him? "The person I saw wearing the coat in the woods is probably the murderer. And it just so happens all the victims have been killed with knives and now my barn knife is missing! And ..." I said, dramatically dragging out the word, "Guess where it was? In *your* pantry!"

"You're crazy. You're out of your freaking mind. I don't know anything about any knife."

Either he deserved an academy award, or he was truly surprised by what I was suggesting. "Maybe you don't, but Louis does."

"Are you insinuating that Louis has something to do with these murders?"

Our eyes met in an unwavering gaze. "What do you think?" I asked.

"What do I think?" He snatched the coat from me and hung it back up. "What do I think?" he asked again, slamming the closet door. "I think you're crazy—an absolute raving lunatic! Just because you saw some guy in a thunderstorm in the woods, now you've got anybody who wears the same kind of coat pegged as a murderer. And you know what? I'm willing to go along with the stupid games you play until you start accusing my brother. Then you've gone too far."

Exasperated, I let him have it. "Can't you put two and two together? Don't you realize he's got Denise pegged for his next victim?" I asked, incredulous that he could be so blind. It was so easy to see.

He looked at me in disbelief. "Just to humor me, why don't you let me in on what gave you that idea? I'd like to be privy to how that pea-sized brain of yours works," he said sarcastically.

Ignoring his insult, I listed the reasons on my fingers, counting them off, one by one. "Two of Denise's necklaces are missing. Her horse head hitch cover is missing. My knife was gone—then it mysteriously reappeared. This killer collects strange little personal items from the victims before he kills them. The only thing that doesn't make sense is why he took *my* knife, and not one of Denise's."

He picked up a stack of mail that lay on the hall table, thumbing through it. "That's not the only thing that doesn't make sense. Don't you think I would have noticed something if Louis was a killer? I live with him!" He began sorting the mail into two stacks. "I can't believe we're even discussing this. It's absolutely ludicrous."

"Wake up and take a look around you! Does Louis seem normal to you?" I asked. It was so frustrating that he couldn't see what seemed so obvious.

"Normal in what way?" He dropped the circulars and junk mail into the trash can.

"He wears sundresses, for starters!" I wanted to grab the mail away from him and force him to look at me. Was our conversation so unimportant to him that he couldn't be bothered to give it his full attention?

"So he's not like you. Who are you to decide what's acceptable and what's not? Do *you* have a normal marriage? Is it *normal* for a husband and wife to barely communicate? I don't think so. But does that make either of you a criminal? Hardly." He tossed the rest of the mail down. "I love my brother dearly and I'll stand up for him no matter what, so don't come around here accusing him of ridiculous nonsense!"

"That's just it. You love him so much that you can't see what's right in front of you." I could tell by the look on his face that he still didn't believe me. I was only wasting my time. I threw my hands up. "Talking to you is like telling the rain to go back up into the sky," I said. "It's totally useless."

With shaking hands I put my shoes on. Stepping off the porch, I heard the door slam behind me.

Marge waited at the door, nervously wringing a kitchen towel. "I've been going crazy. It's been fifteen or twenty minutes since Richard drove in." Her face was blanched white.

"What's wrong?" I asked.

"Denise called. Said Louis was on his way over."

"What?" I screamed, clutching her arm. "What did you say?"

"Denise called and said that Louis was coming over." She said it slower this time, as if I were learning disabled.

There was a strange buzzing in my ears. "Louis is with her?"

"Why do you keep repeating everything? What's the matter with you?"

"Marge! It's him!"

Chapter Sixteen

"Didn't you think that was odd? Especially since we weren't sure of Louis?"

"But we're not sure of anybody, are we?" Marge asked, "And he said Lida needed help. I told her not to go anywhere with him before you or I got there. That's why I was going crazy waiting for you. I figured he wouldn't do anything with one of us there."

"And Todd is gone?" I asked.

Marge nodded.

"Damn her! She was supposed to call us!"

"I know, I know." Marge looked pale and scared.

"I've got to get over there," I said, running to the bedroom. Rummaging unsuccessfully in my purse for my keys, I finally threw my cell phone down and dumped out the contents of my purse on the bed. Spotting the keys, I grabbed them. "Don't talk to anyone until you hear from me."

"What's going on?" Marge ran out the door, close on my heels, her pink flowered dress whipping in the icy wind.

"Go back into the house," I said. The last thing I needed was Marge coming down with pneumonia. Her *don't tell me what to do* look flashed across her face. "It's cold out here and you need your sweater. I don't know what's going on—that's the problem."

*   *   *   *

Gravel spat out from under my tires. Wait until I got a hold of Denise! We told her to make sure she was with someone at all times. Why hadn't she called us before Todd left? Mailboxes whizzed past. I gave a wide berth to two ladies on horseback, slowing only as little as possible. The instant they were in my rear mirror, I pushed my foot down on the gas. There was no telling what Louis may have already done.

There were two miles of country road between my house and Denise's. On horseback it takes about forty minutes, at a snail's pace. Normally, by car, about ten. Today, it took five. I swerved into her driveway, nearly taking out the mailbox, then gunned it up the hill to the house, blowing my horn the whole way. Louis's car was there, but strangely, Denise's truck was gone.

The house wasn't locked. "Denise!" I yelled. Where were they? Two mugs of coffee were on the kitchen table. I felt one. Still warm. "Denise, are you here?" A dog barked, but the barking was muffled. I followed the sound into the utility room in the back of the house. Something was scratching on the door to the basement. Diablo? I felt a moment of trepidation before reaching for the doorknob. Even though Denise's Doberman was a teddy bear when she was around, did I trust a dog that size without her here to control him?

"You're going to kill yourself, driving like that." A voice came from behind me.

I spun around to face Richard. "What are you doing here?"

"Following you."

"Why? I thought I was stupid and crazy and had a pea-sized brain."

"Maybe not. You said something … about the knives. Louis has a knife collection in a glass case at the end of the hall. After you left, I checked it. I don't really know for sure, I never counted them, but it seems like some are missing. I never really paid any attention to it before. But now … I was getting ready to tell you when you flew out of your driveway at ninety miles an hour."

He was only just now beginning to question Louis's behavior? "Denise called Marge, saying Louis was coming over to get her. Something about Lida needing help. Marge tried Lida's number, but there wasn't any answer. It was probably just a ruse. Now they're both gone."

"Son of a bitch." He shook his head, still in disbelief. "I keep thinking that it just can't be. Not Louis. But on the other hand, what if it is? What if my brother has become this horrible, evil thing? When I said I would never let anyone hurt him again, I meant it, but I never thought I should be trying to save the rest of the world from *him*."

He closed his eyes, as if for comfort. What would I do if it were my sister or brother? I couldn't answer that; I could only be thankful it was a decision I wouldn't have to make. "I'm sorry it's turned into this," I said. He was not in an enviable position.

Diablo's barking had intensified at the sound of our voices. "Why would she lock Diablo in the basement?" I asked. "I'm afraid to let him out—something about that dog sends chills up my spine."

"He might lead us to them," Richard said.

"If he doesn't devour us first. Do you know where Louis would take her?"

"I've got an idea. I'll tell you on the way. Let the dog out and let's go."

I opened the basement door just a crack. Diablo went berserk, growling and lunging. Then he shoved his nose through the small opening, pushing the door out of my hand. I screamed. He scrambled past us, his nails slipping on the hardwood floor, and slammed his body into the storm door, breaking the latch from the frame. He catapulted from the porch and squeezed under the bottom rail of the fence. Then he crashed through the cattails on the far side of the property and was out of sight.

"Lot of help we're going to get from him," I said.

Richard sprinted to his truck. "He's headed straight for the woods. Let's go."

"What about Todd?" I asked. "What if he comes home and sees Louis's car and the broken door, and finds Denise gone?"

"We don't have time to worry about it." Richard looked up at the sky. Storm clouds were rolling in from the west. I thought of Marge's comment on the snow and my dire prediction about how quickly that could change.

"I keep hoping we've got this wrong," he said. "That there's something else going on."

"What else is there? I don't think they've gone on a picnic," I said, hoisting myself up into the big dually.

"It doesn't have to be what we're thinking. There could be other reasons."

"Like what?" I asked.

"If only I knew!" He pounded the steering wheel with his fist. "Maybe they really have gone to Lida's."

"Can we afford not to follow Diablo …?" I asked, letting my words trail off.

He popped the clutch and barreled down the driveway, spooking the horses turned out in the paddock. They skittered and bucked, then turned and snorted, watching us. He didn't slow down until we got to the roughest section of the park road. The truck bumped down into a gully, then came up and over a hill. The road narrowed into a deer trail. Richard steered the truck to the edge, skirting an enormous anthill. "Where are we headed?" I asked.

"Haven't they all been found tied to pine trees? I mean *specifically* pine trees?" Richard asked.

I tried to think, but couldn't remember.

"If what I'm thinking is right, he's got to have pine trees. And rain."

I stared at Richard blankly, begging explanation.

"She burned him with cigarettes, then tied him to a tree in the backyard just before a rain. A pine tree. She said the rain would wash away the bad in him." Richard did not look at me, but straight ahead, at the road. The muscles in his jaw were clenched tight.

Rain, rain, go away. A child tied to a tree. I felt woozy, as if I couldn't breathe. *Rain, rain, go away.* Burned flesh. *Come again another day.* He downshifted, shoving the truck into first to make it up a steep hill. The movement jolted me from my nightmare.

"Now it's in reverse—now he's in control—and the woman he perceives as our mother is the victim," Richard said.

"Dear God in heaven, please, no! Richard!" Then I tried to focus. If I let myself become hysterical, I wouldn't do anybody any good. "There's that big stand of tamaracks on the park's west side," I said. Why were we traveling in the opposite direction from them?

"There're pine trees north of the Pinnacle, too," Richard said.

The Pinnacle, true to its name, was the highest point in the park, and on it stood a stone foundation, the only remnant of an old farmhouse. The base of the hill was dotted with pine trees. It wasn't far from the shallow grave Echo and I had fallen into on Sunday. I craned my neck to check the sky.

Richard must have read my mind. "It's not going to rain," he said, matter of factly, as if willing it was all it took. "Pray for snow. He's got to have rain, not snow."

If he was trying to reassure me, it didn't help. "Looks like it could go either way," I said.

"There's something else that might be a factor."

"Richard! I can't believe this. How much more do you know that you're not telling?"

"I don't *know* anything. I'm only guessing, just like you are," he said irritably. Then seeing the hurt look on my face, he squeezed my hand. "Look, it won't help for us to fight."

He was right. We had to work together to find them. "So what is it?"

"We've got until dark. It was always just before dark when she would tie him outside. Never in a million years did I dream Louis would do this."

We were deep into the woods now, and tree branches grazed the sides of the truck as we passed. When we could drive no farther, he parked at the edge of the trail in a sheltered turnoff cut out of the trees. "We'll have to hike the rest of the way."

"But if he brought her here, where's her truck? Shouldn't we keep looking?" I asked.

"There isn't time. We've got to gamble that it's this stand of pines and not the tamaracks." He got out of the truck and reached behind the seat, withdrawing a cloth bag. He untied the string that held the flap closed and slid a pistol out. He checked the barrel, then tucked the pistol into his waistband.

"Maybe we should split up, you check this section, I check the tamaracks," I said.

He shook his head. "I'm sure as hell not leaving you to go off exploring on your own, and since I'm going to the Pinnacle, you're going too. There's no time to argue." He reached for my hand to help me up the bank at the side of the road. I could see no choice but to set off down the narrow trail with him.

"How's your ankle? Can you run?" he asked.

The swelling had lessened each day, but it was still tender and puffy. "I won't break any track records, but other than that, let's go for it," I said.

We started off at what for him was probably an easy pace. It wasn't far to the Pinnacle, or at least it had never seemed so on horseback. Jogging it, though, was quite different. To make matters worse, the trail was becoming more sandy, making the going even slower. Soon I was panting and lagging far behind. "Richard," I called ahead, "I've got to stop for a minute." Cursing myself for having let my body get so out of shape, I sank down on one knee, gulping air. Sweat trickled down my spine.

He backtracked to me. "What's wrong?"

I clutched at the stitch in my side, breathing heavily. "The sand … it's too hard to run … I only need a second, then we can go on." I breathed long, deep breaths, filling my lungs. My ankle throbbed.

Then I saw it. I suppose that because Richard had been running faster than I, he'd missed it. Leaves with dark red blotches on them. I pointed.

He knelt down and scooped up a handful of leaves and sand. He held it to his nose, then crumbled the sand between his fingers, letting it fall. "Fresh blood," he said.

No, it can't be. I refused to believe it. I looked up at the sky, which was becoming more gray and cloudy by the minute. A shiver coursed through me. "I'm calling Sheriff Morton." My cold fingers fumbled in my coat pockets, searching for my phone, but came up empty. Where was it? I retraced my steps from the time I'd left Richard's house, where I last remembered having it.

I'd pulled it out to call Lida when Marge told me Louis and Denise had gone to help her. But Marge had said she'd already tried Lida's number and there was no answer, so I hadn't called. What had I done with it after that? Then I knew. When I dumped out the contents of my purse on the bed, to look for my keys, I'd thrown it down. My cell phone was at home, laying on the bed!

"I don't have the phone," I shouted, angry with myself for having been so stupid. "I don't have the freakin' phone!"

His face was wet with sweat. He looked up at the sky. "I thought she'd be safe as long as the rain held out."

But what about the blood? Whose was it? Had Louis injured himself? I stood up, but my knees felt wobbly. "Go on without me. I'm only slowing you down."

He shook his head. "No. I'll carry you if I have to."

By the set of his jaw, I knew he meant it and arguing would only waste time. We set off again. I concentrated on moving forward, cutting myself off from the pain of my legs, my ankle or my bursting lungs. One foot in front of the other, I told myself over and over. Scanning the sand as it passed beneath my feet, I watched for more traces of blood, finding one spot, then another, then finally a third and we knew we were headed in the direction Louis and Denise had taken.

The next bloodstain, in a three-way clearing in the trail, was noticeably larger than the others. Either the bleeding was more profuse now or they had stopped to rest here. "Which way?" I asked. All three paths wound around and meandered differently through the park, but ended up at Pinnacle Point.

"You check that trail, and I'll check these two," he said, pointing. "Look for blood or tracks, anything that might tell us which way they went. But stay where I can see you," he warned.

Cold and damp, the forest seemed deserted, the wildlife hunkered down for the brewing storm. The tall pines filtered the weak slanting sunlight, deep shadows falling from their boughs. The smell of pine was heavy. There were no signs that my path had been recently traveled.

"Over here," Richard called. "This way."

Backtracking, I joined up with him. He pointed down at the ground, at a dark stain. "You okay?" he asked.

I nodded. My only goal was to find Denise alive. "It's not much farther now," I said, gritting my teeth. Just up the hill was the Pinnacle. I prayed we would find them before it was too late.

Richard stayed twenty feet ahead of me. Even though it was more straining on my good foot, I found some relief from my ankle pain by dragging the side of my injured foot through the sand, rather than lifting it and putting it down with each step. Sometimes I lifted my eyes to watch his back, as he moved easily up the steep and sandy trail. Then with a quick jerk, he stopped. A dark, motionless form lay on the trail. Richard turned to face me and held his forefinger to his lips, motioning me to stay quiet.

I stopped, waiting for a signal from Richard. He cautiously looked around us, then slowly walked toward whatever lay in the path. He knelt by it, then lifted the limp form and turned it over.

"What is it?" I called to him, breaking the silence.

"It's Diablo," he said. "He's dead."

I ran in a stiff, hopping gait, my ankle screaming in agony. A trickle of blood from the dog's mouth had drained into the soil beneath his head. There was a hole in the dog's side, near his shoulder. It seemed such a small wound to kill a big, powerful animal like Diablo. Now I had feelings not only of terror, but also anger. The abused had become the abuser. The cycle had to stop.

"Damn that bastard," Richard muttered only loud enough for me to hear. He pulled Diablo's carcass off the trail, into the trees. "At least we know we're going in the right direction."

"But we never heard a gunshot," I said, confused.

"He's using a silencer." Richard sniffed. "Smell that? It's the sandalwood he wears." He held his finger to his lips. "Quiet," he whispered.

I inched closer to him.

"Let's go the rest of the way up the Pinnacle," he said. "We'll be able to see more up there. Stay close to me."

He needn't have bothered with his last instruction. I had no intention of letting him out of my sight. The woods seemed dark and alien. I imagined a possible hiding place behind every tree, stump, or rock. We crouched as we picked our way up the hill, avoiding disturbing the rock and shale, which tumbled down in tiny avalanches. Once I braced my foot on a boulder to boost myself up and it broke loose, rolling down the hill. Richard's silent admonishment was evident.

Over the crest of the hill we saw the old stone foundation. The only obvious signs of anyone having been up here were hoofprints and mountain bike tracks. The view made it a popular stopping place. The wind blew fiercely.

"Looks like a dead end," I yelled above the wind. "What now?" I asked. My hair whipped across my face.

Richard crouched on one knee, scanning the treetops. "Something tells me we're close. That smell. The sandalwood," Richard shouted.

To get out of the icy wind, I left Richard at the edge of the peak, and went into the remnants of the waist-high foundation. It was separated into three chambers. The smallest had probably been a root cellar, the largest the basement of the house, and the other, most likely where the pump house had been. For a moment, I thought I did sniff a faint trace of sandalwood, but quickly dismissed it. I stooped to pick up a stone that had crumbled from the wall and fit it back into place, like a piece of a jigsaw puzzle.

Suddenly a tremendous force from behind pulled me off my feet, a hand clamping something sticky across my mouth. The hand was close under my eye and on it, I saw a familiar ring. A thick gold band with an inlaid black onyx scorpion. Louis! Then arms as strong and immovable as steel imprisoned mine at their sides, binding my wrists with a rough rope. In fear and confusion, I tried to scream, but only managed a grunt. Then the rope was jerked tightly, tearing the skin on my wrists and pulling my head backward. A sharp pain shot up my spine. He dragged me, on my back, across the graveled base of the foundation. The duct tape on my mouth tore at my lips when I tried to scream. My foot banged hard on a rock as he dragged me through an opening in the foundation.

If I could only yell or somehow make any sound loud enough, I could get Richard's attention. *Turn around,* my brain screamed. He was facing the opposite direction and into the wind. He wouldn't have heard a bazooka blast with the wind howling like this. I struggled frantically in the only way I could, by digging my heels into the ground and wrenching my body from side to side, in an attempt to signal Richard. He didn't turn around.

Trying a new tack, I made myself limp, making it as hard as possible for Louis to move my 130 pounds. Twigs, leaves, and brush were dragged along with me. How had he come up behind me so silently? And where was he taking me?

I remembered Richard's words, "As long as the rain holds off, she's safe." Did my life now depend on the weather, too?

Louis pulled me, head first, to a place about fifty feet below the crest of the Pinnacle. He left me, trussed up like a Thanksgiving turkey, while he pulled brush away from a small opening in the side of the hill, to reveal a cleverly disguised shelter dug underneath the huge tamaracks.

He had used the natural landscape to his advantage by choosing the north side of the Pinnacle, which had more erosion. Some of the tamaracks had already begun to show their roots where the sandy soil had washed away, down the natural slope. He had simply tunneled under the trees, easy digging in this kind of soil, using the massive root systems of the big, old trees as a roof support. Some of the roots were nearly a foot in width and grew through the chamber, into the earth below us, anchoring the space. From the dirt floor to the underneath of the roots was probably six feet high, barely enough for Louis to stand with his head slightly bent. The dugout, roughly twelve-by-fourteen feet, had been braced along its sides with timbers and plywood. The ceiling was similarly braced, by running cross beams through the natural root structures of the trees as supports.

It didn't take an engineer to figure out how easily the sides of Louis's man-made cave could fall in and bury us.

He pulled me into the shelter and propped me against the gnarled roots of a tree. I could see his face now, his black hair a crazy tangle; dark, wild eyes not focusing on me, but rather looking through me, as if I were invisible.

He pulled the brush back in around us, sealing off the entrance to the hideout. Running the bight of the rope that bound me around a stake which had been anchored into the ground, he secured it with a knot. "How thoughtful of Richard to bring you to me," he said, jerking the rope taut. Dirt from the roots rained down on my hair and eyes. His breath spiraled upward in the cold air.

My eyes, I was sure, betrayed my fear, and I wondered if he found pleasure in the terror he had created. The thought angered me, so much so, that I looked away from him, refusing to satiate his ego, even in the smallest way.

"Richard loves you very much," he said, leering down at me.

If Richard loved me, why on earth would he deliver me to Louis? Had I fallen into some plot orchestrated by Richard?

"No one likes it here at first," he said. "That's why I have to tie you. But in the end everyone wishes they'd come sooner. Later I'll be able to take the rope off and you'll stay just because you want to."

Sweet Jesus, deliver me from this madman, I prayed. For a moment I closed my eyes and prayed with intensity, removing every other thought from my brain. When I opened them, my eyes had adjusted to the dark and I looked around my prison.

There was a cut Scotch pine at the back of the dugout which had been anchored into the ground by a heavy stake. Denise sat cross-legged at the base of the Scotch pine, bound to the stake. She was gagged by a strip of duct tape across her mouth and wound around her head. Her eyes were covered in the same fashion. Her face, what I could see of it, was ghostly white.

Dangling like a Christmas ornament from a branch over her head was her Celtic cross. The silver fish was there too, its delicate chain entwined in the tree's needles. So was the hitch cover. There were other things belonging to Denise, too, things I hadn't known were missing. A red and white bandanna she sometimes tied around Diablo's neck. A gold bracelet made of tiny heart links.

She must have heard Louis's coming and going and talking to me, but wouldn't know it was me with her unless she had guessed. There was no way for me to communicate with her. She could hear, but I couldn't speak. She could feel, but my hands were tied.

"Not much longer now," Louis said, checking the binding around Denise's wrists. "Just waiting for the weather to cooperate." He said it as lightly as if we were waiting for snowfall so we could ski or go sledding.

My stomach churned with a sick feeling. The cold dampness of the cave's dirt floor seeped through my jeans and I began shivering. I tried to stop, remembering that although shivering was the body's own way of raising its temperature, it also expended energy reserves. My confused brain tried to unmuddle itself. Concentrate on one thing at a time. What was most important? To get us away from here. How? I tried wiggling my hands free. The rope bit deeper the more I tugged. A better idea might be to work the tape loose from my mouth. But even if I succeeded in yelling, would Richard hear?

Could I even trust Richard? Had he really not known anything about this?

"When the rain comes, you'll be clean again," Louis said to Denise. He wagged his finger at her. "After that you must never be bad again. It upsets mother when you're bad." His voice was small and childlike. "And Richard cannot help you."

He picked Denise's jacket up from the dirt floor and that was when I realized she was bare-armed. The sleeves of her fleece top were pushed up to her elbows, the way she always had them when she did chores around the house. He took cigarettes and a disposable lighter from the pocket of her jacket. He lit a cigarette and inhaled deeply, until the end glowed red.

With horror I remembered what Richard had said about their mother burning Louis with cigarettes. Would he carry this sick reenactment that far? I tensed, new terror filling me. I began to pray again. *Our Father, who art in heaven* ...

"I told her I didn't do those things. Even Richard tried to tell her. But she says I'm bad." He circled the back of the cave, near Denise. "You're bad, too," he said to her. "You need the rain to wash away all the blood and badness. The rain will come."

He took hold of her forearm and pressed the fiery end of the cigarette to it. I cringed and turned my head away as she recoiled in pain. Tied as she was, there was nowhere for her to go except more tightly against the stake. *Hallowed be thy name* ... Again and again the cigarette's tip glowed orange, and again and again he held it to her pale skin. Her muffled cries of pain, though nearly inaudible, rang unbearably in my ears, until I thought I would go insane and now I knew how Richard must have felt. She thrashed her head from side to side, as if that could somehow relieve the pain. Dear God in heaven, make him stop. *Thy kingdom come* ... The words repeated themselves in my mind, like a mantra.

Richard's voice came from outside. "Louis! Let the girls go. Hurting them won't help you."

Get us out of here, please, my heart begged. Frantically, I worked my lips back and forth, trying to loosen the tape. Despite the cold, beads of sweat formed on my forehead. Denise's head was flopped forward, chin to chest, and I wondered if she was conscious. If only she could have seen me! To know I was with her. Richard was our last hope. I had to trust him, and somehow let him know where we were. "Richard," I mumbled, my lips barely moving under the tape. The word came out so muffled I knew it wouldn't be heard outside the cave.

I continued to struggle with the tape. When a small opening formed between my lips, I ran my wet tongue across it, hoping the moisture would break its hold. "Richard," I sputtered, as loud as I could, but still not loud enough.

Louis threw me a threatening stare. He walked over, pulled a pistol from inside his jacket and held it menacingly to the side of my head. My head shook from the tension in my neck. While Denise's fate hung by rituals and symbolism, apparently a plain old bullet was good enough for me. At least it was quick. On the other hand, I'd read somewhere that bleeding to death is like falling asleep. I wanted to believe that, for Denise's sake.

"One more word ..." he muttered in a low voice, his jaw clenched. I recoiled from the gun, turning my face up toward the ceiling. Then I saw it. Cut in the plywood ceiling above Denise, between the supporting jackposts, was a hinged door. It seemed Louis had thought of everything, right down to the way the rain would come in through the opening and wash over his victim. How convenient. But Louis's diabolical attention to detail could also be his downfall: the overhead door provided one more way out of here. Or one more way in. I quickly averted my eyes from the opening, not letting on I'd seen it.

"Louis, don't do this." Was Richard's voice becoming more distant or was it my paranoia?

Louis remained silent. I did likewise. The cold metal barrel, now pressed to my cheek, smelled of gun oil. Moments ticked by like hours.

"Mother's gone," Richard said. "She can't hurt you anymore." Richard was on a fishing expedition, baiting Louis to speak, so he could locate us by the sound of Louis's voice. He may as well have announced his plan with a bullhorn. *It's not working*, I wanted to yell.

As for the sound of Richard's voice, I was not imagining it. Richard *was* getting farther away. Louis knew it too, I could tell by the smile that spread across his face, a smile full of white teeth that in the low light of the cave now took on a wolfish quality.

"No, she's not gone," Louis whispered. "She's right here." He pointed a shaky finger at Denise. Whether his hand shook from fear or rage, I couldn't tell. Surely he'd felt fear at the hands of his mother, but there had to have been anger too, incredible amounts of anger. Stored up for years and now unleashed.

"I know where you are." Richard's voice was faint now. I thought of Elmer Fudd telling Bugs Bunny, "I know where you are, you silly 'wabbit," while Bugs hides behind a tree snickering. *He did not know.*

Louis scowled. "Liar," he said in a low voice. "You didn't think I'd fall for that, did you?" He lifted my chin. His face, only inches from mine, so perfect with its beautiful angles and clear skin, was the face of Satan. "Your beloved Richard is without a clue as to where we are." Again came the wolf's smile.

If Richard knew where we were, what was he waiting for? Was he hoping Louis would give himself away, or release us? I feared the sad truth was that he didn't know where we were, and in that realization, the dank odor of the cave washed over me and I fought to hold my stomach down. Tears ran a jagged path down my cold cheeks.

But in which direction was Richard headed? And why? He must know we couldn't be far off. Why would he leave? I'd pointed out earlier that the pines on the other side of the park could just as easily be Louis's chosen location as this place. Maybe he thought Louis had dragged me off in that direction. But if that was the case, why would Louis have been here to begin with? All signs led us here— the trail of blood and then, finally, poor Diablo's body. *Follow your intuition, Richard. You thought this was the place and you were right.*

Apparently Louis felt the danger of Richard's discovery of us had passed. He retracted the pistol, slipping it inside his jacket. He cautiously pulled a branch away from the entrance, and checked the northern sky. A cold wind swept in and the bleak afternoon light punctured the dark cave. The branches of the tamaracks swayed, dark and gusty, as thunder rumbled in the distance.

He turned around and said, "It will rain soon. Then it will be time." He bunched his fists under his chin, like a child making a wish over a birthday cake. "I do so love this," he said, his anger abated. "It's like going on vacation. Everything is ready, all the plans are made, and you know it's going to be wonderful."

Filthy son of a bitch.

Louis replaced the branch, then began building a fire in a small ring of stones. Bundled twigs and a stack of logs were along one wall. He unwound the twine from a bundle and neatly arranged the twigs within the stones. Using a pocket lighter, he lit the mound. Blowing carefully on the tinder until it glowed orange, Louis then placed a log on it. It smoked for a moment, then ignited with a pop.

From a backpack laying on the dirt floor, he extracted a metal container about the size of a shoe box, a crystal goblet and, to my amazement, the bone-handled knife. He'd been back to my barn again! He moved with the stealth of a coyote, across my property, in and out of my barn, using what he wanted when he wanted to, and putting it back when he no longer needed it. How could I have not noticed that he'd been there?

He added another log to the now crackling fire. "Caliban needs to stay warm," he said, carefully positioning the box near the fire.

Who the hell was Caliban?

When the fire was blazing, he took the knife and held it in the licking and spitting flames, the sharp blade glistening. He appeared mesmerized and didn't notice me watching him. Bringing it close to his face, he scrutinized the tip, then ran his finger along the sharp edge of the blade. He pulled back suddenly and licked a drop of blood from his finger. Though the fire had brought some warmth to the cave, I began shivering again.

Taking the goblet and knife, he went to Denise and lifted her head. She recoiled at his touch and I knew she was conscious. He brushed her hair aside, tucking it behind her ear. With his left hand, he held the cup under her jawbone, in the angle where it curved upward to her ear. In his right hand, he held the knife lengthwise, parallel with the line of her jawbone.

I panicked. There was still time, wasn't there? It hadn't rained yet. While the others had their wrists slashed, he was awfully close to her jugular vein. Why would he stray from his usual technique? There was no time to ponder. Denise's life, and my own, depended on me. Richard wasn't coming back. I could sit here, cry, and watch my friend bleed to death, or I could do something.

My mouth was sealed with tape and my hands were tied, but I had the use of my feet and legs. A star athlete I was not, but judging the distance between the fire and myself, I thought I could barely reach it with the toe of my boot.

I stretched my right leg as far out as I could, aiming for one of the logs. The stiff rope tore the skin from my wrists and sent a sharp jolt of pain up the base of my spine and into my neck. I nudged the log with my foot, then quickly got the toe of my boot under it and brought it forward a little. Knowing I had only seconds until Louis realized what I was doing, I swung my foot back as far as I could, which wasn't much, then brought it up, catching the log fully with my foot. It arched halfway between the fire pit and the cave entrance, coming to rest just short of the brush I was hoping to ignite. Damn! Hurry, try again, I told myself. Faster now, I kicked the last log, savagely pulling against the rope, doing my best to ignore the searing pain it inflicted on my rope-burned flesh. The log landed dead center in the dry brush, sending up a pillar of smoke.

Louis ran to me, his eyes black with rage. "I'll teach you ..." he hissed. I kicked at him, over and over, like an unbroken colt snubbed to a post. He'd gotten the gun out again. I prayed the smoke would rise quickly and the longer I diverted his attention, the more chance there was of someone seeing it.

He pointed the gun at me, as I wrenched my sore and aching body from side to side. Why didn't he shoot me and get it over with? I braced myself for the loud crack and the lightning pain.

Then I knew. A gunshot, even with a silencer, depending on how close he was, would lead Richard right to us. Louis no more wanted to shoot that gun than he wanted me to scream. I had a new surge of strength. Working my lips up and down, side to side, whatever movement I could get, the tape covering my mouth was loosening. Finally, it pulled away from my skin.

"Richard," I screamed victoriously, louder than I'd ever screamed anything in my life. Louis's face screwed up with fury, the muscles in his neck bulging.

He smashed the gun butt against my temple. A sickening pain descended over me. It spread through my skull and down my neck. My vision blurred. "Over here ..." My voice was strangely distant, as if the words were coming from some far corner of the underground chamber.

The hulking blur of Louis stood over me. When he got closer I saw the chrome and wooden handle of Louis's gun as he hit me again, the knuckles of his hand slamming into my right eye.

Chapter Seventeen

Louis's voice woke me.

"Caliban mustn't misbehave," he said.

Fresh tape covered my mouth and circled around the back of my head—this time he'd double-wrapped the tape. My temples throbbed with a fierce pain. Everything was fuzzy around the edges; Louis a dark presence somewhere over by Denise. A shadow circled the dirt around her. He held something long and thin; it undulated, like prairie grass swaying in a breeze. He held it near the top, a small portion of its length sticking out between his thumb and forefinger.

"Carol," Louis said, coming closer. "I was afraid you wouldn't wake up in time to see Caliban's performance. He really loves an audience." My vision was sharpening up fast.

Caliban was an eastern Massasauga rattler, a pit viper, nearly two-and-a-half feet long. Gray and chocolate brown, his tail ended in a button-shaped rattle. Louis held him in mid-air in a pinched hold, his thumb and forefinger behind his broad, flat head.

The enclosed quarters of the dugout were far too small for me to share with Caliban. But even though I was horrified, I sensed that disguising my repulsion might keep me alive.

A metal box, its lid laying in the dirt, told me Caliban had been its most recent occupant. No wonder he'd wanted to keep it warm. The Massasauga rattlesnake, the only poisonous snake in Michigan, normally went into hibernation in October and stayed asleep until April.

Morton hadn't mentioned anything about a snake figuring into the ritual. Was that a part of his investigation that he'd withheld? If so, why? I remembered the snake that had been delivered to my door only days ago and now knew Louis had sent it. Had it been his way of warning me off? Had he felt I was getting too close to Richard, and too close to the truth?

In his other hand, Louis held a crystal goblet. A dark liquid, what I guessed to be blood, filled nearly an inch in the bottom. Whose blood? Denise's? He positioned the glass so the snake's fangs were inside it, then tipping the snake's head, he pressed its fangs against the inner rim. When he had milked the snake of its venom, he set the goblet down and, with care and expertise, placed Caliban back in the metal box, quickly closing the lid. Every movement precisely orchestrated, it was obvious he had done this before.

He held the goblet's foul mixture under his nose and inhaled deeply, as if sniffing the bouquet of a fine brandy. Then, in one quick swallow, he drank the venom and blood. He closed his eyes and swayed slightly. For a moment, I thought he would fall, but then he reached out his hands, as if to clutch onto some invisible wall, and regained his balance.

When he opened his eyes, he spoke slower and more deliberately. He sounded cold, calculating, and in total control. "If you mix the blood of life and venom of death, which prevails?" he asked. Was it a riddle he expected me to answer?

I'd never seen this Louis before. Did he have multiple personality disorder? Dropping to his knees, he clenched a handful of my hair and yanked my face close to his. The dried blood that trailed from the corners of his mouth smelled fetid. His breathing was rapid and shallow. I turned my face away from the putrid odor.

"Death will always prevail!" he snarled like a rabid dog. "Stupid nosy-ass bitch!" he said, shoving my face. "I should have wasted you, instead of listening to Louis's whining about how we mustn't upset Richard."

He kicked me in the stomach. I writhed in agony, struggling to breathe in short gulps. Physical pain and fury filled me. "To hell with Richard and his fairy princess. I'm tired of him bossing me around."

He thrust the knife close to my face. My eyes pinched shut. All the things left to do and say, all the things I loved in this life—Jack, family, friends, cats, horses, home, land—flashed by. My mind closed off the wretchedness and I prayed. The seconds stretched on. If this was the end, so be it.

Instead, in a cool and melodic voice, he said, "Richard can't stop me, since he can't find my newest hideaway." I opened my eyes. He slid the knife into a sheath on his belt and knelt down facing me. A lock of black hair fell over one of his eyes. He shook it back into place and smiled boyishly.

His emotional range, and the speed with which it changed, shocked me. My questioning eyes met his blank ones, straining to see insanity inside them. But in his eyes there was nothing.

His alter ego's voice said, "Louis isn't indebted to Richard. Back then, when things were bad, the only person that could help Louis was *me*," he bragged. "I taught him how to survive the pain. It was *me*, not Richard."

My gaze followed him as he paced the cave.

"I stood in the dark stage wings, mouthing practiced words, while Louis played his part. Louis had to do it; there was no one else. It was the only way."

He nodded toward Denise in the back of the cave. "Richard doesn't care about her. She owes it to Louis—her and all the rest of them. One for each time Louis died. Twenty-seven in all."

Was that his plan? To kill twenty-seven women? I shook my head in defiance.

He backhanded me, whipping my head to the side. At first, the pain drove all thoughts from my brain. Then waves of nausea came.

"How dare you judge us! You weren't there. You have no idea what it was like." He paced the length of our prison. When he stopped in front of me, afraid, I studied the pointed toes of his snakeskin boots. I cringed down into my quilted vest. I'd been knocked down, tied, dragged, kicked, slapped, and backhanded. Every inch of me hurt. Giving up would have been so easy. But when I saw Denise, I was ashamed of my lack of fortitude. If she wasn't giving up, neither would I.

"It would have been simpler if Richard had never met you," he said angrily, jabbing a finger at my chest. "You couldn't leave things alone, could you? There was just no getting rid of your nosy ass, not even my threatening messages did the trick. So now I've got to dispose of you." There was a loud clap of thunder and Louis went to the back of the cave. He removed the plank bracing the overhead trap door, unlatched the handle, and pulled the door inward. The air that swept down on us was cold and held the spicy smell of the autumn leaves.

"Rain!" he screamed, his face contorted. He released the handle, leaving the door to flap open above Denise's head. With his knife, he savagely stabbed the dirt wall between Denise and me. His breathing was loud and rapid, his movements quick, sharp jabs.

Then a movement caught my eye. Someone dropped through the overhead opening and hit the ground with a thump. Louis saw it too, and grabbed me from behind, his left arm wound around my neck, pressing me against his chest, his right hand holding the knife to my throat.

"I'm here now." It was Richard's calm voice. "Don't be afraid, Louis."

Elation! Somehow Richard would make everything all right.

"Don't call me that!" Louis screamed, jerking me backward. He had me off balance, so I was leaning on him, and pulling against the rope which still bound my wrists. If he let go of me, I would fall.

"Put the knife down. You can't do this." Richard slowly took a step forward.

"I'll do as I please. Go away."

"You heard me. Put it down," Richard said, taking another step.

"You control Louis, but you can't control me."

"I'm here to put a stop to this." Richard held his pistol, pointing down, alongside his right leg.

"And just how are you going to do that?" Louis shifted his weight to the left.

"I'll do what I have to." If the bluff didn't work, if Louis didn't back down, did Richard have it in him to kill the brother he had nurtured all these years? If only there was another way out of this!

"You're lying. After she died, you promised no one would ever hurt Louis again. You're not going back on your word, are you?" He jerked my head backward. I felt his breathing rise and fall. "She did this, didn't she? She changed everything."

"Leave her out of it. She has nothing to do with what happened to us. This is about doing what's right. You need help."

"Help?" Louis said with bitterness. "What kind of help should we get? Maybe we should call social services. How about a child welfare agency? Maybe they could find time to respond now, thirty years too late! No, there wasn't any help when it was just Louis and you and I. Nobody gave a damn then. Why should they care now?" He jerked my waist more tightly against his body. "Leave, Richard. If you don't, I'll kill her before you can stop me. I swear I will. She means nothing to me."

Richard slowly stepped forward. "Let them go. It isn't going to rain. You were wrong about the weather. It's going to snow. You know how you hate the snow. Let's go home, where it's warm."

"It's not going to snow. You're just saying that. It'll rain soon. I know it will. It'll rain down on her just like it rained down on Louis. Her blood, mingling with the rain, running down her arms, washing into the earth. But she won't die right away, she'll hang on for a long time, same as Louis. In the end, the weak never survive. Louis was weak and that's why I had to take over."

"Put the knife down." Richard inched closer.

"Or what? You'll shoot me? Go ahead." Louis shoved his wrist tighter against my jaw, the cold, flat edge of the blade biting into my throat. One quick move would slice it open. "You know you won't. You can't. Richard, who never hunted because he couldn't bear to kill an animal? And now you expect me to believe you'll shoot me? Not likely. I know you too well."

"Don't test me. I'll do what I have to."

Louis laughed. "Yeah, you said that before. Trouble is, I don't believe it."

Richard took another step toward us.

"Stay back!" Louis stepped sideways, dragging me with him, his boot nudging the metal box that contained Caliban.

My eyes darted to Richard, trying to tip him off. How could he know what that box contained? I tried to get his attention, but he was intent on Louis, his eyes not moving from Louis's face. If only I could alert him to be wary of the metal container. I wiggled against Louis's hold, mumbling warnings from deep in my throat.

Louis fidgeted, leaning on one foot, then the other, while he slowly pushed the case containing Caliban forward with his right foot.

Richard looked at me. Finally! My eyes traveled to the box, then up to his. But Louis saw what passed between us as well. He kicked the metal case; the impact of his foot sounding in a loud thud. The lid flew off, the snake forming an arc midair.

Richard jumped back, but it was too late. Caliban sank his fangs into Richard's forearm. He grabbed the snake and threw it to the ground, then quickly aimed his pistol and fired, severing its head. The snake's tail continued to writhe on the dirt floor.

Louis raised the knife over me. The blade glinted with the reflection of the flames from the fire pit. The tendons on the inside of his wrist were taut in the grip he held on the knife, his knuckles white.

Richard raised the pistol and pulled the trigger. The sound was deafening.

Chapter Eighteen

The force of the shot blew Louis off his feet and dragged me along. Halfway through the fall, Louis's hands fell slack, releasing the knife. We both fell to the ground. I rolled to the side and looked back to find that Louis had fallen face up, a small hole in the center of his forehead. Blood seeped into the dirt beneath his head. On the earthen wall behind us were bits of bone blown from the back of his skull.

Richard slashed the ropes, unbinding my wrists. Together we ran to Denise. He cut her free of the tree and she slumped forward, semi-conscious. Picking her up, he carried her closer to the fire and covered her with his jacket. Then he knelt over Louis's body. For a moment his head hung low and his shoulders quivered.

I stood behind him, not knowing what to say or do. "Richard …" I started, then broke off.

"I had to aim high," he said. He did not turn around. "I couldn't take the chance of hitting you. He had you in front of him, only he was taller than you. I had to do it. There was no other way."

"No," I said, feeling it was a woefully inadequate reply.

"I broke my promise. I told him I would take care of him." He put his hand over Louis's. "But nothing I could do would save him from this."

"Your arm ..." I said. The sleeve of his shirt was tight where his forearm had begun to swell. I laid my hand on his shoulder and he reached back, grasping my fingers.

"We've got to stop the spread of the venom," I said. He didn't respond, so still unsteady, I took the knife from him and worked it as carefully as I could through his cotton shirt, making a slit close to the shoulder. I ripped the sleeve off and, wrapping it around his arm, above the wound, tied it in a knot. His entire forearm was an angry shade of deep red.

He had not taken his eyes from Louis. "What was left for him?" he asked. "An institution for the criminally insane?"

"What about you?" I asked.

"What about me?" He brushed the corner of his eye with the back of his hand.

"You need to go. Now, while there's still time. You could be gone before they know what happened. If you stay here, you'll be charged with manslaughter. It wasn't self-defense. Just get to a phone and send someone back for us."

"No." His voice was so resolute, so final. I knelt next to him and took his calloused hands in mine. With my finger, I traced the smudge of blue paint across his knuckles. I looked at him.

"The Camaro," he said. "Bahama Blue."

Just the words conjured up a place that was quiet and warm and peaceful. A beach and palm fronds waving in the breeze. When had Richard first told me about painting the car? Had it only been a couple of days? How long ago it seemed. "Richard, please ... *go!*" I begged.

"No." He began to gather up the rope Louis had used to tie us.

Though I tried as hard as I could to prevent it, tears welled up in my eyes. "I've got some money. Not much, but enough. Take it and go."

"Go where?" He brought two logs from the entrance of the cave and propped one end of each up on the wall.

"I don't know. Someplace out of the country. Maybe Mexico, or Canada. You lived in Alaska all those years, you've got to know of a place where a person can get lost."

"I don't want to get lost. I've been lost my whole life. Besides, I'm not leaving without you."

"We could meet somewhere." Was I saying what I thought I was saying? Could I do this? Was this me, practical, both feet firmly planted, hopelessly puritanical?

"Don't you know they'd be looking for you? Do you think that's the way I want you to live your life? Skulking around, always watching your back on account of me? No. There is no honor in that." He went to Denise and felt for a pulse, checking his watch.

A leaf fluttered down through the opening in the ceiling, lightly descending to where Denise had been tied. It was an oak leaf, brown and withered. "You only did what you had to do," I said. "You never had any choices. You shouldn't be punished for that."

"There isn't much time," he said. He measured lengths of rope.

"For what? What are you doing?" I asked.

"Making a travois." He nodded toward Denise. "I'll be able to get her out of here faster than if I carried her. It'll be easier on her, too."

My anger flared. "Have you heard a single word I've said?"

He took my face in his hands and I tried to look away from his eyes, but their intensity overpowered me. "It isn't that I haven't heard you. And there's sense in what you say. But understand me, Carol, I'm not taking any chances with sending someone else back here. What if they couldn't find you? She's in shock and needs a hospital. And what about you? You're not in much better shape. I won't leave you."

His face told me there was no argument, that his mind was set. "Whatever happens after that, I'll deal with it then," he said. "But right now, I've got to get her and you out of here."

I pulled away, selfishly wanting what might be best for him rather than Denise.

"We'll find a way, I know we will," he said, working on the logs, pulling strips of ragged bark from them. "Do you feel strong enough to hold the ends of these logs up, while I connect the rope?"

My head throbbed, but otherwise I was just stiff and sore. My tender cheek meant I'd have one heck of a bruise tomorrow. I stood between the logs, lifting the ends opposite from those propped against the wall. He stood back and assessed the width. "About two feet apart," he said. "We haven't much rope."

I made the space between the logs slightly narrower. He cut eight widths of rope and lashed the shafts together, knotting each end around one of the logs, spacing them even distances apart. Then he took the longest piece of rope and began weaving it in and out, until a loosely woven rope net secured one end of the two logs together. He carried Denise over and laid her on the makeshift litter, then covered her again with his jacket.

"Can you manage to walk alongside?"

I nodded.

"We're set then," he said, taking up the handles.

Suddenly a shadow passed over the opening in the ceiling. With a yelp, someone fell to the ground. For the second time a shot sounded in the cave, as deafening as the first. Jerking my head up in confusion, I looked to Richard. His hand went to his chest and his mouth opened. Red poured between his fingers. He staggered backward. I could not comprehend what was wrong. I called to him, but I don't think he heard. Denise moaned.

I tore my eyes from Richard. There was a gun on the ground—and Sheriff Morton sprawled in the dirt.

"You've shot him!" I screamed in disbelief. "He was going to get us out of here!"

Richard crumpled to the ground, his stunned eyes looking up at the ceiling. He was trying to speak, his lips were moving but no sound came out.

"The safety must have come off when I fell." Wide-eyed, Morton's face bore his shock. His red cheeks glistened with perspiration.

I tore at my coat, ripping the sleeves from my arms in my haste. Blood was pumping from the bullet hole at an alarming rate. Throwing the coat over Richard, I pressed both my palms down over the wound, leaning into him with all of my weight. The blue eyes that had so often mesmerized me, the eyes that only seconds before had held such power, were becoming dull. "Don't do this to me! No!" I screamed.

Morton was yelling to someone over his radio. Within seconds, my jacket was soaked with blood. It gushed from beneath my fingers, pooling at my knees. I didn't know what else to do except keep pressing my hands down, but it was no use. Richard's body convulsed. His torso lifted, then fell. His hand twitched at my side. A milkiness passed over the piercing blue of his eyes, turning them to steel. "Please, dear God Almighty! Somebody help us!" I screamed, pressing harder.

I know exactly when Richard died. It was in that split-second before his eyes changed forever. Just before the snow began to lightly feather down through the hole in the ceiling.

Chapter Nineteen

Jack, in his wrinkled flannel shirt, blue jeans, and boots, dwarfed the waiting room doorway. Stubble on his face told me he'd driven all night. The orange chairs that I'd pushed together had made a hard and uncomfortable bed and, sensing that any movement on my part would be pain-filled, I procrastinated moving anything but my eyes.

"What happened?" he asked.

What happened? A simple question, innocuous and straightforward. But where would I begin to answer it? How did I put it into words? I opened my lips to speak, but instead a tear ran down my cheek. The coward's way out.

Crying was stupid, Jack would say. Nonetheless, I couldn't stop myself. A big hole had been blown through me and everything sucked out; all the energy, emotion, and feeling were gone. Only one thing remained. The truth that right now was still too deep to pull from that innermost layer of myself. Only I knew it was there.

"Marge said something about Denise being kidnapped and I should get up here as quick as I could. That was about it." He knelt by me and brushed the hair from my eyes. "Is Denise all right?"

I nodded. "More or less. Todd is up with her now. Her physical injuries aren't the worst of it. The rest, I don't know." Sitting up, I let the hospital issue blanket fall to the floor. I felt like I'd been hit by a truck. Everything hurt.

"What about you?" he asked.

"Me?" Again I felt the tugging. If I wait, if I don't tell him now, I've made my choice. It's something that either comes out now or stays back forever. No waiting for the right time. How do I tell him six months from now that I'd loved Richard? "Richard's dead," I said simply. "He was trying to help us. Louis was the killer."

"But Morton thought it was Richard and shot him instead of Louis?"

"No, Richard killed Louis."

"Then who killed Richard?"

"Sheriff Morton accidentally shot him."

"Accidentally? How does a sheriff accidentally shoot someone?"

"He fell, and the safety came off his gun."

Jack sunk heavily into the chair I had just vacated, the orange plastic protesting loudly under his 200-plus pounds. "They're both dead?" He covered his face with his hands, then ran his fingers through his thick hair. "Then who kidnapped Denise?"

"Louis. The story goes way back. Richard told me bits and pieces of it. Childhood abuse, broken homes, a lot of moving around. A real nightmare."

"What's that got to do with murder?"

"The abuse was terrible. It warped Louis so badly that he became two persons in an attempt to escape it. When the alter ego dominated, he took revenge on women he perceived as having been like his mother."

I steeled myself for Jack's reaction to my next statement. "I'm having Richard cremated."

Jack's mouth fell open. "Why you?"

"There aren't any relatives," I said simply. "I told Morton I'll take care of the ashes. Frankly, I don't give a damn what they do with Louis, but Richard would want to be with his brother, so Louis is being cremated too."

"How much is that going to cost?"

"Leave it, Jack." My voice was surprisingly icy. I wasn't sure why this was important to me. Richard had loved the overlook on the west edge of the woods, high up on the ridge where the trail narrows and then meanders down to the road. From there I would let both their ashes mingle in the wind. Maybe in this other life, Richard could take care of Louis, like he'd always wanted.

I stood in front of the window. Diamond snow glittered. It would be gone by mid-morning. Tears trickled down my face. "I don't know how to tell you this," I said.

Jack came up behind me and put his hands on my shoulders. "Then don't," he said.

I felt like I'd betrayed him, even though Richard and I had never done anything wrong. But we could have. That was what bothered me. *We could have.* Noticing my sleeve for the first time, I ran my fingers over bloodstains. Richard's blood. I looked at the palms of my hands and didn't remember having washed them. "It's just that I …" I squeezed my eyes shut and drew a long breath. "I—"

"It doesn't matter. It really doesn't matter." He wrapped his arms around me and held me close. I swayed slightly backward, leaning into the familiar crook of his arms, feeling their warmth encircle me.

Maybe it didn't matter. Could we go from here and never look back? Did Jack know what he was forgiving? Did I know?

"Let's go up to see Denise," he said.

*   *   *   *

Lida poked her head around the door to Denise's room. "Lida!" I said, surprised to see her.

"Anybody home? Heard there was a party up here." She kissed Denise lightly on the forehead.

"Some party," Denise said, using the bed rails to pull herself into a sitting position. "We were worried sick about you."

"Yeah, I heard. Perry said, and I quote, 'Those two better stay the hell away for a good long time.' He's hopping mad about something—won't tell me what it is. And he thinks you're a raving lunatic, Carol. Says you got thrown from your horse and when he found you and tried to make a brace for what he thought was your broken wrist, that you were screaming and yelling about him tying you up."

I remembered the dream and now knew that was exactly what it was—a dream.

"Ever since he had that EMT training, he's been dying to use it. He also said something about you wrecking our water softener. How on earth did you manage that?"

"You don't want to know," Denise said.

"Oh, that," I said, dismissing it with a flip of my hand. Her closely cropped dark hair was perfectly coifed, as usual, but there was something different about her.

She took off her coat and, after draping it over the orange plastic chair, sat down. "What are you worried about me for? Looks like you two should have worried more about yourselves. What happened, anyway?"

"Long, long story," I said wearily, not sure I could stomach it again, after having been through it *ad nauseam* with Morton. Denise sank back into her pillow and looked up at the ceiling.

Lida quickly picked up the nuance. "Okay, let's skip it for now. Maybe later," she said.

"Yeah, later might be better," Denise agreed. "Actually, never might be better yet." I wondered how long she was going to be able to shove everything to the back, instead of dealing with it.

Something about Lida was vaguely changed. But what was it? New glasses? "So how is your sister?" I asked, in an effort to move the conversation away from the events of the past twenty-four hours.

"My sister?" Lida asked blankly.

There was something going on here that I couldn't quite grasp. "Perry said you'd gone to visit your sister. Something about her being sick?"

"Oh, yeah. Sure. She's fine. I mean, she's getting better." Lida looked out the window. "Can't believe we got snow in October!"

"What was wrong with her?" I asked.

"Nothing." She smoothed the pink polka dot blouse she wore.

"Nothing?" I asked, confused.

"Oh, you know, minor complaints, stuff like that."

What was that supposed to mean? "But I thought—" I started.

"Well, if you must know, I was at my sister's but it wasn't because she was sick. It's not like I told Perry to lie or anything. He just came up with that on his own." She fingered the drawstring on the hood of her jacket, running the plastic stop up and down the cord.

I didn't say anything and neither did Denise. Admittedly, I was exhausted and slow on the uptake. "Perry lied?" I asked. "About what?"

"The real reason I was at my sister's."

I waited. Denise closed her eyes for a moment, then opened them again. "Okay ..." I said.

"What is this, the Spanish Inquisition?" Lida laughed, too loudly, and shifted in her chair. "I swear, Carol, you have about as much tact as Genghis Khan."

"What did I say?"

"It's the way you stare someone down, like they're being interrogated, like you're expecting something, and come hell or high water, you're going to get it!"

"Get what?" I asked, more than a little confused. Why was she angry with me?

"Maybe Lida doesn't want to talk about it, whatever it is," Denise said, her words soft and billowy, like a cloud hovering over us.

Annoyed, I said, "I'm not making her say anything. Heaven forbid."

Lida scowled. "All right, all right! If you must know, I had a tummy tuck! Are you happy now?"

So that was it. My mouth dropped open. Lida was not the vain sort. She'd never cared a whit about her looks, had always been happy with status quo. Hadn't she?

"I think that's just fine," Denise said.

"Well, I don't," I said. Why on earth would you do such a thing? A tummy tuck. How ridiculous. If something was wrong in your life, your looks or whatever it was, you learned to live with it. Didn't you?

"You sound just like Perry. He's been a nervous wreck and an all-around pain in the behind ever since I decided to do it. He's gone through three bottles of whiskey in a couple of weeks. If I didn't just get it over with soon, the man was going to become an alcoholic."

I thought about the fight Denise witnessed in the grocery store and about Perry's drinking and the worry she must have put him through for something as worthless as vanity. "There wasn't anything wrong with the way you looked," I said, reiterating my position.

"Nothing except a thirty-nine-inch waist."

"Well who cares?" It seemed absurd that Lida would be concerned with such a superficial thing.

She crossed her arms defiantly in front of her. "I do, that's who."

Then suddenly it occurred to me that here we were, arguing about cosmetic surgery, and in its own utterly unwound and mixed-up sort of way, the world had righted itself, at least temporarily. Like shedding a sodden and heavy wool coat, a layer had been pulled away. Immediately I felt lighter. "Whatever," I said, dismissing our argument. It didn't matter. If Lida wanted a smaller waist, who was I to judge? I hugged her, I guess a little too hard, because she winced.

"Careful, I'm still a little sore," she said.

"Sorry. Can we see the scars?" I asked. Denise rolled her eyes in disgust.

"Absolutely not," Lida said.

"Oh, c'mon, I've never known anyone who had a tummy tuck before."

She stood up and modeled for us, then did a theatrical runway half-turn. "Sorry, but that's it. I'm not showing you my scars. Absolutely not."

"Can they really make it so that when you wear a two-piece swim suit, your flab doesn't hang over the top?" My curiosity rampaged.

"I can't believe you asked that," Denise said.

"Believe it. There isn't anything that's beyond this one," Lida said, flicking her wrist toward me.

*   *   *   *

"I'll go with you, if you're afraid," Marge said.

The silver urn, Richard's name etched in script across the front, felt cold in my hands. "I'll be okay." It hadn't occurred to me that I might not like being alone in the woods. Solitary rides on my horses were a way of life that I did not want to change. I would not allow myself the indulgence of fear.

"Sure about that?" she asked.

"Yeah, but thanks anyway." In her offering to come along, I sensed an approval—that if she'd really thought the whole thing about Richard's ashes was wrong, she wouldn't want to be part of it.

"You don't always have to be so strong, you know. Sometimes it's okay to accept help." She scooped up Floreen, nuzzling her nose into the cat's fur.

"That's rich, coming from you, Marge. Miss Independence herself." She meant right, I knew. "I can't allow myself to be afraid. You know what they say about falling off a horse, that you've got to get right back on? If I don't do this right away, I'll never do it. I'll put it off and put it off, until all that's left are excuses and mind games."

"What about Jack? Does he know you're traipsing around in the woods alone?"

"You know Jack. 'Whatever you want to do is fine, Carol.' Mr. Easygoing." Jack went back to his precious warehouse, promising the work would be done by Thanksgiving. Before he returned, though, a lengthy meeting with his boss confirmed there was plenty of work for him within a more commutable distance. He would be home every weekend—maybe even some weeknights. That was a big step for Jack to take, and I vowed to work harder, too, to make this marriage work.

She looked like she wanted to say something, but stopped. Instead, she drew her yellow cardigan tightly around her, hesitated, then spoke. "At least, then, tell me where you'll be, so we know where to look if there's trouble."

"There won't be any trouble," I said, assuring her.

"I don't mean trouble in that sense of the word, like a madman on the loose or something. God help us, I hope we're over that. It's trouble of another sort that I'm worried about. Something I don't think Jack understands at all."

Suddenly my legs were very weary. Pulling a chair away from her kitchen table, I sank into it. I ran my finger along the edges of the carved design, the old wood pitted and scratched from years of use. Somehow the words seemed easier to say if I didn't look at her. "I tried to tell him, but he doesn't want to hear. He wants to act like if I don't put words to it, it never happened, that maybe if we don't talk about it, we don't have to admit it took place." I looked up at her then. Thankfully, there was compassion in her eyes. I don't know what I would have done if she had chosen to rebuke me now. I guess some things are only understood between women. "I wonder what would have happened if Richard had lived," I said, and waited, willing my lips to stop quivering. "I don't think I could have left Jack. We've got too many years together. But even so, Richard was like no one I'd ever known before. Like our spirits connected."

"Just when I think I've got you pegged as hopelessly pragmatic, you do or say something that astonishes me." She put Floreen down.

"Sometimes I feel as silly and awkward as if I were in high school again. Am I having a mid-life crisis?" I thought of my age and how it was a little late for that.

"At some point in everyone's life, there comes a time when you question the decisions you've made. I suspect that, had he lived, and had you stayed with Jack, Richard and you would have become very, very good friends."

"I'm not sure any relationship I had with Richard could have remained on a platonic level."

She shrugged. "Sometimes a relationship evolves. Things change."

For the first time ever, I felt like I was really seeing Marge. Her white curls, the creases in her face, the quivering way her lips moved sometimes. I would always cherish this compassionate woman who had the ability to discern what had happened and put it in a context that not only made it acceptable, but also gave me the grace to forgive myself. All without any explanation from me. "We'll never know, will we?" I asked sadly.

*   *   *   *

After driving to the edge of the woods and pulling my truck off the road, I hiked the three-quarters of a mile up the steep slope to the overlook. All traces of snow were gone, and a southern breeze stirred the grass of the upland meadow and carried the scent of the sun-warmed maples. A leaf brushed past the urn and fell to the ground.

The heaviness in my legs returned and I sat down in the grass, cross-legged. I closed my eyes and didn't move for a moment. When I opened them, I saw a hawk circling overhead. It swooped down, then lifted its wings and caught an upward draft. I stood, removed the lid, and tipped the urn. The wind swirled around my hand; I felt it enter the cup and carry the ashes away.

978-0-595-44271-3
0-595-44271-4

Printed in the United States
89546LV00001B/28-45/A